D1015656

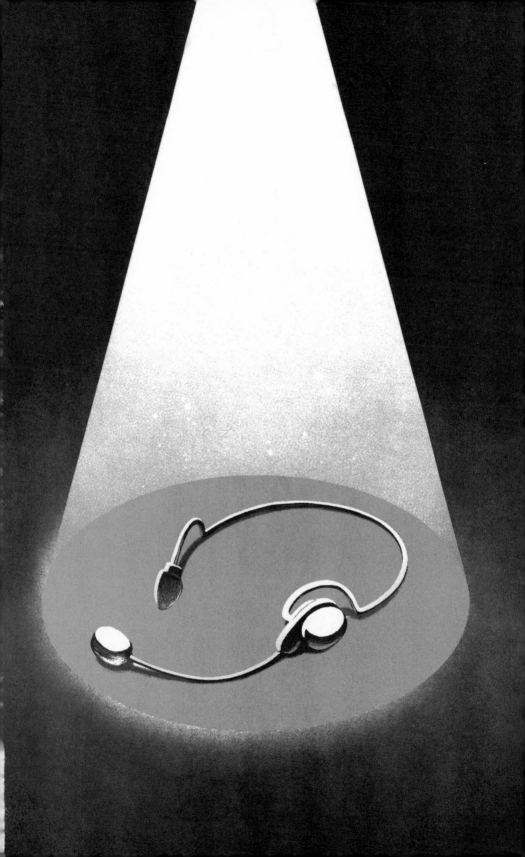

IDOL GOSSIP

ALEXANDRA LEIGH YOUNG

WALKER BOOKS

Text copyright © 2021 by Alexandra Leigh Young
Illustrations copyright © 2021 by Angelica Alzona

First US edition 2021

Library of Congress Catalog Card Number pending
ISBN 978-1-5362-1364-5

21 22 23 24 25 26 LBM 10 9 8 7 6 5 4 3 2 1

Printed in Melrose Park, IL, USA

This book was typeset in ITC Mendoza Roman.

Walker Books US
a division of
Candlewick Press
99 Dover Street
Somerville, Massachusetts 02144

www.walkerbooksus.com

FOR MY GRANDMA ALICE
AND ALL HER UNICORNS

[This page has been translated from Korean.]

12/08

CATEGORY: RUMOR MILL

Top10 Entertainment Scouting New Talent

Like a spider biding her time, I have many eyes on the ground, and those eyes spy something afoot at the famed K-pop mega-label Top10 Entertainment. Sources tell me that Top10's talent scouts have been lurking around noraebangs this month, apparently on the hunt for an English-speaking trainee. Scouts have been spotted in the neighborhoods of Sinchon, especially around the Yonsei University campus; Myeongdong; and, of course, the ex-pat areas of Itaewon.

So, my dear Readers, if you speak English fluently and you fantasize about a nonexistent social life, sleeping a maximum of three hours a night, having a chaperone by your side even when you pee, and undergoing so much plastic surgery that even your own mother won't recognize you, now is your big chance.

+ V +

COMMENTS

dumdeo

Noraebangs?? Is Top10 that desperate??? Don't they have talent scouts all over the world?

Jin-Swoon

I fantasize about living in the same dorm as Jin Soo . . . .

> **XOL**
>
> Or Ye-jun ٩(♡ε♡)۶

Anonymous

Watch out, V will lay spider eggs in your brain if you're not careful.

Inst-110

I saw one in Sinchon! But she didn't pick me because I don't speak English so well :'(

> **zelu-b0t**
>
> Yeh, I'm sure that's why she didn't pick you . . .

Aegyoona

Omg, I can't HANDLE a new Top10 idol rn. I'm still obsessed with Soo-li.

94 MORE COMMENTS>>

One

"LIGHT-UP-LIGHT-UP! YOU SEE ME NOW! NAEGA WONHANEUN GEON NE BICH-IEOSSEO!"

Olivia was jumping up and down on top of a black vinyl love seat in our tiny noraebang booth, screaming her lungs out. The nine members of MSB danced across the TV while the lyrics to "Light Up" scrolled across the screen. I hummed along as I flipped through a phone book–size binder full of song titles.

"OH-OH-OH, HUH-OH!" shrieked Olivia.

I pressed #6403 into the remote, then sat back and watched my little sister finish her song. Olivia always did this move where she flapped her elbows and wagged her ponytail back and forth so it made a fuzzy halo over her head. God, she was such a goofball— even when she was a baby, she could crack me up. I remember this one time when she was, like, two or three years old and she tasted a lemon for the first time. It was hilarious how she sucked her lips all the way inside her mouth because it was so sour, but she kept licking it over and over again and puckering her face just to keep me laughing.

It was Friday, and we had just gotten out of class at our new international school so we were both still wearing our school uniforms. It was the whole prep-school getup—blazer, pleated skirt, and knee-high socks. The only difference was, I wore the high school's color, navy blue, and Olivia had to wear the middle-school color, which was this bright banana-yellow. She looked like Big Bird's niece.

"BUREUL KYEORA, GIRL!" She bent down to put the mic in front of my face, and I echoed the harmony to her melody.

It took Olivia forever to convince me to walk into this place. Not because the front of the building has so many flashing laser lights and blinking LED screens that it looks like a giant slot machine that just hit the jackpot. But because the only karaoke spots I'd ever seen back in America required you to sing in front of a bunch of drunk strangers who would boo you offstage if they thought you weren't doing justice to Journey, or Alanis Morissette, or some other artist that people my parents' age listen to. But Olivia explained we could get our own private booth where we could sing just the two of us, and I finally caved. I had gone six excruciating months without singing—that's how long it's been since I left my voice lessons behind in San Francisco (not to mention most of my earthly possessions and all my friends). A private room in a noraebang wasn't remotely close to the same thing as a voice lesson, but it was the best I could get, and I was desperate.

"LII-IIIGHT ME UUUUUP!"

BA-DA-DA-DAAAAH.

Olivia hopped up on the love seat as the last note faded out, posing with one hand on her hip and the other pointing the microphone toward the ceiling in her best idol impression. I laughed at her, and that made her ham it up even more. One of the best things about moving to Seoul was that I got to hang out with Olivia way more. We barely ever saw each other back home; she was always doing stuff with her friends, and I was always doing stuff with mine. I'd forgotten how much fun we had together—and how hilarious she could be. Honestly, it made living in a city where I knew exactly zero people so much easier.

"Miss Fierce, what a stunning set! How do I dare to take the stage after a performance like that?"

"Har-dee-*har*," said Olivia.

"What was that, your third MSB song in a row?" I teased.

"Fourth, actually." Olivia stanned for a lot of different K-pop groups, but MSB was her bias. She was a die-hard BoM—MSB's fandom—maybe even the die-hardest.

"You are so obsessed."

"I'm not *obsessed!*" she said. "I just have incredible taste."

The TV flickered to the next song, and the quiet opening chords of "Million Reasons" started to play over the speakers.

"Oh, come onnn, Alice," complained Olivia, "you *always* play this song!"

It was true. I probably played "Million Reasons" at least ten or twelve times a day, and when I wasn't playing it on my laptop or my phone, I was singing it. Lady Gaga's was the kind of music that made you wash your hair twice just so you could sing in the shower for two extra minutes. But it isn't just an amazing song—there's something else. This weird thing happens every time I sing something I'm really into: it's like these two polar-opposite feelings fill me up at the same time, this deep melancholy and a total euphoria. The combination completely slays me. It's a pretty rare song that gives me that feeling, but with "Million Reasons," it's guaranteed.

"If you get four MSB songs, I get at least one Lady Gaga," I said, "and get down from there before you fall and break an ankle."

Olivia threw me the microphone and sank down into the love seat to watch me. I stepped up to the front of the room and dramatically turned my back to the screen. I didn't need to read the lyrics; I knew every second of the song by heart. I bowed my head over the microphone, my hair falling around my face as the light from the twirling disco ball in the ceiling danced across my legs. Then I began to sing.

When the chorus hit, I snapped my hair up and over my head, then pounded my fist into my chest, and Olivia busted up laughing. She always brought out my cheesy side; she was, like, the only person who could never make me feel stupid because I know that she knows I'm not.

It's right around the three-minute mark in the song when I start to get that sad-happy feeling. I close my eyes and improvise, singing whatever feels good, whatever feels right. My body starts to take over, like the orchestra made up by my lungs and throat and belly know what to do without my brain conducting. It's pretty much the only time I ever feel truly confident about myself. I think it's because I'm not thinking about how I look or how I sound; I'm just lost in the music.

Half a minute later, the song ended and I opened my eyes to Olivia standing on the love seat again, clapping wildly. "Whoo! Encore! ENCORE!"

I folded my arm across my stomach and took a deep bow. "Thank you, thank you, to all my adoring fans."

"You're getting so good. Like *really* good."

"Nah," I said sheepishly.

"I'm serious. You sound just like Lady Gaga."

"That might be the highest compliment anyone has ever given me."

Olivia looked at me, cocking her head to the side. "You know what I never get?"

"What?" I asked.

"How do you know which notes to sing in that middle part when you're just making stuff up?"

"I don't know, really." I shrugged. It was kind of like asking me how I know that a blueberry is blue. "I just kind of . . . know."

"I wish I knew how to do that."

"Come on, our two hours are almost up. We should hit it."

It was almost eight o'clock, and it would take us half an hour to get home on the subway. I picked up our Mega Coffee empties and snack wrappers and dropped them into a little trash can on the floor. We slipped our shoes back on, then we headed out into the dim hallway. Muffled singing seeped out of other rooms as we walked past.

We had only walked a few steps when Olivia stopped short.

A figure had appeared out of nowhere in the dark hallway. Without thinking, I shot my arm in front of Olivia's chest like a mom who'd just slammed on the car brakes.

The figure waddled up to us, and as it got closer, I realized it was a woman who looked around the same age as my grandma. A faded gray baseball cap with the logo SONY 1985 was squashed on top of her puff of salt-white hair. It was totally bizarre to see someone her age inside a cheap noraebang full of teenagers.

The woman smiled at us and bowed. "Annyeonghaseyo. Jeo-neun Tae So-ri-imnida. Cheoeum boipgesseumnida."

"We don't speak Korean," I blurted out.

It wasn't exactly true. In the six months since we'd been here, I'd learned the basics of Korean. But I'm terrible at learning languages. In fact, Spanish was my absolute worst subject in school back home. And when it came to Korean, I just couldn't tell the difference between the long *eo* and *oo* syllables, and I constantly mixed up the sharp *ch'* and *jj* sounds.

Olivia was like Mom, though; she was a genius at languages. Before we even knew we were going to move to Seoul, she discovered EXO music videos on YouTube and started watching enough K-dramas that she could have entire conversations with her friends in Korean. It used to drive me nuts when her friends would come over and I couldn't understand what they were saying. Of course, now that we lived here it was ridiculously useful, but I didn't want her to talk to some creepy stranger, so I just lied.

"Sorry, we can't help you," I said, trying to move past the woman.

"Ah! Good thing I speak English!" she said. She grinned at us and didn't move an inch out of our way. "I am So-ri Tae. I am with a company called Top10 Entertainment. You know Top10?"

Olivia inhaled sharply and gripped my outstretched arm. "I know Top10!"

"You do?" I said, looking at her with surprise. What the heck was Top10 Entertainment? Did this woman manufacture karaoke machines or something?

"Good!" said the woman, clapping her hands together. "Tell me, please, who is the one with the voice?"

"That'd be her," answered Olivia, pointing up at me.

"American?" asked the woman.

"Uh-huh," replied Olivia.

The lady looked me up and down. "And how old, eighteen? Nineteen?"

"Seventeen, actually," said Olivia.

"Olivia!" I said. This was so not cool. I didn't like this stranger asking all kinds of personal questions about me, and I *really* didn't like Olivia offering answers.

The woman fished a business card and a pen out of the folds of her oversize parka and scribbled *Saturday, 10 a.m.* on the back. "You are a very good singer; I want you to come to our audition next Saturday. You can sing the 'Million Reasons' song. Here." She held the card out to me with both hands, and when I didn't move to take it from her, Olivia took the card with a polite bow.

"Kamsahamnida," said Olivia.

"Kamsahamnida," replied the woman, bowing in return.

"All right, let's go," I said, steering Olivia away by her shoulders.

As I led her toward the exit, I quickly glanced back at the woman. She was watching us leave. "Ciao-ciao!" she said, waving at me with her bony hand.

Ciao-ciao? That was super-weird. Isn't that Italian or something?

I rushed us through the lobby and down the stairs that led to the cramped streets of Myeondong. We stepped out into the maze of beauty supply shops, street food vendors, and mobs of people shopping. A woman wearing an elf costume saw me and tried to press a honeydew face mask into my hands. It's funny, my whole life I've been taught that elves were white. It was good to know that Santa Claus is an equal opportunity employer.

"Oh my god, oh my god, oh my *god!*" said Olivia, barely able to contain herself.

"What the hell was *that* all about?" I asked.

"Al, she was from Top10 Entertainment!"

"Yeah, got that part, but what is it?"

"Are you serious? Come *on*, they're like one of the biggest K-pop agencies in the world. They represent so many big groups, like MSB, EL3MENTAL, and XOKiss!"

"Wait . . . seriously?" I said, stopping in the middle of the sidewalk. Even I had heard of EL3MENTAL, and of course, thanks to Olivia, I knew all about MSB.

Olivia grabbed both my arms. "That woman wants you to audition for the company. Oh my god! What if you become a famous K-pop idol?"

"OK, let's just calm down for a second." I licked my lips, still too skeptical to get excited. Did people actually get discovered in the halls of karaoke parlors? It seemed way too cliché to happen in real life.

"Let me see that business card."

Olivia handed me the card and leaned in next to me so we could both study it. Shoppers streamed past us on all sides, their stuffed shopping bags knocking into us as they pushed past.

The front of the business card was matte black with a magenta Top10 Entertainment logo stamped into it. I passed my thumb over the glossy 10, which was slightly raised. Flipping the card over, I checked the address, which was in Gangnam, a super-ritzy area in Seoul I had never been to.

"The auditions are next Saturday. You have to go," said Olivia.

"I don't know. You know I could barely get through auditions back home . . ." Actually, I *hated* auditions. All the judging, the rejection—it was the worst part of wanting to sing professionally.

Whenever my voice teacher suggested I go to one back in San Francisco, I found an excuse not to go.

"Well, that woman will be there," pressed Olivia, "and she called you a quote-unquote very good singer."

"Yeah, true . . ." I turned the card over in my hands a couple times, letting the excitement work its way in just a tiny bit. "I guess if it's just the one song it's not so bad."

"Well, you might have to dance, too," said Olivia.

"Welp, that settles that," I said, the excitement instantly gone. I crumpled up the card, stuffed it into my jacket pocket, and turned to start walking again.

"Alice! What're you doing?" Olivia snatched the balled-up card out of my pocket and tried to smooth it back out. "What do you mean 'that settles that'?"

"Liv, I can't dance! There's no way in hell I'm going to that audition."

"Well, I'm only guessing! You might not even have to! And obviously that woman didn't think it mattered if you could dance or not anyway."

"Don't care. Not going."

Thick white flakes began to drift down from the sky, and we picked up the pace toward the subway stop.

"But this is your dream!" said Olivia, jogging to keep up with me.

"It's not my dream to be an idol. K-pop is *your* thing, not mine. Remember?"

"OK, but it *is* your dream to be a professional singer."

"Yeah, a professional singer like Lady Gaga. Not like a member of a Korean girl group."

"Come on, Lady Gaga isn't *that* different. She sings pop music and dances with a whole troupe of backup dancers just like idols do!"

"You know what I mean!"

"I just don't see the difference between . . ."

I wheeled around to face her. "Look, I'm not going to look like an idiot in front of a bunch of talent scouts from some famous company. I'm not doing it, so stop trying to convince me!" I really didn't mean to be so aggressive, but it felt like Olivia was putting so much pressure on me all of a sudden. I just needed her to back off.

"All right, all right. *Jeez.*"

When we got to the subway station, we tapped our T-money cards at the turnstiles and didn't talk the rest of the way home.

We got back to our apartment about an hour later, where it was nice and warm. I peeled off my soggy parka and shoes and flexed my bare toes on our heated wood floors.

I loved our apartment. It was a perk of my mom's new job at the American consulate: a condo on the twenty-sixth floor of a brand-new building that overlooked Namsan Park, which is kind of like Golden Gate Park and Central Park all rolled up into one. With its milky-white wood floors and 360-degree windows, it was way more modern than our apartment back home.

Stepping into my slippers, I left Olivia in the hallway and walked into the living room where Dad was lying on the couch. I stood facing the giant flat-screen TV—another perk of Mom's job—and crossed my arms.

"Streaming American news?" I asked.

"Mmm," he grunted. "Get this, Al. They had to exhume a dead woman at this cemetery in Colma? But they accidentally dug up a different woman with the exact same name. Gross, huh?"

"Morbid," I said.

Dad raised the remote and changed the channel. "Did Olivia finally talk you into going to that karaoke parlor?"

"Yeah, she did," I answered.

"She's a pushy one, your sister."

"God, tell me about it."

"How'd it go?"

"Honestly, it was pretty fun. Felt good to sing again, even though we had to do it inside a karaoke parlor."

"That's great, Al."

I bent down and picked up a stack of American newspapers Dad had left on the floor and straightened them into a neat pile on the glass coffee table. "Where's Mom?"

"She's hosting some dignitaries from Hong Kong. She shouldn't be home too late tonight, though."

I let my eyes drift down to Dad's face. His thin, sandy-blond hair radiated out over the pillow under his head, and his dark-blue eyes looked even bluer in the bouncing light of the LED screen. Before we moved to Seoul, Dad was just as obsessed with work as Mom, maybe even more. He was a web designer, but for him it wasn't just a tech job, it was more like an art form. He used to draw his designs by hand first, and he had millions of sketchbooks all over the house in case inspiration struck while he was shaving or making coffee. He hadn't gotten a job in Seoul yet, though, because of some issues with his work visa, so this was where I usually found him, on the couch in front of the TV. I think he was feeling kind of depressed.

"K. Dinner?" I asked.

"You guys mind fending for yourselves tonight?"

With Mom being so busy with her new job and Dad being so busy with . . . the couch, I'd been taking care of dinner almost every night recently. "Sure," I answered.

I shuffled out of the living room and found Olivia sitting at the kitchen counter in front of her laptop. She was looking at the Top10 Entertainment website.

"Not going to happen, Liv."

"I'm just looking! God!"

There were still some dirty dishes left out from breakfast, so I gathered them up and dropped them in the sink. "Chicken or beef tonight?" I asked.

"Ummmm, chicken."

I opened the cupboard, grabbed two packages of chicken-flavored ramen, and put some water on to boil. Our kitchen was my favorite place in the entire condo. It was like something out of *Minority Report*, all smooth and glistening in its newness. The appliances were bright white and made by Samsung (until we moved to Korea, I didn't know Samsung made anything except televisions and phones). We even had two refrigerators, one next to the stove and one on the little balcony off our kitchen. Mom told us the one on the balcony was supposed to be for storing kim-chi, but we mostly kept soda in there.

"Al . . ."

"No." I tore open a package of noodles and pulled out the little foil flavor packet.

"Oh, come on, I just want to tell you *one* thing!"

"Are you going to tell me even if I say no?"

"Uh-huh."

"Fine," I relented. I was feeling kind of bad about blowing up at her after karaoke. "What's the *one* thing you want to tell me?"

"OK, *so*," said Olivia, clearing her throat dramatically. "It looks like next weekend is going to be an open audition—girls on Saturday, boys on Sunday. I guess Top10 invites the public to try out once a year."

"What, like *American Idol* or something?" I asked.

"Yeah, I think so?"

"So there's going to be a million people there."

"Um, yeah, I guess," she said, frowning.

"Great. Strike two. Anything else?" I plunked two thick blocks of dried noodles into the simmering water and stirred them to break them up.

"It also says there are three parts to the audition: singing, which you'll nail, choreography, and a short interview."

"Strikes three and four. You know the old saying, four strikes and you're out."

"OK," said Olivia, "what about this. If you make the cut, it says you get to attend their boarding school full-time—for free!—*and* you get daily voice lessons with some of Korea's top voice teachers."

I stopped my spoon midstir. "Daily voice lessons?"

"Yeah!" said Olivia, taking advantage of my momentary lapse in skepticism. "And if you live in the boarding school, you'll be surrounded by other people who love singing just as much as you do."

It did sound amazing . . . but the idea that I would somehow get through the auditions and land a spot in this fairy-tale land where I got professional voice lessons every day seemed pretty far-fetched. "OK, but then who would take care of *you*?"

"Mom and Dad. Obviously," said Olivia.

I snorted. "Oh, you mean like tonight?"

As if on cue, the front door crashed open. "Hey, everyone, I'm home!"

"Hey, Mom!" Olivia and I shouted in unison.

"Hey, Mom," echoed Dad in the living room.

"Someone come help me; I have a ton of leftovers from this dinner."

Olivia ran to help her, and I turned off the stove, sighing. Mom was always doing this; I'd have everything under control and she'd barge in with a totally new plan.

Mom and Olivia came back into the kitchen each carrying a bag overflowing with plastic food cartons. Mom dropped hers on the counter, kissed me on the head, then immediately whipped out her phone.

No matter how busy she was, Mom always looked immaculate. She wore her jet-black hair cropped exactly parallel with her square jawline, its razor-sharp edge maintained by a monthly trip to the hair salon. She had a permanent ring of black eyeliner around her eyes, too, which pinched downward like sideways apostrophes. The joke in our family was that Olivia and I both look exactly like Mom, but we looked nothing like each other. I look way more like the Chinese side of our family—brown-eyed, stick-straight hair, and a wide nose—whereas Olivia got all of Dad's European genes. Sometimes people didn't even realize we were sisters.

"Are you going to eat with us, Mom?" I asked hopefully.

"Oh, I don't think so, hon," she said, still staring at her phone. "I already ate at the event. And now I have hundreds of emails to reply to."

"I thought this was going to be Chinese food," said Olivia,

riffling through the food cartons. "Didn't Dad say you had a thing with Hong Kong delegates tonight?"

"Yes, but we served Korean barbecue," replied Mom.

Olivia frowned. "I *miss* eating Chinese food."

I pulled out one of the cartons and opened it up to find three pieces of thinly sliced raw beef. "Is this all just raw meat?" I asked. "I still have to cook this."

"Hmm?" said Mom.

"Never mind."

"Oh my god! Mom, mom, mom! Guess what?" Olivia said suddenly. She was hopping up and down, jiggling Mom's arm to get her attention.

"What, sweetheart?"

"Alice got discovered today!"

"Discovered?" Mom said, finally looking up from her phone.

"Today, at karaoke, a talent scout heard Alice singing and she asked her to audition for this K-pop company. And the company is *huge*."

I couldn't help smiling at Olivia; she had this ability to make the tiniest accomplishment seem like a really big deal. And when she put it that way, it did sound pretty exciting.

"Is that true?" Mom asked me with the amused look we sometimes gave each other when Olivia really worked herself up about something. "You landed an audition today?"

"Yep, my life is now officially the plot of a Hollywood movie."

"Well, that's extremely exciting! Do you think you'll go?"

Before I could say no, Olivia said, "Alice is definitely auditioning, and she's going to be amazing."

"I haven't decided if I'm going yet," I corrected.

"Well, I really think you should do it, Alice," said Mom. "It'd be so good for you to get back into singing again."

"Yeah . . . we'll see."

"Just tell Dad and me before you go so we can discuss it, OK?"

"I will—*if* I go."

"OK, I have to get back to work. You two eat up and let me know when you're heading to bed so I can come say good night." She kissed Olivia on both cheeks and rubbed my shoulder. "Congratulations, hon. Really."

We listened to the sound of her phone clicking down the hallway until her office door shut, then I flipped the heat back on the pot of noodles and dropped in a couple slices of beef. Olivia sidled up next to me and stared into the pot. "So you're thinking about it."

I cracked an egg on the rim of the pot, and we watched as the yolk swirled around in the boiling water. "Yeah, I guess I'm thinking about it."

Back home, I barely knew anyone who had their own bedroom; I even had a friend who had to sleep in her family's living room. The only thing that separated her bed from the couch was a velvet curtain she bought at Urban Outfitters. People think that living in a big city is really glamorous, but it's not; it's just cramped.

So when Mom told Olivia and me that we had to share a room in Seoul, I didn't really think anything about it. Tonight was different, though; I needed space to think. But there was Olivia, sitting on her bed mere inches away from mine, determined to talk about the audition.

"You don't have to do it . . . I mean, I think you *should* do it, but you totally don't have to," she said.

"I think I do want to do it," I said slowly.

"You do?" said Olivia, her face lighting up like a slot machine.

"I mean, I want to be a singer. And it's not like another talent scout is going to randomly overhear me singing karaoke again."

"Yeah, that's for sure," she said.

What I didn't say was that I wanted to be a *famous* singer. Secretly, I hoped one day I'd perform in front of tens of thousands of people in a massive arena. But there was something kind of embarrassing about admitting that, even to Olivia. Fame was something that was supposed to just *happen* to you if you had enough talent; you weren't supposed to actually wish for it. That seemed way too vain.

Olivia flopped forward onto her stomach and cradled her chin in her hands. "So why do you seem like you don't want to do it?"

"I don't know. I guess I just look at myself, and then I look at the girls in those K-pop videos you watch, and I can't even imagine being on their level. They're so perfect. I mean, look at me, Liv." I squished my cheeks together. "I have a jillion zits. This is not the face of an idol."

"Yeah, but do you know how photoshopped everyone is?"

"Mmph," I grunted. "Not the point."

Olivia suddenly sat back up and grabbed her phone. "You know, you should really watch *Produce 101.*"

"What's that?"

"It's this K-pop competition show. A lot of the girls are pretty amateur when they first start out, but they train superhard, and by the end of the season, you can't even believe how much progress they've made."

Olivia was silent for a minute while she scrolled around, then she leaned over my bed and handed me her phone.

In the video, three extremely nervous-looking girls were standing in front of a panel of judges. The girls did this whole dance routine, then the judges graded them one by one. When one of them got a D, she looked like she was going to puke.

"Ugh, see, this is exactly what I don't want to go through." I tossed Olivia's phone onto her pillow and went to lie back on the bed with my hands under my head.

"But you didn't even see their transformation yet!" she pleaded.

"Maybe later. I don't think I can stomach watching that right now."

"You're going to have a huge advantage over everyone else, you know," she said. "I bet most of the people who show up next weekend won't have a personal invitation from a Top10 talent scout."

"Yeah, but as soon as they find out I'm America's Worst Dancer," I said, dragging my thumb across my neck, *"krrrcht."*

"Hello, have you ever heard of dance lessons? They can teach you how to dance."

"Can they teach me how to have a new body?" I asked.

"I mean, yeah, kinda. Besides, there are tons of idols who don't dance. Mostly idols do whatever they're best at. I'm sure the dancing part of the audition is just to see what you're capable of."

I rolled my head away from Olivia and let my eyes travel up the wall to the bulletin board hanging over my bed. The edge of the board was fringed with dozens of concert tickets: Adele, Janelle Monáe, Beyoncé, and a bunch of local bands from the Bay Area. Embarrassingly, there was even one from a One Direction show, my very first concert (you can't throw away the ticket from your first concert!). There're a million concert venues in the Bay Area, and my friends and I used to spend all our money on shows.

Sometimes, when I go to shows, I pretend it's me onstage. I'm the one singing for a crowd who knows all my lyrics by heart. I imagine that my backup dancers and musicians are as passionate about making music as I am, and we're so tight-knit that we can read one another onstage just by making eye contact. And then after the show, we're all hopped up on adrenaline, and we head backstage to celebrate our amazing set that we worked so hard on.

Pinned right in the center of my bulletin board were ticket stubs from the two times I saw Lady Gaga. I had saved all my babysitting money for those tickets; I even did some filing at my mom's office so I could afford seats that weren't in the nosebleed section. The funny thing was, at one of the shows, she'd had a K-pop girl group open for her. They were extremely talented and so fun to watch. Honestly, Olivia was right . . . if I could be in a group like that, I would be really happy performing K-pop.

"It's not like they think you're going to walk in as a fully formed superstar already."

"Huh?" I had spaced out while Olivia was talking.

"All I'm saying is that you don't have to blow their minds with your dance moves. You just have to do good enough to seem passable."

"Or maybe I'll suck so bad that everyone will gouge their eyes out, and then Top10 will have to shut down forever."

Olivia reached over to me and poked me right in the middle of my armpit.

"Hey!" I laughed, clamping my arms down.

"You're being annoying!"

"Oh, I'm sorry. Am I being annoying?"

"Yes!"

I rolled off my bed and pinned her to her mattress, tickling her in the place under her ribs where I know she's the most ticklish. Olivia tried to squirm away, but I was way too strong for her.

"Say I'm not being annoying!"

"You *are* being annoying! It's just a dumb audition!" She was giggling like a total maniac now.

"Say it! I'm not being annoying!"

"OK, OK! You're not being annoying!" she finally squealed.

I let go of her and slumped against the wall, and Olivia lay there with her arms and legs splayed out like Wile E. Coyote after falling off a cliff.

Olivia looked up at me and grinned. "So are you gonna do it or what?"

I sighed. There was no way she would ever lay off unless I said yes.

"Yeah . . ." I said, "I'll do it."

"Yesss."

[This page has been translated from Korean.]

12.17

CATEGORY: REVIEW

1XTRA's Comeback Video: "Mega Crush"

Do you remember when you were in middle school, and you would pick out an outfit and you'd get all excited to walk out of the house in it, but then your mother would take one look at you and make you change into something that *she* picked out? That, dear Readers, is what the members of 1XTRA look like in their latest music video—like their mothers dressed them.

Yes, 1XTRA's comeback music video was leaked to me today by an inside source that, for obvious reasons, I cannot name. The nine-member boy band has come full circle, from their motorcycle-themed bad-boy concept to this fresh travesty, a cute concept for their new single "Mega Crush." The video opens with the boys playing with toy dinosaurs on the floor of a playroom. Like round little toddlers, 1XTRA is dressed in pastel overalls and oversize sweatshirts, with cheeks as pink as a cherry blossom past its peak bloom. And then, through some random power of imagination, the boys shrink down to miniature, their toys come to life, and they're chased around the playroom by someone dressed in a low-budget dinosaur costume. Please, someone fetch me a paper bag—I might be sick.

Longtime readers know that I'm not a fan of male Aegyo (to say the least), so let us move past the visuals to the heart of the matter, shall we? If I played this music video on mute, I could have guessed the melody. The video opens with the sound that K-pop fans have become all too familiar with. You know that groan-inducing whine, a distorted vocal pitch that vaguely sounds like a dolphin? And it only gets fishier when the tropical house beat drops and the auto-tune kicks into overdrive. My dear Readers, I cannot go on. I've written this exact review so many times before, and I am tired. So, so tired.

KP Entertainment, please, do have a seat. You cannot simply give Hyun-ki jaw-reduction surgery, stick him in a pair of OshKosh B'goshes, throw on an overplayed dancehall beat, and call it a day. A modicum of creativity is expected. I suggest you return to your playroom and don't come out until you've grown up a little bit. And please, when you do, have an original idea in hand; 1XTRA fans all over the world will thank you for it.

+ V +

💬 COMMENTS

sad jaya
Hyun-ki got plastic surgery?!?! V, you can't just throw that in like a side note, you have to prepare a girl!!!

> **EXOBTS**
> He doesn't need plastic surgery, he is the bidam of the group

baekhyun babygirl
If V keeps leaking videos she's gonna get shut down one of these days . . . . . .

> **tinytiny**
> Unless she's working with the entertainment companies (o_O)

> **+ V +**
> Oh, honey, you're flailing. And your ignorance is showing.

> **Kwang-hee4Me**
> ㅋ ㅋ ㅋ ㅋ ㅋ ㅋ

Garmy
Is it just me who loves Aegyo concepts?

> **Oh_Hyun**
> I love them toooo! I also have a whole playlist of tropical house. People always complain about it but I can't get enough~~~~~~

Suga_Stan
Haven't even watched the video yet but I guarantee G2K's is better.

G-Power
Sneak-peek reviews are the besssst. How does she do it every time????

💬 **81 MORE COMMENTS>>**

Two

THE LINE WRAPPED ALMOST ENTIRELY AROUND
the building. It was so long the two ends almost touched, like that
snake that's eating its own tail. Before I even had a chance to gripe
about it, Olivia shoved me toward the back of the line.

On the subway ride over, Olivia explained that we weren't going
to the main Top10 Entertainment building, the one where girls
stake out the coffee shop across the street in hopes of spotting an
idol, the one with the sign so big that you can see it from the Seoul
Sky Observatory. That building was a few blocks away from where
we were now, next to the Cartier and Louis Vuitton storefronts on
the main strip in Gangnam.

Instead, we ended up in front of the Top10 Entertainment Star
Academy, the place where trainees and some of the younger idols
lived—and where all the Top10 artists rehearsed and recorded. It
was a four-story cream-colored building with caramel-tinted windows. It looked like any other luxury apartment building in the
neighborhood. You wouldn't have even noticed it if it weren't for
the snake of people wrapped around it. There wasn't even a sign
out front.

Olivia and I joined the back of the line and hunkered down for the long wait. It was one of those freakishly sunny winter days that seemed warm until the wind rudely reminded you that it was actually zero degrees outside. The whole line was shivering in their winter jackets as they peered up toward the front. There were hundreds and hundreds of girls, some with their parents, most looking like they were in middle or high school.

The few times I went to auditions back home, I tried out for singing parts in TV commercials. My voice coach was constantly pushing me to do it, even though I would inevitably be the youngest person at the tryout. It was so stressful going up against adults because I knew they had way more experience than me. Every time, I completely bombed and I never got a single callback. Now I stood out because I was the only foreigner in line. I might as well have been wearing a red, white, and blue clown wig and an American flag draped across my chest.

Of course Olivia had already started up a conversation with the girl standing in front of us. Turning back to me, she said, "Hey, did you see those tents when we walked up?"

"Yeah, why?"

"This girl says the people at the front of the line have been waiting since five a.m. yesterday morning. I guess they slept here last night—in the *snow*."

"Damn," I said as I shoved my mittened hands deeper into my jacket pockets.

The girl in front of us said something else in Korean that made Olivia frown.

"What's wrong?"

"Um. Nothing." Olivia shook her head.

"No, come on, it's something. Just tell me."

Olivia got up on her tiptoes to get a better view of the crowd. "So, since we're this far back in line, we're probably not going to make it in today."

"All right then!" I said, a wave of relief washing over me. "Let's get out of here before my extremities fall off."

"Um, no-o." Olivia crossed her arms tightly across her chest.

"Look, it's freezing out here, and it sounds like we're not getting in anyway. So let's just try again next year," I said.

I started backing out of our spot in line, but Olivia grabbed me by the front of my jacket and pulled me back in. "Come back here. I have an idea."

She fished around in her backpack and pulled out the crumpled Top10 business card.

"You kept that?" I asked.

Olivia didn't respond. She had that I'm-up-to-something expression. "Don't move," she said, then disappeared around the corner.

The girl in front of us asked me something in Korean, but I made a big show of shrugging. "English," I said. She nodded and turned to lean against the wall with her friend, while I took out my phone and started scrolling through Instagram.

It's not that I didn't want to be there. I just wanted to skip past the audition, past the part where Top10 would inevitably scrutinize the crap out of me, past the part where all the other people auditioning would compare themselves to me—and me to them—and shoot right to the part where I got to sing every day. But instead, here I was turning into an icicle, scrolling through pictures of my friends in California eating ice cream on the beach.

About ten minutes and a hundred or so selfies later, there was some commotion in the line. A huge man in a black suit and one of those walkie-talkie earpieces was walking right toward me, and people were pointing.

"Alice Choy?" he said.

"Uh-huh?" I said, nodding.

"Ijjok-euro oseyo."

Like a cuckoo in a clock, Olivia popped out from behind him. "He says to come with us!"

I stared at them, too shocked to move, until I noticed everyone gawking at me, probably wondering what the hell made *me* so special that Top10 would send this guy out to get me. I quickly shoved my phone back in my pocket and got out of line so I could follow the man toward the entrance.

"Oh my god, this is so embarrassing!" I whispered to Olivia.

"I kind of can't believe it actually worked!" she said gleefully. "He's going to let you cut in front of everyone!"

"Perfect. Now they're all going to hate me."

"They're going to hate you anyway when they hear you sing."

"Oh god, don't even say that."

When we got to the entrance, the man stretched his arm out in front of the girls who were first in line, pushing them back to make room for us. A security guard opened up the door at the main entrance and ushered us inside.

We stepped into a cavernous black-marble lobby. All along the walls, framed faces of Top10 idols gazed down at us in soft-focus like pictures of saints in a church. Down at the other end of lobby, four receptionists sat underneath a massive Top10 Entertainment logo, its magenta glow reflected off the black-marble walls and making the lobby look like the inside of a yawning mouth.

"Holy shit, Liv. You did it. We actually made it inside!" I said, wrapping my arm around her shoulders and drinking in the lobby. I didn't expect to feel so . . . awestruck, but there I was, struck as hell.

"No big deal," said Olivia. "We're only standing inside the academy of the biggest K-pop agency in the entire world. You know, just a totally normal day."

"That is definitely where we seem to have found ourselves."

"Do you know how many girls would die to be inside this building right now?" asked Olivia.

"I think we just cut in front of at least five hundred of them," I said.

"At least."

The man who brought us inside had disappeared, leaving us to fend for ourselves in a crush of people trying to check in at two registration tables. We picked one and got in line.

When we got to the front, a woman with a clipboard spoke to us and Olivia translated. The woman took down my personal information—my address and phone number—then handed me four safety pins and a coated piece of paper with the number 385 printed on it.

"That's your number. You have to pin it to the front of your shirt," explained Olivia. "They'll call it when it's your turn to audition."

After I was all checked in, the woman directed us to a marble corridor that veered off from the lobby. It was lined with framed album covers and tour posters for artists like Full Heart, G2K, and Soo-li.

Olivia stopped in front of a blown-up album cover with a blue frame. On it were five perfectly sculpted faces, each one wearing an old-fashioned top hat. It was MSB.

"Do you realize . . . ?" Olivia trailed off midsentence to stroke the photo of a boy wearing a monocle. "That we are currently in the same building as Joon Kwon right now? He could have walked down this same hallway like an hour ago. We could be breathing the same air as *Joon Kwon*."

"Liv, seriously, you sound like a deranged stalker."

Olivia's eyes had sort of glazed over, and she kept her hand pressed against the picture. "For Joon, I would drop out of school, denounce my family, and sell all my belongings."

"That seems a little drastic."

"You wouldn't understand unless you had an 'ultimate bias.'"

"All I understand is that you are bonkers. Come on, let's go," I said as I tugged on the back of her hood.

Olivia dropped her hand and sighed. "You know, *you* could be someone's ultimate bias someday."

"Let's see if I get through this audition first."

We walked through a pair of double doors that said SOUNDSTAGE and into a massive studio the size of a warehouse. It smelled like hot rubber and fresh paint. In one corner was a giant white backdrop lit up by dozens of spotlights. It looked like a blank movie set before they added any of the scenery or props.

At the edge of the stage, a group of important-looking men and women sat at a long row of tables.

"Those must be the judges," said Olivia, nodding at the tables.

"Ugh." I had somehow momentarily forgotten that there'd be judges, and now I didn't even want to look at them.

"Oh!" Olivia was pointing to the end of the table. "There's the woman from the noraebang!"

"OK, I see her." I pushed her hand down so she wouldn't draw attention to us, but actually, I was kind of relieved to see the woman.

At least there was one person here who knew I could sing. She was still wearing her Sony baseball cap, and she looked totally out of place next to all the suits sitting next to her.

We headed over to the side of the stage opposite the judges' panel, where auditionees were stretching and practicing dance steps. Seeing the girls without their winter hats and coats, I realized that most of them had their hair and makeup professionally styled. Some even had on cute little outfits like a leather jacket with ripped jeans or a frilly skirt with heels. It was like they were going for a certain look, like "the sexy one" or "the girl next door." I, on the other hand, was very unfortunately wearing my standard audition outfit: a white button-up tucked into black slacks, and a pair of scuffed running shoes for the dancing segment. If anyone asked, I guess I could say I was going for office-worker chic.

I grabbed Olivia's arm and we slinked to the very back of the group, where I hoped no one could see me while I pretended to stretch.

Eventually, a man walked to center stage and called out something in Korean. Everyone fell silent and took seats on the floor, and after some sort of announcement, the man started calling out numbers. Twenty or so girls stood up from the crowded floor and made their way over to the stage. I looked to Olivia, who shook her head—they hadn't called my number yet.

After the girls had organized themselves into two rows on the stage, a woman in a sports bra and leggings emerged from behind the judges' panel and started demonstrating choreography. First, she pointed the toes of her left foot out in front of her and sort of gyrated her hip around as she slid her hand up the side of her body. Then she thrust her hand forward and wagged her finger as if to say

"No, you don't." She sauntered forward a few steps, then jumped in the air, landing with both feet forward and her hands behind her neck, whipping her head side to side.

As she went along, she yelled out instructions until finally she said, "FIVE-SIX-SEVEN-EIGHT!" and all the girls snapped into action, dancing along with her. It was the only thing she ever said in English. It had never crossed my mind that this whole thing would be extra-difficult because I didn't speak Korean; I was just so used to having Olivia translate everything for me.

In other words, I was screwed.

"Liv," I whispered, leaning my head in close to hers.

"Yeah?"

"This looks impossible."

"It's not impossible! See, you're lucky, they only have a few minutes to memorize the routine, but you get to sit here and learn until it's your turn!"

Was it actually healthy for one human to be so optimistic? "*Lucky* is *not* the word I'd use to describe my current situation."

"Shh!" A very serious-looking mom who was massaging her daughter's calf shushed us.

"Sorry," I offered as the lady huffed and turned back around. Olivia crossed her eyes at the back of the lady's head, and I had to stifle a laugh.

The dance instructor went through five rounds of different combinations, while I sat there trying to memorize them. When she was done, she walked back to her seat behind the judges' panel, leaving the girls standing alone on the stage. Unlike the girls in the video that Olivia had shown me the week before, these girls looked confident as hell.

Suddenly, a bone-rattling beat exploded out of a stack of speakers hanging from the ceiling. Without missing a step, the girls danced out the choreography they had just learned. Then, just as abruptly as it had started, the music cut out and the dancers were left hanging in midstep—the song hadn't even played for a full minute.

The judges huddled together, and when they were done, the same man who had called the girls up to the stage stood and yelled out three numbers.

Three girls screamed, thrilled that they got to move on to the next round, but the rest looked utterly shattered. The unlucky ones trudged back over to our side of the stage, picking up their stuff to leave, some of them looking like they were about to burst into tears.

"Nope. I can't do this," I breathed at Olivia, "we gotta go."

"Wait, wait!" she begged.

I reached for my coat, but Olivia threw herself on top of it. The mom in front of us whipped around to shush us again.

I stood up and yanked at my jacket with both hands, ripping it free from under Olivia's body.

"Three eighty-five!" gasped Olivia.

"What?"

"He called your number. Three eighty-five!"

I was so busy freaking out that I had completely missed the guy call out another round of numbers, and now a new group of girls was making their way up to center stage. I looked down at Olivia in a panic.

"Alice, we came all this way," she said.

I shook my head, unable to speak.

"You have to at least *try*."

I could see something like disappointment starting to creep into Olivia's eyes, the light of her usual admiration dimming. Seeing that shadowed look on her face was somehow more unbearable than just sucking it up and getting the audition over with.

I let my jacket fall to the ground, tucked my hair behind my ears, and walked toward the stage. I joined the back row, making sure to stand behind the tallest girl for extra coverage. The girl directly to my left shot me a look that contestants on *RuPaul's Drag Race* get, right before they eviscerate their opponent in a lip-sync battle. This was not going to be pretty.

The lady in the leggings got up in front of us, and it was immediately clear I was in deeper trouble than I thought. She was teaching us entirely new choreography.

"FIVE-SIX-SEVEN-EIGHT!"

The whole group moved together with the instructor, except me, the girl who had inconveniently lost control of all her limbs. I could feel the girls next to me losing patience as I tried not to dance right into them.

"FIVE-SIX-SEVEN-EIGHT!"

We moved on to the second combination, and I instantly forgot the first one. By the time the instructor had shown us all five combinations, I was completely out of breath. She walked back to the judges' panel, and before I could get my breathing under control, the music blasted back on above our heads.

When I was a little girl, my mom got this gag book for her birthday that had step-by-step instructions for surviving extreme situations like an avalanche or a circling shark. I've always remembered the page about escaping quicksand because the instructions seemed so counterintuitive. When you're sinking into a pit of quicksand, your instinct is to struggle, but the more you try to dig yourself out, the faster you sink into the pit. That's exactly what I felt like now.

I desperately tried to keep up with the rest of the group, but the harder I tried, the faster I fell behind. When I kicked my leg up, everyone else had moved on to waving their arms above their heads. But when I put my arms up, they were already on the ground with their feet in the air. I had no clue what my feet were even *doing* most of the time.

The book says you're supposed to stay calm and make very "slow and deliberate" movements. But that seemed like terrible advice right now, and how the hell are you supposed to stay calm when you're sinking into a literal pit of quicksand anyway?

By the time the music stopped, my shirt was pasted to my back by the cold sweat of sheer and utter panic. I bent over, trying to catch my breath, while the other girls stood frozen, their eyes glued to the judges' panel.

The judges huddled again, then the man stood up and called out a single, lonely number. The lip-sync queen next to me screamed.

Of course she was the one who made it through. I sighed and looked over at her, but her face was buried in her hands. She was sobbing. She had screamed because the man *hadn't* called her number.

Hopefully, I looked back at Olivia, but I could tell by her expression that he hadn't called mine, either. I couldn't help it; even though I knew I had bungled the entire thing (and that was putting it mildly), I was still disappointed.

I dragged myself back to Olivia, ready to get as far away as possible from this studio of broken dreams. Olivia got up off the ground and tugged gently on the edge of my sleeve. "Sorry," she whispered.

"No biggie," I said, trying to muster up a smile for her. "Let's just get outta here."

I bent down to pick up my jacket, and a familiar voice started speaking to the room. When I looked up, I saw it was the woman from the noraebang. Her announcement was short, and when she finished, Olivia was practically vibrating.

"Alice, oh my god, she says you can stay!"

"Wait, what? Are you serious?"

"Yes! She wants you to sing!"

I looked over toward the judges. The entire studio was staring at me, including the shushy mom, who was frowning so hard her mouth looked like it would fall to the floor.

"I knew it, I knew it!" whispered Olivia.

"It's just . . . I don't believe it."

"I *told* you they were going to let you sing!"

"I just can't believe they're going to let me stay after . . . whatever the hell that was." I waved my hand vaguely at the stage.

"I don't think it was as bad as you think."

"Oh, I'm pretty sure I was," I said, relieved to see her looking at me with her usual approval again. I could have done the running man for five straight minutes, and Olivia still would have thought I did a good job.

I pulled my wet shirt away from my sticky skin and sat there for a second, letting myself feel excited all over again. After my debacle of a dance audition, I really wanted the judges to know that I was good enough to be there. The thought was like a hard little corn kernel in my popcorn nerves.

My shirt eventually dried out as we sat through hours and hours of dance auditions. We watched the daughter of the shushing mom perform and then get dismissed, and her mom grabbed her by the back of her arm and dragged her out the door like she was the world's biggest disappointment. When the dance segment of the auditions was over, there were fewer than forty of us left.

We broke for lunch, and Olivia and I ran to an Angel-in-us Coffee a few blocks away and wolfed down a few tiny egg sandwiches. Then we sprinted back to the soundstage, where we sat back down to wait for my turn. One by one, the girls around me were called up to the stage to sing, but this time, no one was dismissed. We all had to wait until the end to find out if we could go on to the next round.

Finally, my number was called. I squeezed Olivia's hand for good luck, then grabbed my thumb drive with my music on it and walked up to the stage.

After handing over my drive, I stepped back into the ring of lights and bowed toward the judges, just like I had seen the other girls do.

"My name is Alice Choy, and I'm going to sing 'Million Reasons' by Lady Gaga," I announced in English (because I had no idea how to say "Million Reasons" in Korean). I straightened my back, smoothed my shirt, and unfocused my eyes. Then I nodded at the man with my thumb drive, and that familiar piano chord swelled into the soundstage.

A few verses in, the hard corn kernel that appeared after my dance audition rose into my chest and I focused in on it. I had complete control over my body now, and my voice came out clear and strong, just the way I meant it to. By the first chorus, I was traveling with my voice, ricocheting off the walls and reverberating through all the bodies in the room. I didn't need to hide behind anyone anymore; I wanted the judges to see me, so I locked eyes with them. By the end of the song, all my popcorn anxieties had un-popped, as if the mean mom who shushed us, my lame outfit, and my quicksand dancing were all settled back down at the bottom of my stomach.

No one clapped or anything when I finished, but the woman from the noraebang smiled at me. I returned to my seat on the floor next to Olivia and couldn't help but kiss her right on the top of her head.

She grabbed me back hard. "It was so, so good. You seriously blew everyone away."

"I felt really good up there, Liv. I think that was the best I've ever sang it." My adrenaline was back in a big way, and I could feel it radiating off of me like waves of electricity.

"I thought the same thing! The judges looked so impressed the whole time."

"God, I really hope so."

There were only a few people left to audition after me, then the judges got up and exited through a door on the other side of the stage. The room was wound tighter than it had been all day. No one really spoke, and we all kept looking anxiously at the door that led to who knows where.

It was almost a full hour until the door swung back open, and a new guy who hadn't been on the judges' panel walked out. He sauntered over to the row of tables and dropped down into the first available seat without ever lifting his eyes from his phone. He was wearing these weird half-moon glasses with tangerine-tinted lenses, and he looked less than thrilled to be there. When the rest of the judges came out behind him, it sort of seemed like they were trying to avoid him.

Once everyone was seated, the guy who had made all the announcements stood up, and Olivia and I grabbed each other's hands.

"Alice Choy ssi malgo-neun modu dolagasyeo-do josseumnida."

He said my name.

He said my name.

I clamped both my hands over my mouth in disbelief. Olivia shrieked and grabbed me around the waist, hugging me tight. I didn't even care that we were laughing like we had just won the lottery.

"What did he say?" I whispered.

"He said everyone else is excused except for you!"

"Holy shit . . ."

Slowly, the others around us picked up their stuff and shuffled toward the exit. They were like deflated parade floats, all drooping and sagging, as they limped out of the room. I wanted to feel guilty, but I just couldn't; I was soaring.

After everyone else had left, the judges motioned me up to their table.

"Alice Choy, it is a pleasure to meet you," said a woman in a maroon blazer. Her hair was swept up into an elegant knot, and her lipstick was exactly the color of her blouse. "My name is Jackie Kim, and I oversee the girls' wing of Top10 Entertainment's residence for trainees and idols. Many of the English-speaking residents call me Miss Jackie." She extended a hand with long red fingernails so glossy that they looked wet.

"Nice to meet you," I said, shaking her hand.

I continued down the row of judges, exchanging handshakes as I went. The woman from the noraebang cupped my hand in between her palms and said, "Good job, Alice Choy." She had a kind of squinty, wistful expression, like the one my mom gets when she's really proud of me.

When I reached the end of the table, Miss Jackie introduced the man with the orange glasses, who was still busy on his phone. "And this is Kim Sungmin, or Mr. Kim. He is Top10 Entertainment's founder and CEO." Mr. Kim offered me a limp hand and a grunt, then returned to his texting.

"Please, tell us, where are you from?" asked Miss Jackie.

"I'm from California."

"Northern or Southern?"

"San Francisco."

"And do you speak any Korean?"

I looked down at my scuffed-up shoes. "Um, no, not much."

Miss Jackie smiled tightly. "That is quite all right. Language can be taught, stage presence cannot. I take it you've had several years of voice training, yes?"

"Yes," I said, lifting my eyes back up to meet hers. "I've been taking voice lessons since I was about eight. I was also in a chorus back home."

"Alice, I am going to cut to the chase," said Miss Jackie. "You have a singular voice the likes of which this panel only encounters once or twice in a career."

I stood completely still, trying not to blink, for fear of missing even one syllable of what she was saying.

"However, to be perfectly frank . . ."

Uh-oh, here it comes, the dancing.

"Your dancing is subpar."

Shit. I knew the dancing would screw me. I could almost see the wavy lines forming as the dream sequence melted back into reality.

"We are searching for the fifth and final member of a debut girl group, and the hope was that she would be a capable singer *and* dancer." Miss Jackie paused to consider me, pursing her maroon lips. "However . . ."

Oh, thank god, there was a "however."

"It would be foolish not to accept you into the program considering your immense singing talent. I have seen dancers in similar shape rise to our standards with the proper training, but to meet the level of excellence we require of our idols, you would have to commit to a rigorous dance-training schedule. Is this something you would be willing to do?"

"Yes! Yes, I am." I was so relieved they were still considering me that I probably would have agreed to tattoo *Top10 Entertainment* on my forehead.

"Very good. We spent some time deliberating on the matter, and we are confident that under our instruction you have the potential to become one of Top10 Entertainment's brightest stars."

I hadn't moved, I hadn't blinked, and now I wasn't breathing. I could see the woman from the noraebang out of the corner of my eye, and she was leaning forward, nodding in agreement.

"Thus, we are prepared to offer you an artist contract," said Miss Jackie.

"Oh, thank you . . . thank you so much!" I gasped.

This was one of those instant-classic moments in life, the kind you tell your grandkids about and they say, "We know, Grandma, you've told us a million times already." I couldn't see Olivia from where I was standing, but it was so amazing that she could have this memory, too.

"As you know, Top10's Star Academy is an elite training center where only the dedicated succeed," continued Miss Jackie. "Only a fraction of our trainees debut, and then only a fraction of those become idols."

"I understand," I replied. The soles of my feet were practically hovering off the ground. "It's enough just to know that I'll be able to train with your voice teachers."

"Becoming a Top10 idol can change the trajectory of your life." Miss Jackie placed her folded hands on the table in front of her. "But make no mistake, the life of a trainee demands huge sacrifices. As such, we recommend you take some time to consider our offer and to review the terms of our contract."

She nodded to a woman sitting next to her, who handed me a thick stack of paper with a black business card paper-clipped to the top page. I took it from her delicately as if she were handing me my own beating heart.

"That is a generic contract and my business card. If you and your parents approve of the terms, our lawyers will draft a personalized contract, and once signed, you will move into the Star Academy immediately."

"Thank you again. Really," I whispered. I stood there in front of them holding the contract tight to my chest; the weight of it seemed to be the only thing keeping me tied to planet Earth.

"So where is this star center thingy again?" Dad pushed his glasses higher up on his nose as he squinted into his laptop screen.

"It's called the Star Academy and it's in Gangnam," I answered.

We were all sitting around the kitchen table, scraping out the last of the food from takeout boxes onto our plates. It was snowing again, and big flakes danced around in the white city lights outside our kitchen window.

"Oh, that neighborhood is so enviable. If we had a few extra million dollars lying around, I'd buy one of those gorgeous modern homes," said Mom to no one in particular. She had her head down as she leafed through the Top10 contract. The muscles in her jaw tensed and un-tensed as she pored over the legalese.

"Maybe when Alice gets rich and famous she'll buy us one," said Olivia.

"I'm going to buy you a whole block of houses when I'm rich and famous!" I declared. Ever since we left the auditions, I'd been in the best mood. All my anxiety and hesitation had melted away, and now I was floating in some kind of glittery dreamland. The way everything had happened—being discovered, landing a contract—it felt a little bit like destiny.

"HOW YOU GONNA GET ME, BOOOY?"

Dad's laptop abruptly sprang to life. We all jumped except for Mom, who was too focused on the contract.

"Ah! Sorry, sorry!" Dad banged frantically at his keyboard until the sound dropped down to a listenable volume.

"HUH-UH. HUH-UH. HOW YOU GONNA GET ME?"

"Oh my god, Dad! Are you watching an XOKiss music video?" squealed Olivia.

"Well, I'm trying to."

"You can't watch that. That's, like, way too weird for me to handle," said Olivia.

"I'm just trying to see what kind of musicians this company represents," said Dad.

"They're not *musicians*. They're *idols*," she corrected.

"Well, I'm trying to see what kind of *idols* this company represents." Dad turned back to the video and his face soured. "I don't know, Al, this is some pretty provocative stuff."

"Ew, Dad, stop!" cried Olivia.

He tapped the space bar and the music quit. "These girls are what, seventeen, eighteen years old? And they're prancing around with half their bodies exposed, doing all these sexy dance moves."

Olivia slapped her hands over her ears, letting her metal chopsticks clatter onto her plate. "Dad, gross! Please stop talking!"

"It just doesn't seem very much like *you*, Al. That's all I'm trying to say."

"I know I'm not really the prancing type," I admitted as I traced a spiral on my plate with a chopstick. "And I was worried about that stuff, too, at first. But this is a really huge opportunity, Dad. I don't mind making a couple compromises if it means I get to focus on my art full-time."

"It's more than just a couple compromises, don't you think?" pressed Dad.

"Yeah, maybe. I don't know; they're not *all* prancers. And the more I think about it, the more I'm realizing that being an idol isn't *that* different from my dream. I mean, there are so many incredible K-pop singers."

"That's true, Dad," said Olivia knowingly.

Before I had a chance to say any more, Mom emerged from the thick stack of papers. "Alice, honey?" she said, switching into the voice she normally only used at work. "Have you actually read this? This contract is binding for six years. This can't be right."

"I know about this," said Olivia matter-of-factly. "Six years isn't even that long; some idols are under contract for, like, ten or twelve years."

I kicked Olivia's leg under the table. Mom had been poking holes in the contract ever since she cracked it open, and I didn't need any extra input from the peanut gallery. "I'm not really worried about it, Mom," I said as nonchalantly as I could. "I think it's a good sign Top10 wants to commit to me for so long; it means they believe in me."

Mom shot Dad a look that said "Can you back me up here?"

"Mom's right, Al," Dad said. "Six years is a long, long time. There's a very good possibility Mom could get reassigned in that time, and we could all move back to the US. In six years, you might be a completely different person. Heck, you might not even *want* to sing anymore by the time you're—what? Twenty-*three?*"

"OK, of all the futures you just made up, me not wanting to sing anymore is the least likely," I said. "Besides, if you think about it, college usually takes four years; this is only two years longer."

"Speaking of college . . ." said Mom as she licked her finger and peeled back another page in the contract. "Have you thought about that at all? How are you going to attend college if you're training full-time?"

"I don't know . . ." I said, pushing my empty plate to the middle of the table. I knew what I was about to say next might freak my parents out a little. "Maybe now I don't have to go to college."

Mom and Dad raised their eyebrows at each other in surprise. "Oh, now you don't want to go to college?" asked Dad.

"I mean, it's not like I've thought this all the way through or anything. It's just that I was planning to study voice and music theory in college anyway. So now that Top10 wants to train me . . . doesn't college seem like kind of a waste of money?"

Mom placed the contract on the kitchen table seriously. "Alice, college is *not* a waste of money. College is where you learn to think critically and figure out how to navigate the world as an adult."

"What makes you think I can't learn those things at the Star Academy?" I argued.

"I'm sorry, but singing and dancing lessons are no replacement for a strong liberal arts education. You really need to think about what you're saying here." This was the worst part about talking to my mom, the diplomat—she always had to walk through every single possible scenario until she was satisfied; she could never just let me dream about something. This contract *was* a really big commitment, but why couldn't she just trust, for once, that I knew what I was doing?

"I *am* thinking seriously," I argued. The glittery dreamland I'd been living in all afternoon was starting to fade away. "This could be a huge leg up for my singing career. The rest of it I can figure out when I get there."

"That's not good enough, Alice," said Mom, her voice rising. "This isn't something that you can just make up as you go along. We're talking about the next six years of your life here."

DING-DONG.

"Who's *that?*" asked Olivia.

"I don't know, but it's pretty late at night for a visitor," said Dad, his eyebrows raised. He walked over to the little screen that showed who was at the door and peered into it. "It looks like a little old lady."

Olivia and I jumped up from the table and ran over to look at the screen. "That's the woman from Top10!" said Olivia.

"What's she doing here?" Dad asked me.

"I have no idea," I said.

"Well, we can't just let her stand out there in the snow." Dad pushed the button on the screen, and we watched her walk through the building's front door. About four minutes later, there was a loud knock, and the four of us crowded around the front door.

"Ah, Alice, la bonne étoile!" said the woman when I opened the door. "And the little sister."

"Hi!" said Olivia.

The lady dumped her wet jacket into my arms and took her shoes off, then walked into the apartment like she'd been there a million times. Bowing deeply to Mom and Dad, she said, "Hello, I am So-ri Tae. I am from Top10 Entertainment; I find your daughter. I am here to make sure she comes to study with me. Where we can talk?"

Mom and Dad, looking kind of flabbergasted, introduced themselves and led her into the living room.

"I'm sorry," said Mom once we were all sitting down, "but what did you say that you do at the company?"

"I am head voice teacher," replied So-ri, grinning right at me. I blinked and turned to Olivia, who looked just as shocked as I felt. I never in a million years would have guessed that she was a voice teacher. She was just so . . . *old*.

"So! Tell me how you are thinking," said So-ri, folding her hands into her lap.

Mom chimed in first. "To be perfectly frank, we're very worried about this contract."

"We're not worried," I said, trying to soften Mom's response. "I think my parents just have some questions."

"Ohh. Yes, this contract very strict," So-ri agreed knowingly. "Please, I answer all your questions."

"Well, one of our main concerns is that Alice very recently transferred to a new school. It was difficult finding a place for the girls on such short notice, and she is only a year and a half away from graduating high school—we don't want to interrupt her education again." Mom glanced at me before continuing. "And we'd very much like her to attend college when she's finished."

"Aha! But she can get her diploma while she trains with us. We have excellent tutors who instruct in English, and students at the academy study with them five hours every day," said So-ri. "And she will speak very good Korean when she is done."

I looked at Mom's face again to see if that satisfied her, but it was clear it didn't. "But that doesn't address our concerns about the length of this contract. I don't see how we could ever commit her to six years. We might have to go back to the States in the next few years. We can't just leave her here."

I snapped my eyes back to So-ri, afraid that all of Mom's worries would scare her away and she'd take my contract with her.

"Two years, then. Done. Any other questions?" So-ri looked around at us expectantly, still smiling.

"I'm sorry, but are you able to make that decision?" asked Mom doubtfully.

"Mmm," hummed So-ri, like she knew it was time to get a little more serious about the whole thing. "Top10 does not take students without my approval. I decide who is up to our singing standards, and I will make sure they make such a change to her contract."

Now it was Dad's turn to question her. "Can I just ask . . . you came all the way over here tonight, and you're willing to significantly change the terms of this contract. I know my daughter is an excellent singer, but why are you willing to do all this for her?"

So-ri paused to think about it, tapping her knobby thumbs against each other. "When I hear your daughter singing, I know she have a very special voice, and I know right away I want to be her teacher. She have a gift . . . Students like her is *why* I teach. I don't care for how long. If I only get to have Alice for two years," she said, shrugging, "that is enough."

"We appreciate that, but still," said Dad, hesitating, "even at two years, this seems like a really huge commitment."

"Mom, Dad," I said, clasping my hands and turning to face them. "We came all the way to Seoul so Mom could work at the consulate here." Mom put her hands up to interrupt, but I pushed on. "I know that we talked about it as a family, and we decided to do this together, but we had to sacrifice a ton. Dad had to put his career on hold and might not get back to work for a long time because of all the visa stuff. Olivia and I had to start all over again at a brand-new school, and I had to give up the voice teacher that I'd been working with my whole life."

"Alice," said Mom, her eyes darting uncomfortably to So-ri then back to me. "We've talked about this. A lot. I am very aware of and grateful for all the sacrifices you each have had to make, but . . ."

"My point isn't that you owe me this," I interrupted. "What I'm trying to say is that I have a dream, too. I've wanted to be a singer since before I can even remember. I know we didn't expect it to happen this way, but my chance to do something literally just knocked on our door."

Mom shook her head, but I could tell that something I said had gotten through to her. "I don't know, Alice . . . There's a lot we need to think through; we just found out about this today."

"Mom," I said, placing my hand on top of hers, "this is the first thing I've asked for since we moved here. It's only two years; you have to let me at least *try*. Please."

Mom looked up at Dad, and they did that parent-to-parent telepathy thing. Sighing, she turned her palm up and laced her fingers with mine.

"Alice, do you really want this? I mean, do you *really* want to do this?"

"Yes, Mom. I really want this."

She looked at Dad again and he nodded.

"OK, then . . . If this is what you truly want, we'll help you do it."

"Thank you," I said, practically whispering. "I love you."

"I love you, too," she said, her voice breaking. My tough, diplomat mother was fighting back tears.

[This page has been translated from Korean.]

12.19

CATEGORY: RUMOR MILL

Top10 Entertainment Auditions Rundown

Today was one of the most competitive days of the year. And no, I'm not referring to the annual Suneung exams. I'm, of course, referring to Top10 Entertainment's winter "cryouts," the company's cutthroat auditions for poor souls possessing infinite dreams and zero chances. Early yesterday morning, frigid wannabes began lining up in the snow for the girls' audition segment, only to await their disappointment. Sources tell me the line wrapped around the entire perimeter of the Star Academy like icing on a funeral cake.

Of the thousand or so snow bunnies, less than a quarter passed through Top10's hallowed front doors. These lucky few were ushered into Top10's soundstage, where such music videos as MSB's "W1NNA" and Full Heart's "More than Us" were shot. The hopefuls were allowed less than five measly minutes of surprise choreography and—*if* they survived—one song of their choosing in front of some of the world's most discerning talent scouts. By the end of the day, the masses were whittled down to one. That's right, my Lovelies, no need to rub your eyes, you read that right. Out of hundreds of hopefuls, Top10 only anointed a single chosen one. (Kisses to @sad_jaya for the inside scoop.)

There are oh so many questions, dear Readers, oh so many. Where will this newest addition to the Top10 family be placed—that is, of course, if she ever debuts? As a new member of an existing girl group? As a member of a yet unknown rookie group? Or does she possess the oh-so-rare star power to become the next Top10 solo artist?

We shall see . . . And until then, bundle up, snow bunnies.

+ V +

💬 COMMENTS ═══════════════════════════════════

Chingutie
These auditions are so BRUTALLL!!! I could never do it.

....

23444219
God, who would sleep in the snow just to become a pawn of the entertainment companies?

....

^1XTRA^
I waited in line but I never made it inside πΔπ

> **Mina-Moo**
> Omg, me toooooo. Will you try again in the summer?

> **^1XTRA^**
> Yeah, definitely, but I'm going to get there a lot earlier next time.

Hallyu_VIP

I honestly don't understand the Top10 audition process. They never sign anyone from open auditions, why don't they just stick to working with the modeling agencies? That's how they find most of their talent anyway.

> **+ V +**
>
> I ask myself the same question every year. But apparently this baby trainee has proven us both wrong.

Kwanghee21

F@&k the chosen one. I'm the chosen one!!! ㅋㅋㅋㅋㅋㅋ

 **87 MORE COMMENTS>>**

Three

"IF YOU TALK TO CHINJEOL FROM MSB, MAKE SURE
you don't mention his brother. They're not talking anymore."

"OK, got it."

"Oh, and Eun-jin is obsessed with planets and constellations
and stuff like that. So if you can bring up outer space or something,
she'd be really into it."

"It's hard to imagine that coming up naturally in conversation."

Olivia, my parents, and I were in a rental car, on our way to the
Star Academy. It was all happening so fast, like time and space had
collapsed, and things were moving at light speed.

"Oh yeah! And Soo-li is deathly allergic to strawberries, so don't
get near her with them."

"Don't throw strawberries at Soo-li. Check."

"Alice, food allergies are a matter of life or death!" Olivia looked
at me with this dead-serious expression.

"OK, OK, I know," I said, laughing. "I'm only kidding."

In the three weeks since I officially signed with Top10, Olivia had
transformed into the Wikipedia of K-pop. She incessantly listed off
random facts about Top10 idols, and I knew so much about MSB

that I felt like a secondhand stalker. It was kind of a nice distraction, though. Ever since I woke up this morning, I had that scattered feeling, the one where you start walking across the room to do something, but on the way there your brain vomits up so many new thoughts that you completely forget why you started walking in the first place. I felt like a giant ball of excitement and anxiety all rolled together.

"All right, Olivia," said Dad, who was sitting shotgun. "I'd like to have a turn with my firstborn daughter before she's officially out of my charge." He turned toward me in his seat with this kind of mushy, sentimental look in his eyes. The last time I'd seem him like this was at my middle school graduation.

"Dad, what?" I half laughed.

"I just want to say that I can't believe this day has come. I always imagined that one day we'd drop you off at some big college campus, but this seems much more fitting for you—a music academy!"

"Aw, Dad, that's really nice." Hearing him say it like that—*a music academy*—made me feel excited all over again.

"I'm going to miss you, daughter o' mine. I know you've been helping out around the house a lot and taking care of your sister since we moved here. You've really made the transition to Korea so much easier on your mom and me. I'm just . . . really proud of you." A couple tears rolled out of Dad's eyes, which made me feel like I was going to tear up, too.

"Thanks, Dad. I'm gonna miss you guys, too," I said.

We pulled up to the academy's underground parking garage, and a security guard opened the electric gate and waved us through. Mom parked near the elevators and turned the engine off, and the car went quiet.

"Alice," said Mom seriously, "we really are proud of you. And we will *be* proud of you, no matter what."

"What do you mean, 'no matter what'?" I asked.

"This is a very competitive world you're about to step into, honey. You're going to train with some of the most successful singers and dancers in the country, which means you might not be the most talented student there. And that's OK; you never have to beat yourself up about that. And if at any point you feel like it's not the place for you, it's OK if you want to come home."

"It's my first day here, Mom. I haven't even walked in the door yet. I don't really want to think about failing right now."

"That's not what I'm saying, Alice," she said. "Coming home would not be a failure, not at all. I'm saying you never have to feel like you're stuck in a situation that you don't want to be in, contract or no. I just want you to know that we're always here for you." She put her hand on my knee tentatively.

"I know you are," I mumbled.

"And your dad is right—we're going to miss you so much."

"You too."

She rubbed my knee with her thumb. "Well . . . are you ready to go?"

"Yes," I said. "Very."

We all piled out into the cold and huddled around the trunk to watch Dad pull out my two suitcases. "You want help getting these inside, Al?"

"No, I got it. It's really not that much stuff." Mostly, though, I just didn't want to do the whole farewell pageant in front of anyone at the academy.

Suddenly, a whimper came from Olivia's direction. We turned

to look at her, and her face was all red and splotchy. She had been crying silently to herself, and I hadn't even noticed.

"Hey, come here." I pulled her in for a hug and she pressed her soggy face into my chest. Her little head fit right into the hollow spot in my sternum, like two interlocking puzzle pieces. As she sobbed, I started to cry, too. I knew this moment was coming, when I'd have to say goodbye to her, but it was still so painful. Part of it was because I was scared to walk into a brand-new school in a foreign country without her. But more than that, in Seoul, Olivia was my best friend, and I was about to leave her behind.

"Don't go!" she cried, her hands kneading into my puffy jacket.

"This was your idea in the first place," I teased gently, trying to regain my composure.

"I know, but I was wrong. I take it all back."

"What are you talking about?"

"It's just . . . I'm never going to see you anymore!" she sobbed.

"That's not true," I said, squeezing her tighter. "I'll be home in a few months for Children's Day."

That made her cry even harder. "A few months is *forever!*"

"No-o," I said. "I promise it'll go by so fast you won't even notice I'm gone."

Though, in the history of us being sisters, which was basically most of my life, a few months *was* kind of like forever. The longest Olivia and I had ever been apart from each other was when I went to performing arts camp one summer, and that was only for, like, fifteen days. I actually had no idea what it would be like to be away from her for longer than a couple weeks.

"You're going to meet all these new people and make all these new cool friends, and I'm just going be stuck at home all by myself," she said.

"Liv, come on, you make new friends in your sleep. You make friends with people who don't even like having friends!"

"That's not the same thing," she cried.

"Hey," I said, bending my knees a little so I was at her level. "I was being serious, you know, when I said this was all your idea. I owe this all to you."

"Really?" she sniffed.

"Yeah, really."

Olivia calmed down a little, and when she finally stopped crying, I wiped her cheeks with my jacket sleeve.

"You have to promise to text me every single night before you go to bed," she said, sniffling.

"I promise to text you every night. And multiple times a day."

"And you have to promise to Snap me every time you see an idol."

"That seems like a little much, but I'll try."

"And promise you'll dedicate your first solo album to me."

"I mean, obviously. Who else would I dedicate it to?" I framed an invisible picture with my hands. "'To my little sister, Olivia.'"

Her face twitched like she was going start crying again, but instead she collapsed back into me for one more hug. Mom and Dad wrapped their arms around us so our heads were all smashed together. I could feel Dad's glasses dig into my temple, but I didn't care; I needed this.

As we stood there holding on to one another in the cold, an elevator door scraped open and the staccato click of high heels tapped toward us. It was Miss Jackie, flanked by two men in gray suits.

I let go of Olivia and wormed my way out of my parent's arms to grab my suitcases. We finished up our goodbyes, then one of the gray suits took the suitcases out of my hands.

The three of them packed themselves back into the rental car, and Olivia immediately rolled her window down.

"Love you!" she called out.

"You too," I said, waving.

When the car had disappeared, a hand dropped onto my shoulder; I could feel how cold it was, even through my thick parka.

"Come," said Miss Jackie. "Time to meet your new family."

We rode the elevator up two floors, and the doors slid open to reveal a room that made the marble lobby beneath it seem like it was from an entirely different building. It was bright and sunny—and full of modern furniture in soft pastels. Kids my age were scattered around the place, reading at one of the little study areas or hanging out on couches. There was a big bulletin board next to the elevators, collaged with newspaper and magazine clippings featuring the faces of Top10 idols. It was just like a dorm from one of the college brochures that started showing up in the mail my sophomore year, except the kids here were some of the most famous people in the world.

"Boots off, please," said Miss Jackie, gesturing to a row of shelves stuffed with shoes and house slippers. I pulled off my winter boots and replaced them with a pair of terry cloth slippers. "This way," she said.

With a flick of her fingers, Miss Jackie sent the two men off to deliver my suitcases as she led me farther into the building.

"As the head of the girls' wing, it is my responsibility to ensure that every girl at the academy measures up to Top10's standards. You will have many teachers while you are here, but my job is to oversee your orientation and training. I will keep an eye on your progress in your dance and voice training, your education, and your fitness and diet."

We walked into a sort of indoor courtyard, where three wide doors opened onto a busy cafeteria. "That is the cafeteria, where you will take all three of your daily meals. Like in every home, the kitchen is the heart of the Star Academy, and the dormitories sit on either side of it, boys on the left and girls on the right."

Two hallways shot off from the courtyard and cafeteria. The left one was painted baby blue and the other was peach, like the colors in a hospital nursery.

"You will be expected to follow all the rules at the academy, but perhaps our most uncompromising is that you are never to visit the boys' dormitory. And you are *never*, under any circumstance, to fraternize with boys alone. That goes especially for boys outside the academy."

I couldn't imagine any of the boys at the academy, or any other idol for that matter, wanting to "fraternize" with me, but I nodded anyway.

"It goes without saying that we do not permit drugs and alcohol on campus. Any trainee caught with such items will be disciplined— or worse." Miss Jackie shot me a look to make sure I was paying attention, so I nodded again. "The soundstage, wardrobe room, and styling studios on the first floor are off-limits to students without permission. You are, however, permitted to leave campus on week-ends and in the evenings after your lessons. But you must check in with the security guard in the garage as you come and go. Curfew is ten p.m. sharp. If you miss curfew once, your off-campus privileges will be revoked for thirty days."

A squeal erupted from somewhere above us. It got closer and closer until a girl wearing a preppy white sweater and a pink skirt burst from a stairwell nearby. She skidded to a stop in front of us and proceeded to bow over and over, making her corkscrew ponytail bounce up and down like a yo-yo.

"An-nyeong-ha-se-yooooo!" Her voice was so high-pitched it was hard to believe it came from a human.

"This is So-hyun Song. She is late," announced Miss Jackie in an annoyed tone. "So-hyun began training at the Star Academy when she was fourteen. Now she is a member of XOKiss."

When So-hyun's head popped up from her bowing, I realized that I recognized her. Olivia explained to me that she's XOKiss's maknae, which means she's the youngest member and kind of like the baby of the group. My first celebrity sighting—Olivia would lose her mind.

"It's so nice to meet youuuu!" So-hyun said in perfect English. She grabbed my right hand, shaking it and smiling so wide I could see almost every single one of her teeth.

"Nice to meet you, too," I said, trying to get my hand back from her.

"And how old are *you?*"

Kids in Korea were always asking how old you were. They did it because there was a whole different vocabulary you were supposed to use, depending on whether someone was older or younger than you.

"I'm seventeen," I said.

"Oh, me too!" she squeaked, putting both her hands to her mouth in surprise. It was hard to believe she was my age; she acted like she was even younger than Olivia. "My birthday is in April. When is yours?" she asked.

"Um, I just had mine, in December."

"Oh my gosh!" she gasped. "Happy recent birthday then, Alice!"

Miss Jackie placed her hand on So-hyun's shoulder as if she was trying to reign her back in. "Even though So-hyun has already debuted, she is not of age yet, so she still resides at the academy. And since she is currently in between albums, she has the time in her schedule to be your guide during your first weeks at the academy. You can think of her as a big sister. You should consider yourself very fortunate, Alice."

So-hyun clasped her hands together as if Miss Jackie had just said she was getting a new puppy. "I cannot wait to get to know all about youuu!" she sang.

"You, too," I said politely.

So-hyun was . . . a lot. I like to think of people as having a specific volume, not like how loud they are, but more like how much they're turned up personality-wise. My volume is usually around a four or a five, and Olivia is usually a seven or an eight, but So-hyun seemed like she was completely off the scale; she was turned all the way up to twenty.

"So-hyun," said Miss Jackie, "please take Alice around the campus and show her which areas are off-limits. And be sure to return her to her dormitory at five p.m. sharp." Turning to me, she continued, "Alice, you will meet the four other trainees in your group then, the same girls you'll be dorming with." Miss Jackie made a quick bow, then click-clacked back to the elevator.

"So," said a raspy voice. "Welcome to Hell Academy."

I looked around, but there was only So-hyun. Her cheesy grin had disappeared, and she stood there with her hands on her hips.

"Um, I'm sorry . . . What did you just say?"

So-hyun doubled over cackling. "Oh my god, I'm totally kidding! I just thought it would be a super-dramatic thing to say."

I shook my head as if I was somehow hallucinating the change in her voice. "Your voice . . . What happened?"

"Oh, *that*? Girl, that was just my stage voice! You didn't think I actually talked all high-pitched like that, did you?"

"I guess I didn't really know," I said sheepishly.

She laughed again. "It's so extra, right? I barely even notice switching in and out of it anymore. It just automatically happens when there's an adult around." Her voice rattled pleasantly, like a marble rolling inside a glass jar.

"So what's so hellish about this place?" I asked, letting this new version of So-hyun sink in.

"OK, honestly, there *are* some hellish things about the Star Academy—waking up before the sun rises, training a hundred hours a day, having all your social media monitored. And you know what the worst rule is?"

"What?" I asked.

"Under no circumstances are we to fraternize with boys," she said, mimicking Miss Jackie's stern tone.

I laughed; her Miss Jackie impression was perfect. And it was kind of a relief to hear her make fun of someone who was actually pretty scary.

"She's kind of draconian, huh?" I said.

"Uhhh, that is like the biggest understatement in the whole G-D universe. Let me tell you something: if you want to make it here, just make sure you do whatever Miss Jackie says."

"Will do," I said.

"OK, but besides Miss Jackie, you're seriously going to love it here. Like, where else do you get to immerse yourself fully in your art and make music with your best friends every day? Nowhere."

I practically shivered; it was just so incredible to hear So-hyun describe the academy this way. "That's so cool. I think I've always dreamed of a place like this."

"Well, stop pinching yourself, girl, because you're not dreaming anymore! Come on, I'll show you around." So-hyun pulled me toward the stairwell next to the cafeteria, and we headed up to the next floor.

"So, OK, what's your passion? What's the thing that you came here for?"

"Well, I love singing. That's what I really want to train in," I said.

"Ugh, yes, girl! Freaking *love* singing!"

When we got to the top of the stairs, she steered me to the right. "Let me show you the recording studios, then."

The studios were all the way at the far end of the third floor. The hallway was lined with metal doors, and each one had a little glass window cut into it. As we walked past one, I stopped to peek inside.

Two men sat in front of this giant spaceship-control-panel-looking thing. It had all these knobs and buttons and flashing lights. Behind the control panel was a booth with a big glass window, where three boys in headphones were huddled around microphones. They were obviously singing, but I couldn't hear a thing.

"So these are our recording studios," said So-hyun behind me.

"We have twelve of them. Some of them are big enough for fifteen singers and a full band. Cool, yeah?"

"Really cool," I said.

"Here, this one is empty," said So-hyun, shoving her whole body through one of the heavy doors. The studio had dark, felted walls and a ceiling padded with black egg-crate foam. So-hyun let the door whisper shut, and suddenly the room sounded dead. It wasn't quiet like when you're home alone and all you can hear are cars driving by or the fridge running; it was the kind of quiet where you can almost hear the fluids in your brain sloshing around. It was the sound of absence.

So-hyun watched my face as I listened to the silence. "So quiet, right?"

"Scary quiet," I said.

So-hyun sauntered up to a microphone stand and cradled it as if she were going to lay a fat kiss on it. "The best part about these studios is you can be as loud as you want AND NO ONE CAN HEAR YOOOU!"

I laughed but couldn't help looking over my shoulder to see if anyone heard her.

"That's why I always videochat in here, so I can make sure no one is listening," she said.

"That's smart. And you're allowed to come in here whenever you want?" I asked.

"Oh, hell no." She slipped back into her Miss Jackie impression. "Trainees are *strictly* prohibited from the recording studios unless an adult is present!" Returning to her natural, gravelly voice, she said, "So you have to do it on the D-L."

"Got it," I said.

"Here." So-hyun held out the microphone to me. "Let's hear that voice everyone keeps talking about."

"Oh, that's OK. I can try it another time," I said, backing away from the microphone.

"Come on, it's really cool to hear your voice on an expensive mic." She pushed the microphone into my hands and walked over to the board with all the buttons and knobs. "Put those headphones on so you can hear yourself."

"K," I said, giving in. I was actually super-curious about what I would sound like.

I plucked a pair of headphones off the back of a music stand and pulled them onto my head. They sealed over my ears and made my skull feel heavy.

"OK, say something," said So-hyun's voice in my headphones.

"Um, hello? . . . Whoa!" I could hear my voice in my ears crisper than I'd ever heard it, as if my whole life I'd been hearing it through a long-distance telephone line.

"Try singing something!" she said.

"Um, I don't know! This is so weird!"

"Come on, sing! This is what you came here for, right?"

"OK, uhh, gimme a second. I have to think of something." I twirled the drawstring on my hoodie, mentally scrolling through all the songs I knew by heart. Finally, I opted for one that didn't really require any music: Rihanna's "Higher."

I sang the first couple verses with my eyes closed so I wouldn't have to think about So-hyun watching me. Hearing myself so clear and raw sent shivers up my spine. I could hear every waver, every vibration in my voice. I sounded *good*.

For a moment, I lost myself in the song.

"Shit," said So-hyun in my headphones.

I ripped the headphones off my head. "God, I didn't warm up or anything, and I never sing that song except in the shower! Sorry!"

"Ummm, do *not* apologize. You're, like, ridiculously good. No wonder they signed you so fast."

"Well, thanks," I said, smiling at her gratefully. There was something so easy about So-hyun, and not just because she was complimenting me on my singing. She reminded me of my friends back home.

"God, just think of all the incredible music you're going to record in these studios."

"I literally can't wait."

"All right, come on, let's keep this tour moving; there are so many more things I want to show you," she said, pushing me out the door.

We left the recording studios behind and explored the rest of the third floor. So-hyun showed me mirrored dance studios and rehearsal spaces, with music pouring out of each one. There were little rooms with music stands, sort of like phone booths, where you could practice your singing. On the fourth floor, there were teachers' offices and regular classrooms where I'd do my last year and a half of high school. Inside one of the classrooms, a teacher was writing *Subjunctive Mood* on the white board—it was an English lesson.

I knew from the outside of the building that the Star Academy was the size of an entire city block, but I didn't realize just how massive it was. Every time I thought we had gotten to the end of the tour, So-hyun would take me down another hallway or into another rehearsal space. I couldn't get over the fact that I lived here now; I felt like I was Harry Potter walking through Hogwarts for the first time.

When we finally circled back to the stairwell, So-hyun stopped and pointed above us. "So, up there? You won't be going there unless you're 'summoned.'"

"Why, what's up there?" I asked.

"It's like a restricted staff area, but it's also where Mr. Kim's big-ass office is."

"Mr. Kim, as in Top10's owner?"

"The one and only," So-hyun said, nodding.

"What's he like?"

"Let's just say compared to Mr. Kim, Miss Jackie is like a soft little baby kitten."

I craned my neck over the rail to try to get a glimpse of the floor above us but all I could see were more stairs. "Yikes."

"Yikes is right." So-hyun linked her arm with mine. "Come on, let's go to my favorite place—the cafeteria!"

As we walked back down the stairs, I asked So-hyun the question I'd been wondering all afternoon. "So, where are you from?"

"I'm from a town kinda near Busan."

"So you're Korean."

"Yep, I'm a true original," she declared in a posh accent, pronouncing it like *ori-jahn-ahl*.

"So how is your English so perfect?" I asked.

"It's good, right?" she said, flipping her ponytail.

"Really good."

"First of all," she said, "I watch a *disgusting* amount of American YouTube." Well, that explained all of So-hyun's funny slang. "But the real reason is my parents started sending me to an English tutor when I was really little. I'm the oldest of four and, like, I think they thought I'd be everyone's ticket out of our small town."

"It seems like you did pretty well for yourself," I said.

"Well, they probably would have been happier if I ended up a CEO or something, but I fell in love with singing and dancing when I was little, so they agreed to send me to a rando K-pop training center. That led to auditions, and now here I am." She tilted her head to the side and perched her chin on top of her fingers like she was posing for a close-up.

"So you've always known you wanted to be an idol?"

"Oh, for sure. I swear I came out of the womb singing and dancing. Plus, it's a hell of a lot better than being in business or whatever my parents originally planned for me," she said.

"I think my mom secretly hoped I'd get into international studies," I said. "She's a diplomat; that's why I'm here in Korea."

"Oh, I know, Alice Choy. I know *everything* about you."

"Creepy," I teased.

"Yes, Alice. I am a low-key creep. Better to learn that now."

Right then, it hit me that So-hyun and I were bantering. What a stupid word—*banter*—but that's what we were doing. It was something that I had totally taken for granted back home, but now that I was living in a country where I didn't speak the language, it felt like every conversation was a gigantic struggle. Talking to So-hyun was so effortless that I wanted to keep doing it forever.

"You're from California, right?" asked So-hyun.

"Yep."

"That's like beaches and tanned boys and all the schools have lockers, right?"

"Uh, sorta, yeah," I said, smiling to myself. Everyone I met in

Korea thought that that's what California was like. "They don't really have all that stuff in San Francisco, where I'm from, though. Have you ever been?"

"Nope. Never even been to America . . . Sigh, one day."

"I bet you would really like it," I said.

"Oh, guaranteed," she said. "So, I know you don't speak the language, but are your parents Korean?"

"No, I'm actually half Chinese and half 'miscellaneous.'"

"Half miscellaneous?" So-hyun laughed. "What does that even mean?"

"So my dad is all kinds of white; we just don't really know *what* kinds. There's some Irish and some French and some other things."

"Ah, oui, c'est la vie, as So-ri always says."

"Does she?" I asked. "What's her story?"

"So-ri? That woman has traveled all over the world and can speak a million languages. She's like the freaking owl in Duolingo. I think she's spent more time outside of Korea than in it," she explained.

"Huh, I had no idea."

We headed into the cafeteria, which was almost completely empty now. It was brightly lit, with row after row of long white tables and benches. There were cartoony nutritional posters hanging all over the walls, like one of a man riding a bike made of fruits and vegetables.

"So on a scale from one to ten, do you give Korean food a thumbs-up or a thumbs-down?" asked So-hyun.

"Ummm, not sure how to answer that," I said with a laugh. "But I really like it. Especially bibimbap."

"Bibimbap is your favorite Korean dish?" said So-hyun, aghast. "Girl, that's basically just meat and vegetables on rice. We have way more interesting food than that! Have you ever had honey brick toast?"

"Mmm, no."

"Oh my god, you'll die."

She led us deeper into the cafeteria to a long counter in the back. "This is where you pick up your meals. Miss Jackie is going to be watching you like a hawk when it comes to food, so if you want to eat anything outside of your meal plan, don't let her catch you."

"Meal plan?" I asked, surprised.

"Yeah, she and the nutritionists will put together a meal plan for you every day."

I frowned. "So you're telling me I don't get to choose what I eat?"

"Yeah, no."

"Is the food good here at least?" I asked hopefully.

"Yeah it's pretty good actually," she said.

"Well, that's something, I guess."

"Oh shit." So-hyun was looking up at the clock on the wall; it was almost five. "You have to go meet the other members of your group!"

I followed So-hyun into the girls' wing, which opened up into a big common room with overstuffed couches and chairs in the same Easter egg colors as the ones in the lobby. We passed by a communal bathroom before we hooked around a corner and So-hyun came to a stop. She pointed at a door in the middle of the hall. "OK, you're in that one."

"You're not coming in with me?" I asked, sounding way more anxious than I meant to. I was feeling nervous all of a sudden, like I was about to walk into a final exam or something.

"Nope. You're on your own from here."

"Where's your room?" I asked, reluctant to leave her.

"I have a single, closer to the bathrooms," she said, pointing her thumb behind her back like a hitchhiker.

"You get your own room? That's so lucky."

"I guess . . . it's just that all my other groupmates live in an apartment, and it makes me feel *so* left out," she said, sighing. "But I'll get to move in with them once I graduate from high school."

"You guys are close?"

"Girl, I'm closer to them than my actual sisters!"

I looked back at the closed door, hoping I would feel the same way about whoever was on the other side.

"All right, stop stalling! You're late!" So-hyun took me by the shoulders and turned me back around to face my room. "These girls are going to love you, I promise. You're all gonna bond so fast you won't even remember who I am by the end of the week."

"I hope so. I mean, not the forgetting-you part, obviously."

"I'll find you later, K? Okaaay, byeeee," she said, shoving me one last time toward the door.

"Bye," I said half-heartedly.

I took a long, deep breath, then walked slowly up to the pink door, number five. Just as I was reaching for the knob, it flew open, revealing Miss Jackie.

"AN-NYEONG-HA-SE-YO!" sang four girls who were standing behind her. They bowed in perfect unison and I quickly bowed back.

"Welcome to your dorm room, Alice," said Miss Jackie.

The room was tiny—way too small for five girls. Four plain wooden bunk beds were pushed up against the left and right walls, and there was a single twin bed shoved under the one window in the room. There wasn't even enough wall space for a single poster.

Jammed right in the middle of all the beds was a little table with a jumble of makeup, school supplies, and other random stuff piled on top. I don't know, I guess because everything else at the academy was so sleek and spacious, I expected my room would be a little more . . . luxurious. This was more like the cabin I slept in at summer camp, only half as big.

"Alice, I would like to introduce you to Top10's up-and-coming girl group and your new groupmates: A-List."

I had prepared myself for the possibility that the girls in my group were going to be pretty, but these four girls were *stunning*. They were all taller than me and slender and what makeup commercials call *effortlessly beautiful*. They were the kind of girls that the clouds part for so the sun can shine on them, while the rest of us mortals watch from the darkness. A-List was the perfect name for them.

And there were my arms, on cue, crossing themselves over my chest and hunching me over because it was as close as I could get to hiding.

Miss Jackie nodded at the girl who somehow managed to stand out from the other three. "This is Aria, A-List's leader. She is both the main singer and a lead dancer."

Aria looked directly at me with her golden-hazel eyes. She had long black hair with strawberry highlights that framed her face in soft waves. Right then I realized it was totally possible to be starstruck by someone you'd never heard of. There was something about the way she carried herself or the way the air swirled around her—I don't know; she just screamed celebrity.

Aria stepped forward in one confident stride and held out her manicured hand. "Hello, Alice. We're so happy to welcome you to the group." She had the slightest accent, but otherwise her English was immaculate. "We hear that you have great talent."

"Thank you, it's so nice to meet you." I shook her hand, feeling like I didn't do it right, even though I knew that was ridiculous.

"This is Hayan, the group's main dancer," Miss Jackie said, referring to the athletic-looking girl with jet-black hair and blunt-cut bangs. Hayan lifted her pointed chin and smirked confidently.

"Nice to meet you," I said.

Hayan took my hand and pumped it up and down a couple times. "You too," she said in a thick Korean accent.

"And this is Yuri. She is a lead dancer." Yuri was as tall as the others, but everything about her seemed small and delicate, except for her big brown eyes. She reminded me of these porcelain dolls with huge eyes that my grandma used to collect; I think they were called Blythe dolls. I always wanted to play with them when I was little, but my grandma wouldn't let me because they were too fragile.

Yuri pulled at her orange-blond ponytail and gave a shy little wave. "Hi."

"Hi," I said, waving back.

"And finally, Seol, whose specialty is rapping." The other three had on skintight workout clothes, but Seol was wearing a cutoff tee and baggy sweatpants that sagged around a pair of boxer shorts. She was the only one who didn't have long hair, too. Instead, her hair was dyed a faded navy blue and styled into a cute bowl cut.

Seol tried to say "Hello, how are you?" but started cracking up at herself before she could get all the way through. Her laugh was super-goofy, like a cross between a hiccup and the sound a donkey makes; it was so disarming and lovable that it was impossible not to laugh with her.

"Good, how are you?" I laughed back.

She shook her head, still cracking up. "English not so good."

The other girls were giggling now, too, which made Seol laugh even harder. It was nice laughing with everyone and a relief that we were all getting along so quickly.

But then Miss Jackie snapped her fingers, and our laughs fell to silence. "Sit," she instructed.

The girls and I sat down at the table, and Miss Jackie stood over me with her hands laced in front of her. "Alice, as you may have gathered, you are to be A-List's fifth member. It is a position that has been long vacant, and we are grateful to have you."

The girls beamed at me like I was the answer to all their hopes and prayers.

"The group is slated to debut this spring," continued Miss Jackie. "In the next few months, the five of you will launch your first concept, promote your single, and eventually debut at one of K-pop's most anticipated events, the Dream Concert. This year's concert has already sold out and will be held at the Seoul World Cup Stadium, a venue that boasts more than sixty thousand seats. It is scheduled for May twenty-second, leaving you less than five months to prepare."

Five months.

Five months until I was singing on a professional stage—a stadium no less!—in front of tens of thousands of living, breathing humans! I thought I'd have to wait at least two years for that, if ever. Five months was nothing! I licked my lips, almost tasting how soon it was.

"The other girls have been rigorously preparing for their debut for close to a year now. To ensure that you perform at their level in such a short span of time, your training will be accelerated."

Miss Jackie pressed her fingers together, her red nails meeting exactly at their tips. "The next few months will be grueling and will require great commitment from you. You must set your sights on this one goal and let nothing distract you."

I nodded, hoping I looked like I was up for it.

"Good. Now, Alice, please acquaint yourself with your schedule. You may take this evening to settle in, but your training begins first thing in the morning. If you have any questions, the girls will be more than happy to answer them."

Apparently done with her speech, Miss Jackie squinted ever so slightly, which made the girls jump from their seats. I scrambled up from my chair to join them.

"Goodbye," Miss Jackie said.

"ANNYEONGHI-GASEYO," we said, bowing in return.

When the door clicked shut, Aria motioned for us to sit back down at the table. I took the same seat as before, and Yuri quickly swept aside a bunch of the makeup and other stuff to make more room for me.

"Thanks," I said, smiling at her nice gesture.

Yuri giggled nervously at herself. "You welcome."

"Alice, how old are you?" Aria asked politely. There was that age question again.

"I just turned seventeen."

"Oh, seventeen is such a fun age." It would have come off as condescending, but Aria just seemed like one of those girls who'd been an adult since she was in kindergarten.

"Se-beun-teen!" groaned Seol, dramatically smacking herself in the head. Everyone laughed, and I did, too, but I didn't really get what was so funny.

"Seol will turn seventeen in the summer, so it looks like she will forever be the baby of the group," explained Aria. She smiled warmly at Seol, who actually seemed pretty happy about it. "Hayan and Yuri are both eighteen. I turned nineteen this year, so you can call me Unnie, OK?"

I didn't know what Unnie meant, but I figured it had something to do with Korean honorifics. I nodded and made a mental note to ask Olivia about it later.

"So," said Aria, tossing her hair over her bare shoulder, "since you're part of the group now, the girls and I want to tell you something. It's something we've been talking about for a really long time." She looked around the table at the other girls, her eyes shining like she was about to let me in on the deal of a lifetime. "Have you ever heard of a light-stick ocean?"

I actually had; Olivia had shown me pictures from an MSB concert.

"Yeah," I said, "it's when fans wave a group's light sticks at a concert, and it kind of turns the stadium into a sea of lights?

"Yes, exactly!" said Aria. "Our goal is to gain enough fans by the time we perform in May that we'll have an ocean at the Dream Concert. Of course it won't be a huge ocean, since there will be so many other fandoms there, but can you imagine thousands of people cheering for us and waving our light sticks? Wouldn't that be amazing?"

"That would be incredible," I said, marveling at the idea. Although I was still so shocked that we were supposed to perform in five months that it was hard to even comprehend the idea that we'd have thousands of fans by then, too. "Do you . . . I mean, do we have a color yet?" I asked.

The girls all shook their heads.

"Top10 is designing our light stick now, and they promised they'll announce our color soon," Aria explained.

"Oraen-gi ocean!" exclaimed Seol.

Hayan clicked her tongue as if only a moron would like the color orange. "Aniii! Labendeo ocean."

"Hot-pink ocean," said Yuri quietly, like she was making a wish.

"No matter what our color is," said Aria, focusing us back onto the main point, "it's going to be a lot of work. Most rookie groups only have a couple dozen fans in the audience, and that's not enough to create an ocean. If we work hard enough and perform well enough, we can be the first group to pull it off."

We all nodded at one another like it was inevitable. Somehow, it felt true if Aria was saying it.

"So," said Aria, moving right along. "Miss Jackie told us that you are a very accomplished singer."

"Hah, well, I don't know about accomplished, but I took vocal lessons in America for about nine years."

Smiling, Aria explained my answer to the other girls, who thankfully seemed impressed.

"How about you all, how long have you been training?" I asked Aria.

"Well, we've only been training together as A-List for about ten months. But we've all been at the academy for years."

"Oh wow."

"Hayan and Yuri started dancing when they were practically babies." She reached over to Yuri and affectionately squeezed her shoulder, and Yuri's heart-shaped lips spread into a smile. Something about their familiarity with one another made me slightly uncomfortable; it was like the four of them had already done all their bonding years ago and I'd probably never catch up.

Hayan said something in Korean and Aria nodded. "She wants to know what kind of music you like to sing."

This question always worried me back home because I never knew if people were going to like what I was into. "I guess I like to sing a lot of pop music, like Lady Gaga and Rihanna. But sometimes I also like singing opera. I know it's kind of weird, but it's fun to use my voice like that."

Hayan nodded approvingly. "Rihanna is so good."

"Back in America," Aria asked, "did you perform in a group or as a solo artist?"

"Oh, neither."

She flinched ever so slightly, and I felt like I had to explain myself. "I mean, I was in a chorus, but other than that I haven't really performed much in public . . . unless karaoke with my little sister counts," I added, laughing a little too hard at my lame attempt at a joke.

Aria blinked twice and clearly decided not to translate my answer. "And how many years have you trained in dance?"

"Oh, um, I've never trained in dance," I admitted, looking down at my hands. Shit, I didn't think I'd have to admit that so soon.

Now Aria actually looked a little concerned, and the others started to notice. Yuri anxiously threaded her fingers through her ponytail, waiting for Aria to translate, but she never did. "Top10 told us our new member would also dance . . . But I'm sure they wouldn't have signed you if you didn't have great potential," she said diplomatically.

"I don't know about that; I was kind of a disaster at the auditions . . . Honestly, I'm a pretty crappy dancer!" Where was all this coming from and why couldn't I stop?

Aria looked deadly serious now. "And acting? How much training have you had?"

"Um, none!" I sputtered. My nervous laughter was spiraling out of control now as if I were on a sinking ship and thought that laughing hysterically was going to magically produce a life raft.

"Well," Aria said slowly, "as Miss Jackie said, you should unpack and get settled in. We have a lot of work ahead of us." Aria was like a light bulb of approval that had suddenly clicked off. She stood up from the table and the others followed after her, confused.

What a complete and utter disaster. That had to be one of the top ten worst first impressions of all time!

There was nothing I could really do, though, so I slinked over to the bunk bed where my suitcases were laid out and tried to make myself as inconspicuous as possible. On the lower bunk next to my things was a stack of folded sheets and towels, as well as a schedule printed on a laminated sheet of paper. I searched for my voice lessons—two hours a day!—and scanned the rest quickly: Korean classes, dance lessons, study time. I tossed it on my pillow. I was too worked up to really take it in.

There was also a silver school-issued laptop that I was supposed to use for studying. I didn't even open it. So-hyun had told me it was so full of parental controls I wouldn't even be able to access YouTube. "Don't even try to message someone or make a phone call; you won't be able to download the app," she warned.

I unzipped my suitcases, and the first thing I pulled out was a photo of Olivia and me. We had taken it in one of those photo booths where you can use filters and change the shape of your face. Olivia had added a bunch of sparkles and made our eyes huge so that we looked like a couple of anime characters. There wasn't really anywhere in the room where I could hang it, so I just tucked it into one of the slats under the top bunk, positioning it right above my pillow. I put So-ri's Top10 business card right next to it as kind of a good-luck charm.

I had my back to the girls, but I could hear them start to talk behind me. It was obvious they were trying to keep their voices down even though I couldn't understand most of what they were saying. When I worked up the courage to look back at them, they were all huddled around one another in a circle. Aria noticed me looking, and she flashed me a tight smile. Yuri, who was in the middle of a sentence, stopped and looked away, embarrassed.

It didn't matter what language you spoke; that was the international sign for "We're talking about *you*."

Dinnertime could not come fast enough. So-hyun came and got me, and I nearly jumped into her arms. I couldn't wait to get out of my room where I had become a social outcast in the matter of an hour.

The cafeteria was packed, and So-hyun introduced me to all seven of the other members of her group and about a million other people, but I was too distracted to keep track of anyone's name. I kept playing the conversation with Aria over and over in my mind. It was like having an annoying song stuck in my head, except instead of lyrics, it was Aria's disappointed face playing on repeat.

It's not like I had planned to admit that I was a bad dancer on my first day here, but there was a part of me that wanted to tell them what they were going to find out anyway—that I actually *was* a crappy dancer (or whatever is ten times worse than crappy). I don't know why I was always doing that, pointing out the stuff I was bad at and downplaying the stuff I was actually good at. I guess I just didn't ever want to be a disappointment.

By the time I got back to my room, I was sure that the girls would have thrown all my stuff out the window in protest, but everything was right where I left it. They were already in their cute pajamas—Yuri in a pink spaghetti-strap tank and polka-dot shorts, and Hayan and Aria in lacy little tops. Seol was lying on her stomach in the bunk above mine, wearing headphones and leafing through a fat textbook.

I walked over to the little wooden dresser where I had stored all my clothes and pulled out my faded Gaga tour shirt, the one I've been wearing to bed for years. As I was looking through the drawer for sweatpants, Yuri padded up to me in a pair of fuzzy slippers.

"Alice?" she said tentatively.

I winced, expecting the worst. "Yeah?"

"Do you like rabbits?"

"Rabbits?" I repeated, totally stumped. What was this, some kind of weird test?

"Yes." Yuri giggled, then pointed at her bed, the top bunk across the way from mine. "Is my collection. See?"

I stood up on my tiptoes so I could see over the rail and saw a mountain of stuffed bunny rabbits piled up on top of her pillows.

"Ohh, you collect stuffed animals," I breathed, relieved. It seemed like a funny collection for someone her age to have, but then again, I did bring my teddy bear with me when we moved to Seoul. It was this dingy old panda bear called Andy-pandy that I'd had since I was a baby. I just couldn't stand leaving it behind, all alone in a storage facility. "How many do you have?" I asked cautiously, still unsure if this was a trick.

"I have maybe twenty-two? And see," she said, pointing to Hayan's bed underneath hers, "Hayan has music pin collection."

I stooped down to get a look at Hayan's bed, and there were dozens and dozens of metal pins stuck into the wood frame. A lot of them looked like merch from other K-pop groups, but I recognized the pins of some old-school bands: the Kiss logo and the Rolling Stones tongue.

"Wow, she has so many," I said.

"Do you have a collection?" asked Yuri.

"Um, I collect concert tickets and movie stubs and stuff like that."

"Ah, cool! You have a lot?"

"I think I have like sixteen or seventeen concert tickets? And then movie stubs—I probably have more than a hundred. I don't know; I need to count them again."

"Wow! You like movies!" she said excitedly.

I smiled at her, relaxing a little bit. "Ha, yeah, I guess I do."

"What kind?"

"I mostly like dramas and romance, especially older films, like from the thirties and forties. I'm not a huge fan of action movies or anything like that."

"Mmm, what about *Itaewon Class*. You like that?"

"Um, I don't know what that is."

Yuri bit her lip and looked up at the ceiling like she was trying to think of the right words. "Euhh . . . *Itaewon Class* . . . a K-drama. You can watch with us?"

"Oh, uh . . ." I stuttered. I looked over her shoulder at Aria and Hayan, who were watching us talk. It was obvious they had sent Yuri over to me to kind of bury the hatchet. I wanted to say yes, but the truth was that they had all really intimidated me earlier, especially Aria. They reminded me of these three senior girls who were super-popular in my old high school. They had everything— confidence, boys obsessing over them, teachers loving them, and all the awards and stuff. Plus flawless hair and skin. It wasn't like they were mean or anything; I just felt this weird pressure when I was around them, like they were so perfect that I had to be perfect, too. Besides, all I really wanted to do was text Olivia and forget that the last few hours had ever happened.

"Thanks, but I'm OK," I said to Yuri.

Yuri had this mildly panicked look on her face that I'd noticed Koreans sometimes got when they didn't understand what I was saying; it was usually my cue to end the conversation. I made like I was yawning and stretched my arms above my head. "I'm tired; I'm going to bed."

"Ahh," she said, nodding. "OK. Good night."

"Night."

I got into bed and pulled my phone out. I had nineteen missed text messages from Olivia, half of which were just the question mark emoji.

ALICE
Hiiii.

Olivia started typing before I even hit send.

OLIVIA
OMG finally!!!!!

ALICE
Sorry been a busy day

OLIVIA

That's ok! How is it?? Who have you met???

I'M DYING TO KNOWWW

ALICE

I met So-hyun from XOKiss. She's really nice.

OLIVIA

WHAT. TELL ME EVERYTHING!!!!

ALICE

I also met my new group. We're called A-List.

OLIVIA

Omg I love that name so much!!!

How are the other girls in the group??

ALICE

They don't seem to like me very much

OLIVIA

Orly why do you think that?

I glanced across the room. Hayan, Yuri, and Aria were scrunched up around a phone in Hayan's bottom bunk, and Yuri was squeezing one of her stuffed bunnies under her chin. Apparently *Itaewon Class* was a drama because they all had tears running down their faces.

ALICE

I think because I told them I can't dance

OLIVIA

You told them that?

ALICE

Yeah, I'm dumb

OLIVIA
But they haven't heard you sing yet, right?

ALICE
Not yet

OLIVIA
Sorry, that sux. But I bet they'll get over it as soon as
they hear you sing.

As I was typing my next text, a hand wagged in front of my face. I looked up and saw Seol's face peeking over the edge of the top bunk. Smiling like a goof, she pointed at herself to show me that she was the one who'd be sleeping above me. I smiled back and gave her two thumbs-up. Seol hooked her hand under the bottom of her bunk and stuck something small and pink next to the photo of Olivia and me. I sat up to see what it was and found a Post-it note with *Welcome to A-list!* ♡ *Seol* scrawled on it.

I smiled up at her gratefully and Seol grinned back. She dropped her hand down for a high five, which I slapped as softly as I could so we wouldn't bother the other girls.

The note was so simple and silly, but something about it really got to me. I shoved my phone under my pillow with my text to Olivia still unsent and cried until I fell asleep.

[This page has been translated from Korean.]

01.09

+ ABOUT V +

My mother keeps a pot of plastic orchids next to the cash register in our family's gift shop. We can't grow real plants because our shop is located underground, in the Bupyeong subway station. The orchids, white and slender, are perfectly formed plastic replicas of the real thing. (Except they're not exactly perfect; if you look close enough, you can see the seams running along each stem.) They never wilt or brown, and when they get dusty, my mother cleans them off with a microfiber cloth. If something ever happened to them, if the pot got knocked off the counter and broke, she could easily replace them with a new set of fake orchids and no one would ever know.

About eight years ago, I convinced my mother to start selling K-pop photo cards in our shop. This was back when I was in middle school and thought that K-pop idols were god's greatest creation, back when I was an OMEGA. Yes, dear Readers, I stanned for MEGAONE, and I'm ashamed to admit that I actually thought Ji-hoon and I would end up together one day. (I actually believed I was saving my first kiss for him, not that I had any other prospects at the time . . .)

To my mother's complete surprise, the photo cards were a huge moneymaker. Kids flocked to our little underground stall on the weekends to get their hands on the latest Girls Generation or BIGBANG stickers, and we would rake in the cash. My mother even constructed a huge display rack that could hold hundreds of photo cards, which she placed front and center in our little store. Of course I always made sure to position the MEGAONE photo cards in the most visible spot on the rack.

With the money we earned, I bought an expensive DSLR camera—and about a dozen lenses—and started designing my own photo cards. Instead of studying at yaja like the rest of my classmates, I followed MEGAONE to all their public appearances, photographing them and photoshopping their images. When I wasn't designing photo cards, I was chatting on Instiz or MEGAONE fan-cafés. I was so wrapped up in idol gossip that I preferred talking on forums to talking to my actual friends. Eventually, the MEGAONE fansite began referring to me as Master-nim, and that only made me even more devoted. I took the title seriously, spending hours translating variety shows into English for their international fans and shipping my photo cards overseas, sometimes at a loss, just for the good of the group.

But then, my K-pop bubble . . . popped.

It happened the day that Ji-hoon killed himself. I don't like talking about it. In fact, this is the only time you'll see me write about his death on this blog. After the shock of his suicide wore off, I began to question the entire K-pop system, and I took a deep look into the reality of what goes on inside my once-beloved entertainment companies. I realized that everything was faked—idol personalities, their relationships, their noses and jawlines, even the gossip itself—all of it as artificial as my mother's plastic orchids.

Of course no one can be as perfect as plastic. The pressure got to Ji-hoon, and his death was the result.

I began this blog four years ago as a referendum against (or perhaps a rebellion against?) the current state of K-pop. On this blog, you won't find curated leaks from the entertainment companies. I source real information from a network of savvy netizens who don't mind breaking the law now and again to reveal the truth. I am dedicated to exposing the real side of idols in hopes that no one else is ever consumed by the K-pop machine.

You can still find a photo card stand in our store because my mother insists it makes money, but it's much smaller now. It sits, semi-obscured, by my mother's orchids.

+ V +

#ForeverONEJi-hoon

LOCKED

Four

ALL THE LIGHTS IN THE ARENA HAD GONE DOWN,
but I could still make out the crowd waiting anxiously in the dark.
There must have been over ten thousand people out there.

"Are you ready?" asked Aria, her face blank and emotionless.

I nodded, but I was hiding something from her: I didn't know
a single step of choreography. Five months had somehow flown
by, and I hadn't gone to any of my dance classes. I wasn't even
remotely ready.

The crowd was starting to get out of control, stomping their feet
and hollering for us to start the show. We couldn't make them wait
any longer. The girls stepped out onto the dark stage, and pure terror drove me out after them.

I stumbled to a random spot on the black stage floor. My breath
felt scratchy and erratic as I tried to keep from hyperventilating. If I
could have caught my breath, I would have screamed.

How could anyone think I was ready for this? Didn't they know
that I was completely unprepared?

The lights flashed on, blinding me. I clamped my eyes shut in terror, and when I opened them . . . I saw Miss Jackie flipping on the light switch in our room. It was morning.

I slid my phone out from under my pillow to check the time. 5:15. It took me a second to comprehend just how early that was, and by the time my eyes focused on all the texts Olivia had sent me the night before, Miss Jackie was clapping her hands together, ordering us out of bed.

"Ileona! Up, up, up!"

Tucking my phone back under my pillow, I dragged myself out from under my sheets and stood up. I felt like a bag of concrete.

"No time for a shower this morning, Alice," said Miss Jackie. "Put on your workout clothes and running shoes, and be at the elevators in ten minutes."

Seol dropped down from her top bunk, yawning loudly. When she saw me looking at her confusedly, she moved her arms and legs up and down like she was running on a StairMaster. I shook my head, too sleepy to understand, but she just shrugged and headed over to her closet.

I threw on a T-shirt and some yoga pants and grabbed my sneakers, then headed into the hallway, already crammed with other girls who were dressed and ready for the day. I followed my roommates to the elevator, and we rode down to the underground parking lot where a white van was waiting for us. There were a bunch of other girls in the van already—and when Aria, Hayan, Yuri, and Seol got in, they took up an entire row, so the only seat left was next to Miss Jackie. After we all buckled up, two men got into the front seats and drove us out of the garage.

"Have you ever been to Namsan Park, Alice?" asked Miss Jackie.

"Yes, I live—uh, lived—right next to it," I said.

"There is a very fine hike up to Namsan Peak that I like to do with the girls. You can see almost all of Seoul from there."

I nodded. A hike would have sounded nice if it weren't so freaking early.

"You can expect to do this hike every morning before your lessons begin," she explained.

"Every . . . morning?" I repeated, shocked.

"Yes, every morning. This," she said, dragging a maroon fingernail across my belly, "must go by the time of the Dream Concert."

I looked down. I never really thought much about my weight, and I certainly never thought about my stomach as something that "must go."

We hiked for almost two hours through the empty park, climbing hundreds of concrete stairs that zigzagged up to the peak. Miss Jackie made us run up and down each set of stairs multiple times.

It is a huge understatement to say that exercise isn't really my thing. I never got into sports, and PE at my school back home was kind of a joke.

At first, the other A-List girls tried to wait up for me, but I was so slow that eventually they just went ahead. Only Seol stayed in the back with me the whole time. She kept clapping and yelling funny things like "You can DO it!" or "Go to the top!" When we did finally get to the top, we didn't even stop to look at the view Miss Jackie liked so much; we just did fifty jumping jacks and turned right back around.

On the way back down, I actually caught sight of our apartment building. I could picture Mom and Dad and Olivia all warm inside, eating breakfast without me. Probably scrambled eggs or something.

It took all of my willpower not to break off from the group and just run home.

By the time we made it back to the parking lot, I was starving and my lungs were burning from breathing in the freezing air. I settled into the heated van with everyone else, and as my sweat turned into a clammy film, I started to shake with hunger. Sitting there in the silent van, I got a weird trapped feeling, like I'd be stuck inside this awful morning for the rest of my life.

Thankfully, Miss Jackie dismissed us for breakfast as soon as we got back. I nearly ran to the cafeteria, where I found So-hyun standing in line with a few other girls from her group.

"What the hell happened to *you*? You look like you spent the night in the back of a garbage truck," she said.

"I don't want to talk about it. If I don't get food in me right this second, I might literally die."

"Oh shit, did you go on one of Miss Jackie's morning hikes?" she asked.

"Mm-hmm," I grumbled, grabbing a tray off the stack.

"Lord. Her workouts are notorious." So-hyun told the other XOKiss girls about the hike in Korean, and they all gave me sympathetic looks. "Did she tell you that you have to lose weight?" asked So-hyun.

"Yes," I said, "apparently, all this has to go." I pressed my fingers into my stomach and it rumbled back at me.

"Don't take it too personally," commiserated So-hyun. "Everyone has to lose weight when they first get here. She had me running up and down the stairs when I started while my group watched. It was humiliating."

"Ugh, that's cruel," I said.

"It was. But then the girls started running with me, even though they didn't need to." She bumped hips with Hana, one of the dancers in her group, who grinned and gently tugged on So-hyun's ponytail.

I frowned picturing Seol clapping me up the mountain, the only one who stayed behind with me. "Yeah, people kind of gave up on me today."

"Ah, you guys'll get there. Just give it some time."

We got to the front of the line, and a woman behind the counter handed So-hyun a plate heaping with rice and pickles, crowned with a golden omelet. My stomach growled so loud I swear everyone in line could hear it.

When it was my turn, the woman looked my name up in a little tablet, then walked back into the kitchen to get my breakfast. She came back with a cup of tea and a plate with six leaves of wet-looking cabbage on it. I held the plate out, expecting her to drop an omelet on top, but she had already moved on to the person behind me.

I stood there staring down at my plate, not wanting to believe that was really all I was going to get, when So-hyun put her hand softly on my arm. "Come on, you can have some of mine."

I followed her and the other girls to an empty table, still coming to terms with my so-called meal, when Miss Jackie walked past us and disappeared into the kitchen.

"Shoot." So-hyun scrunched up her face like she smelled something bad. "I can't give you any food while Miss Jackie is lurking around, OK? She'll lose her shit if she sees."

"OK," I whimpered. I was starting to shake again. I slid my trembling chopsticks around a piece of cabbage and lifted it to my mouth. The table in front of me started to fall away, then my stomach dropped and I watched the world turn over.

Then there was only black.

$\text{\textperthousand}$

"Whoa, hey there."

"Ughh."

My head was pounding. I pushed my palms into my eyes, and when I opened them I saw an absolutely perfect face hovering above me. It was the kind of face that an artist would sculpt so that in a thousand years humanity would know what beauty looked like at the beginning of the millennium. The corners of his coffee-brown eyes ended in graceful points, and the long bridge of his nose met the deep well in the middle of his soft upper lip. And his mouth— oh, that pouting mouth—was set in a jaw that wasn't too square but wasn't too round, either. His face wasn't human—it was the face of an angel.

"You all right?" asked the angel, his bleach-blond bangs just barely touching the top of his black eyebrows.

Suddenly, I realized I was lying on the cafeteria floor. I tried to lift myself up, but the angel gently pressed me back onto the floor.

"Just chill for a second. You fell pretty hard," he said.

"Did I faint?" I asked groggily.

"Yeah, I was sitting behind you, and you crashed into me." He pushed his bangs back with the heel of his hand and let out a glorious laugh.

"Sorry. I've never done that before," I said, rubbing my throbbing head.

"It's no biggie. I'm Joon, by the way."

"Joon . . . from MSB?" I said way too loud. How did I not

instantly recognize him? I must have hit my head or something.

"Yup, that's me," he said, smiling.

He bent his head closer to mine, squinting his bright-brown eyes. He smelled brand-new, like he just got out of the shower and put on clothes straight from the wash. "You seem OK now," he said, scooping his hands under my arms and slowly lifting me into a sitting position.

"You're my sister's ultimate bias," I blurted. Welp, this was it. I was officially starstruck, which apparently meant losing complete control of my mouth and brain.

"No way! That's so sweet; I wanna meet her someday," he said.

"Oh god, she'd kill me if she knew I told you that," I groaned.

"Nahh. Don't worry about it; I'm a lot of girls' ultimate bias." Joon wagged his eyebrows up and down at So-hyun, who was standing over us.

So-hyun rolled her eyes. "Joon is the worst; don't feed his already enormous ego."

"Nahhh, my ego is pretty average," said Joon. "Come on, let's get you off the ground." He and So-hyun each grabbed an arm and pulled me to my feet.

"You're Alice Choy, right?" asked Joon.

"Yeah," I murmured. I was still dazed from fainting, and my head ached.

"And you're from the States?" he said.

"Yeah, California."

"That's cool. I'm from Seoul, but I went to school in New York. Man, I really miss it." Olivia, of course, had already told me all this. She also told me that his mother is Korean and his dad is American, that he plays the guitar, that his favorite sport is basketball, and that he has a cat named Vega that has over fifty thousand Instagram followers. But I nodded as if everything he was saying was brand-new information.

"How're you liking the Star Academy? Is it . . . knocking you off your feet?" Joon wagged his eyebrows at us again, which made So-hyun groan. God, he was so . . . *charming*, or at least that's the word my dad would have used. I bet parents loved him.

"She just got back from a Miss Jackie hike," So-hyun explained.

"Ohhh, shit." Joon's grin faded and he crossed his long arms across his chest. "No wonder you fainted."

"I guess when she called it a hike, I envisioned more of a calming 'watch the sun rise over a new day' sort of experience," I said.

"No way. Her hikes are infamous here," he said. "I wouldn't even call them hikes; they're more like death marches. You're definitely not the first trainee to pass out after doing one."

"Thank god, I thought it was just me. I figured I was wildly out of shape."

"Definitely not just you," said Joon, shaking his beautiful head. "But aside from the faint-inducing hike, how's your first week going?"

"It's been OK, still kind of figuring things out, I think."

"For sure. Don't worry, though, you're gonna love it here. It's the best training you can get."

"Alice already has a debut date," said So-hyun. "She's going to perform at the Dream Concert with us."

Joon rocked back on his heels like he couldn't believe it. "Already! You just got here; that's, like, unheard of! Congrats on that, seriously."

"Thanks," I said, smiling bashfully, "but it's pretty nerve-racking."

I was slowly coming back to reality now, and I started to notice that everyone in the cafeteria was staring at me, the girl who just fainted. Great, now I was going to be *that* girl. Like Talia Hellmann from ninth grade who everyone back home referred to as "the girl who broke her leg" because on the first day of school she tripped in the parking lot and fractured her ankle.

I went to pull my hood up, but Joon stopped me. "Wait!" He reached his hand up to my face and peeled a fat cabbage leaf off my cheek.

"Oh god," I uttered, burying my cabbage-slimed face into my hood.

"Don't worry about it. I'll toss it on my way out." Joon knocked me lightly on the shoulder with his fist. "Nice meeting you, Alice. Try not to faint on any other unsuspecting boys."

"I won't," I groaned from behind my hood.

"Ganda!" he said, waving at us.

"Byeee," rasped So-hyun.

So-hyun and I sat back down in our seats, and I dropped my head onto the table. "Ugggghh."

"Come on, it wasn't *that* bad," she said.

"See how you feel when you have cabbage all over your face and fall headfirst into the most gorgeous being on earth."

"*Joon?*" she gasped, horrified. "Joon is *far* from gorgeous."

"Uhh, you're joking, right?"

"OK, I mean objectively, *yes*, he's hot . . . I guess he's just not my type."

"If *he's* not your type, what exactly *is* your type?" I asked.

"I mean, someone who doesn't live in a dorm?"

"*You* live in a dorm!"

"I *know*. That's why I have to hook up with someone who doesn't," she said.

I took a big swig of my tea, drinking the whole thing down in one gulp. "OK, so we don't like Joon because he lives in a dorm and he has an enormous ego?"

"What, no! Joon is such a king; I was just messing with him. Besides, my ego is at least twice the size of his," she said.

"It's amazing an ego that size can fit inside a body as small as yours," I teased.

"Excuse *you!*" she cried. "Watch it, or you'll never eat anything but cold cabbage for breakfast again." So-hyun nudged my plate toward me, where mysteriously, half an omelet had appeared.

If I hadn't been so distracted and actually looked at my schedule like I was supposed to, I would have been more mentally prepared for the rest of the day. I had two hours of Korean with a teacher who basically wanted me to memorize the entire Korean dictionary by the end of the week; a few hours of math and science; three hours of one-on-one dance instruction, in which I was a total nightmare disaster; and this class they called humble lessons, with Miss Jackie, who literally pulled my lips back with her fingers to show me how much teeth to expose when I smile. When it was finally time for the one thing I had been looking forward to—voice lessons—I was almost too exhausted to care.

Miss Jackie shepherded me down a hallway on the fourth floor that So-hyun had somehow missed on my tour the day before. At the end of the hall, there was an open door. A mesmerizing hum poured out of it, like the sound of an opera singer performing deep in the belly of a submarine.

Inside, the room was a mess. Towering bookshelves leaned every which way, each crammed with stacks of songbooks and yellowing sheet music, which poked out between the stacks like spinach between teeth. It looked like no place else in the academy.

"Alice-yah, Nǐ hǎo," said So-ri, who was perched on top of a rickety old stool. She was eating a bag of shrimp chips, and her oversize T-shirt had collected crumbs like an apron. There was a faded Mickey Mouse on the shirt that said SHACKFORD FAMILY'S ANNUAL DISNEYLAND ADVENTURE.

"Alice, I believe you know So-ri Tae, one of South Korea's national treasures," said Miss Jackie. "So-ri is one of the grandmothers of teu-ro-teu-style music, having popularized the genre nationally throughout the nineteen sixties. Her records sold millions of times over worldwide, and she was the first Korean artist to ever appear on US pop charts."

So-ri, this tiny woman wearing used clothing covered in shrimp-chip dust used to be a famous pop star? It was almost unbelievable. But if it was true, I was infinitely more excited to train with her.

"She is a recipient of the prestigious Order of Cultural Merit, and she has performed on television shows and stages on almost every continent."

So that's what So-hyun meant when she said that So-ri was a world traveler!

"So-ri has trained hundreds of students in contemporary singing," added Miss Jackie. "You should consider it an immense honor to be included in those ranks."

I stared at So-ri, amazed.

"Come here, my mezzo-soprano," she beckoned, smacking her lips mischievously. I walked up to her stool, and she took my chin in her hand. I could feel little salt particles trapped between my face and her fingertips. "Anyeong-hi ka-seyo!" she said to Miss Jackie over my shoulder, keeping her eyes pinned on my face. Miss Jackie bowed without a word and left me in the literal hands of my new voice teacher.

"Bienvenidos, Alice! Only adults call me So-ri. *You* call me Seon-saeng-nim."

Seon-saeng-nim meant *teacher* in Korean; it was what all the teachers wanted me to call them.

"OK, Seon-saeng-nim," I said through my teeth, my jaw still pinched shut in her soft hand. She smiled with her winking eyes, then released me.

"So, chica, I want to know why you choose singing. Tell me."

"Well, I . . ." I faltered. No one had ever asked me that before. "I wouldn't say I really *chose* singing. I guess I love singing because it makes me happy?" It came out more like a question than an answer.

"Mm." So-ri slipped a chip into her mouth and munched on it thoughtfully. "How about I ask what does singing make you *feel?*"

I didn't even have to think before answering. "Singing is the only thing that can make me feel fearless. I love how when I perform something I've practiced a lot, I can shut my brain off and the song just pours out of me. I love how when I hit certain notes, like really hit them, I get this powerful feeling, like my heart is breaking but in the most euphoric way. I don't know . . . does that make sense?"

"Mm, yes. I know these feelings. Like you cannot hold on to your heart almost?"

"Exactly!"

"I hear that when I listen to you, Alice. Your singing . . . it remind me of myself."

"Really?" I said quietly.

"Come, I show you something." So-ri popped off her stool and led me over to her desk, a mess of sheet music and crumpled papers. She picked up a framed photo and held it out toward me. It was a black-and-white picture of a woman onstage in a packed outdoor stadium. She wore a polka-dot dress and had a beehive hairdo, and she was singing into one of those old-fashioned chrome microphones. Her mouth was wide open, eyes squeezed shut and arms thrown back, belting something out like her whole life depended on it.

"Is that you?" I guessed.

"It is me."

"Wow, it's amazing. I had no idea you were so famous."

"And see that one," she said, pointing at another framed picture on the wall. "That one is when I am on *The Ed Sullivan Show*."

"Oh my gosh!" I'd heard of *The Ed Sullivan Show*; it was this really popular variety show my grandparents used to watch on TV. Big artists like Elvis Presley and the Beatles performed on the show, and So-ri had too!

"When I am your age, singing come so easy. I have a beautiful, beautiful voice just like you—everyone say so. Singing give me a heartbreak feeling, too, only for me it feels like flying."

I knew exactly what she meant; sometimes I felt like I was flying when I sang, too.

"But . . ." So-ri reached her pinkie into the side of her mouth and fished something off a back molar. "Singing professionally is not only good feelings. You cannot shut your brain off all the time. Many times it is difficult to perform—takes discipline. It is good you say you feel fearless when you sing because training—learning discipline—can be very painful. You know this already, yes?"

I nodded even though I couldn't really imagine singing being painful; at least it never was when I trained back home.

"Top10 expect so much from you, almost like a perfection. And so do I. Singing is not just about voice; it is about how you live. So, in this room we work on voice but also on many other things. That sound good?"

"It does," I promised. It seemed like I had been waiting my whole life to meet someone who took singing as seriously as I did, and here she was.

"Good," she said, patting me on the cheek. "OK, time for warm-up, ma chérie!"

I could tell right away that So-ri was going to push me further than any other teacher ever had—she wasn't joking about having high expectations. She picked apart all the bad habits I'd developed in the months since my last lesson, and she had me do these breathing exercises I'd never done before. And they were *hard*. At one point, she had me crouch on the ground for almost half an hour so I could access my diaphragm better. It felt so good to really use my voice again, though, and by the end of the lesson, I was sounding better than I had in more than a year. It was almost like going home again. Almost.

On the way out of So-ri's office, I was riding so high that I didn't notice someone else waiting in the hallway.

"Alice, do you have a second?" asked Aria, tapping me on the shoulder with two fingers. She had somehow found time in the day to shower and change out of her workout clothes. Her hair was swept up in a long, graceful ponytail with a little corkscrew curl at the end of it, and she had on a pair of high-waisted skinny jeans and a satiny top. I glanced down at my own shirt and realized I hadn't washed it before packing it up in my suitcase.

"Oh . . . hi," I half squeaked.

"Sorry, I didn't mean to scare you."

"No, it's OK, you didn't." Suddenly, I was very aware that I was alone with Aria; at least with the other girls around, I didn't feel so on display. "Um, so what's up?"

She looked down at the floor like she was thinking hard about what she was going to say. "I wanted to say that I know things got a little awkward yesterday."

"Oh, no, it was totally fine!" I lied. I didn't want her to know that I was upset or bothered in any way.

"Well, it's just that we've all been waiting so long to debut, and when I heard that you didn't have that much training, I . . . I got worried." She dropped her chin like she was ashamed for saying so.

"No, I totally get it," I assured her. "I'm just some random stranger barging my way into your group. It makes sense that you would feel that way."

"Right, but, Alice, that's not fair of me. I shouldn't—I *don't* believe it's just my group; we're all supposed to be in this together. I feel awful about how I reacted yesterday; that's not how I wanted us to start off with you."

Of course Aria was amazing at apologizing; she could probably make tripping on her shoelaces look like a graceful swan dive. If only I could prove to her that I was worth the apology. "Aria, I mean it when I say I'm dying to perform at the Dream Concert. I'm going to do whatever it takes to make sure I don't mess it up for any of us."

"I know you will. But thanks for saying so."

"Yeah, of course."

We stood there for a second, listening to the faraway sound of people singing behind closed doors.

"Hey," she blurted, "can we just start over?" Aria locked eyes with me, waiting for my answer. Her eye contact was so intense, like there were a million and one expectations in it. I wished we could start over, too, but I already knew I was a disappointment to her. Our whole relationship was going to be about me trying to prove I was good enough to be in A-List, and I already knew I would never be as good as she hoped I would be. But I couldn't say any of that, so I just said, "Sure."

"Great," she said, sighing. It was a melodious sigh that ran down an entire octave of notes. "I'm really glad we talked about this."

I looked down at my shoes so I wouldn't have to keep the eye contact going. "Me too."

"So," she said, her voice bright, "the girls and I are going to get boba right now. You should come with us!" Aria affectionately reached for my elbow, and I flinched.

I knew I should go. I knew she was trying to help me "bond" with the group. But after the high of my voice lesson—the first time I'd felt like I truly belonged here—I wasn't ready to take on my role of the D-list member of A-List! "I . . . Actually, I have a ton of homework tonight. I've got, like, ten pages of Korean to memorize."

"It'll only take a few minutes; we're going to a place right down the street."

"I don't think I can. But I'll see you in the room when you get back."

"OK . . ." she said, pulling her hand away from my arm. "I'll just bring one back for you, all right? Good luck with studying, Alice."

"Thanks."

I waited till she was gone, then I ran to our room, grateful to finally be alone.

ALICE
Hiii!!

OLIVIA
omg hi!
what happened? you just disappeared last night.

ALICE
sorry, I had kind of a rough night and then today my schedule was all over the place and I couldn't get to my phone at all.

OLIVIA
it's ok!!!
What happened on your first day, did you get to sing at all??

ALICE
yeah! That part was pretty great. So-ri is so, so amazing. She's super-challenging but I can already feel myself getting better.

OLIVIA
That's so cooool!!!

ALICE
I also found out that she's a former pop star???

OLIVIA
WHAT!!!
Omg, I just googled her and she sings trot! That's really coming back right now, a lot of idols are singing it now.

ALICE
Really?? That's exciting.

OLIVIA
What else did you do? Did you meet any more

IDOLS?????

ALICE
Well, I had to wake up at 5:15 to go on a 2-hour hike.

And then I fainted in the cafeteria . . .

OLIVIA
OH NOOOOOO

Are you OK????????

ALICE
I'm ok

Don't tell Mom, k?

OLIVIA
I won't

promise

ALICE
But Liv guess who I fainted ON?

OLIVIA
WHOO?????

ALICE
. . .

You're going to die

OLIVIA
omg tell meeee

ALICE
. . .

Joon Kwon

OLIVIA

😱😱😱😱😱😱😱

ALICE

lol

OLIVIA

R U SERIOUS????

ALICE

the most serious :)

OLIVIA

DO NOT TAKE A SHOWER UNTIL YOU COME HOME SO
I CAN SMELL HIM

ALICE

loool you are ridic

OLIVIA

I AM NOT JOKING

"This is going to be so *fun*," exclaimed Aria.

This was not going to be so fun. It was not going to be even remotely fun.

"Yeah, I'm, um . . . excited," I said.

I was not excited.

The five of us were heading up to our first group dance lesson. I was exhausted—and not because I'd been waking up at the crack of dawn every morning for the past week (although that didn't help); I was just so anxious about having to dance in front of the girls that I barely slept the night before. I kept imagining myself tripping and falling flat on my face while the girls watched in horror. If Aria was worried about my dancing before, she was going to lose it when she actually saw me attempt to do it.

Hayan was leading us toward the dance studio. She was wearing high-waisted spandex shorts and a black-and-silver sports bra with straps that created a woven lattice across her back. She looked amazing, like a fitness model. "This is my favorite teacher," she said to me over her shoulder, "Moon Seon-saeng-nim; he is a very good dancer."

Seol elbowed Hayan in the ribs and said something in Korean that made Hayan scoff, but everyone else laughed.

"Seol thinks Hayan has a crush on the instructor," explained Aria. Aria was also in a sports bra and shorts, but hers were fuchsia and had little diamond-shaped cutouts running down the sides. She leaned in conspiratorially and lowered her voice. "Actually, we all have a little crush on Mr. Moon; he's gorgeous. Just wait till you see his arms."

Seol flexed both her biceps like The Rock, but her slim arms made only the tiniest bumps under her mesh top. "Mr. Muscleman," she joked. Everyone laughed all over again, even Hayan. One thing I'd picked up right away about Hayan was that no one was allowed to tease her except Seol.

"Ha," I said weakly. It was all I could muster at the moment; I was getting so nervous I had apparently lost the ability to form words.

Hayan must have noticed my nervous energy because she slowed down until we were walking next to each other. "I will help you today, OK? No worries." She placed her hand squarely between my shoulder blades, almost pushing me down the hallway.

"Thanks," I croaked.

"How are your private lessons? You like them?" she asked.

My private lessons were an attempt to fast-track me through years of technique that the other girls had already mastered. The instructor also had me do something called conditioning, which mostly involved systematically torturing my calves and thighs. "Um, they're fine," I replied. Actually, I was pretty sure the instructor thought that I was hopeless.

"I can practice with you after class. Help you get better."

"Yeah, all right, sounds good."

"Today in class, just copy me and you will be fine."

"OK."

It was not going to be OK.

The studio was bright and airy, with big windows and even bigger mirrors—and long ballet barres that ran down the length of one wall. The wood floors had been waxed to such a high gloss that they reflected the white light of snow that hung on tree branches just outside the windows. Who knew that hell would look so cheery?

Aria wasn't kidding; Mr. Moon had seriously ridiculous arms— and muscles in places I didn't even know you could *have* muscles. He didn't speak English, though, so Aria and Hayan had to act as my dance translators.

"Since this is your first class with us, he just wants to see how your style fits into the group dynamic," explained Aria. She was smiling at me with those expectant eyes again. "He says to just use your body naturally, whatever feels good."

"Sure," I said. Leaving and never coming back would feel good; was that an option?

Mr. Moon had us line up in front of the mirrors and used a remote to turn on the music, a laid-back hip-hop beat.

"This is for the warm-up," said Aria, "so just rock from foot to foot."

OK, this I could do. I stepped from one foot to the other, back and forth, back and forth. Simple.

Mr. Moon circled around the group once, stopping next to me. "He say the hip-hop posture is more curving the back," said Hayan. "Like lazier." Hayan rounded her back and let her arms hang by her sides and I did the same, still moving side to side. "You got it," she said.

All right, so far, so good.

"Now add your arms," instructed Hayan. She made her hands into fists and then began opening and closing her arms on each quarter note. The strappy lattice on her sports bra rippled over her back muscles each time her arms expanded and contracted. Even though we were doing the easiest thing imaginable, it was obvious that Hayan was built for dancing. She was so sure of herself and moved so precisely, like she had control over every single atom in her body.

It took me a few tries to get the rhythm right, but once I did, I was pretty much able to stay on beat. Mr. Moon, who was still watching me, nodded in approval. "Nice," he said. Somehow, this was going better than I imagined.

Mr. Moon called out more instructions. "Time to add a move now," said Aria.

Opening and closing my arms to the beat was one thing, but adding another move changed everything. The move was so basic, just a little slide on the downbeat while I pushed out with my hand, but now I had to keep count in my head so I didn't miss the beat.

Was it possible to sweat from overworking your brain? Because my armpits were somehow soaked already.

I was able to keep up through a couple easier drills, and then Mr. Moon called out "Bring it in!"

"He wants us to make a circle," said Aria. "It's just for fun, but I love it when he lets us improv!"

Improv? I only knew three dance moves, and I had literally learned them all in the last twenty minutes!

The five of us formed a wide circle and continued stepping from side to side, this time adding a clap with every step. "I'll start us off!" said Aria. She leaped into the middle of the circle, landing with her feet wide. Smiling seductively, she clapped her hands high above her head, then she slowly rolled her head in a semicircle, letting her auburn-streaked hair hang low over her chest.

It wasn't that she was an incredible dancer, even though she was, it was more that she was captivating to watch. She had what my old singing teacher called stage presence, the ability to put an entire room under her spell.

Aria improvised a few more moves, then pointed at Seol and blew her a kiss. It was her turn. Seol eagerly jumped into the center of the circle, her baggy sweatpants billowing as she popped and locked. She ended with the robot, pretending to power down until her arms and head drooped like she had run out of batteries. It made the other girls crack up, but I was too busy freaking out. What was I going to do when it was my turn? I had no plan whatsoever.

Seol faced Yuri and mimed like she was shooting an orb of light out of her cupped hands, and Yuri pranced into the circle. She was light on her feet and moved her arms gracefully like a ballerina.

When she danced, it was like all her normal hesitancy left her body; she was just a blur of flowing motion.

The beat seemed to be getting faster and faster somehow, and every time we clapped, the bass shattered like thunder. After Yuri, there would only be two of us left, Hayan and me. My nerves were on the move, like a million tiny pinpricks shooting up from my stomach into my chest. Yuri was twirling in circles, her arms sweeping around the circle and pointing at each of us like she was the silver ball in a roulette wheel. Who was she going to land on, Hayan or me? She lengthened her arms above her head like a swan princess, then extended a single finger out in front of her. It was pointed directly at me.

I tugged nervously at my drenched T-shirt and stepped forward. Now everyone's eyes were glued to me as they waited to see me dance on my own for the first time. I moved like I was going to step to the left, when all of a sudden my nerves lurched into the back of my throat. It wasn't nerves—I was going to puke.

"I have to go to the bathroom!" I shrieked. I broke away from the circle, ran out the door, and sprinted blindly down the hall to the nearest restroom, bursting into an empty stall just in time. Dropping to my knees, I heaved into the toilet until I had nothing left to give. When I knew for sure nothing else was going to come out, I yanked a wad of toilet paper off the roll and wiped my mouth and my sweat-slicked forehead. My mouth tasted like a dumpster, which was fitting because that's where I felt like I belonged.

"Alice . . . ? Are you OK?"

I froze. It was Aria; she must have come in while I was puking. I didn't even hear the door open.

"I'm fine!" I called, trying to sound as nonchalant as humanly possible.

I could see her feet under the door, elegant in her black jazz shoes. She took a few steps closer to my stall. "Are you sure? Do you need some water?"

"No, thank you, I don't need water! I'm really OK!"

"I can stay with you until you feel a little better."

"No!" I yelled. I just wanted her to leave. I couldn't bear the thought of her seeing me post-puke, my hair all raggedy and my face pale and damp. I had to think up an excuse. "I—I must have eaten something funny at lunch. I think I, um, just need to go lie down."

Aria took another tentative step toward the stall. "Oh . . . so you don't think you can come back to class?"

"No, I don't think I can." It was cowardly, and I hated myself for simply giving up, but I just couldn't show my face in that dance studio now that she knew I was vomit-level nervous about dancing.

"Well, what if you come back and take it a little easier? We can slow down a little—I honestly think it would be a shame if you missed out on our first class together."

"I really think it'd be better if I sat this one out. I still feel pretty queasy."

"But what if you just watched?" she persisted. "You can sit on the floor and . . ."

"Like I said, I don't feel well."

"OK . . ." she relented. The disappointment in her voice made me feel even more cowardly; we were supposed to be starting over and I was already letting her down. "I can tell the teacher you're sick . . . Are you sure you don't need anything?"

"I'm sure!" I called, desperate for her to just leave already.

"Feel better, Alice."

"I will!"

Under the door, I watched her feet pivot around and head toward the exit. The door swung open and she paused in the doorway for a second, then she was gone.

I flushed the toilet twice, just to be sure, and quickly cleaned myself up. When I got back to our room, I threw myself onto my bed and buried my head under my pillow. So now I wasn't just the girl who fainted during her first week of class at the Star Academy, I was the girl who fainted *and* puked during her first week of class at the Star Academy. If the girls were worried about me before, now they were probably on hands and knees begging Miss Jackie to find them a different groupmate.

I must have fallen asleep, because the next thing I knew, the room was dark and the door was opening. I pulled the pillow off my head and rubbed my eyes as the light from the hallway spilled into the room.

"Dinnertime," said Yuri, her voice quiet like she was talking to a convalescing hospital patient. "You are hungry?"

I squinted at her in the semidarkness. I was actually pretty hungry, but I wasn't ready to face the girls yet. "I don't think so. I'm still feeling kind of sick." I tried to sound as pathetic as I felt so she'd just leave me to my misery.

Yuri grabbed something I couldn't see off her bed and brought it over to my bunk, crouching down so we were on the same level. "I am nervous, too, when I come to Star Academy."

"Oh, I'm not nervous," I lied. "I'm just a little sick to my stomach."

"Mm-hmm," she said. I could only make out the edges of her orange-blond hair in the hallway light. She was nodding, but it was hard to tell if she believed me. "Umm . . . here. For you." She held out her hand, and in it was a tiny baby-blue bunny rabbit with a white heart for a nose. "This one make me feel better when I miss home."

"Oh, thank you," I said, sitting up on my elbows. She was being so nice, but I just needed to be alone. I put the rabbit on my pillow and kind of patted it on the head, hoping that would satisfy her.

Yuri sniffled and rubbed her nose with her open palm; she almost looked like a rabbit herself. "So you not eating dinner tonight . . . ?"

"No, I just need to rest, I think." I went to lie back down and put my hands together under my face to show her what I meant.

Yuri reached her hand out and tenderly propped the rabbit's ears so they both stood up straight. She smiled crookedly at me, then headed for the door, saying good night as she left. When I was sure she was gone, I put the rabbit on the end of my bed next to my feet and pulled my pillow back over my head.

Later that night, when everyone came back to the room, I pretended to be asleep. Eventually, I fell asleep for real, completely starved.

[This page has been translated from Korean.]

02.09

`CATEGORY: SCOOP`

An Explosive Departure

My darling Readers, I would like to pose a simple arithmetic problem: 12−1=??

"Eleven," you say?

"V, please, I placed in the top two percent on the CSAT; I think I know how to solve a remedial math problem," you say?

Alas, the math is not so simple when the 12 I'm referring to is J-Star Media's own Bomb-POP, and the 1 is none other than Korea's favorite little sister herself.

Yes, Zaya will be announcing her departure from the group this evening. But do not worry your little heads, Zaya stans, your beloved bias will be striking out on her own. As of this summer, she will be going solo.

If you'll allow me an indulgent stroll down memory lane, the cracks began forming between Zaya and her sisters early last year, back when this very blog was shook by news of a fight between her and Eun-a. You remember that fated day, when the two got into a screaming match over—irony!— a pile of dirty laundry that Zaya so carelessly left on the floor of their shared dorm room. Well, my Lovelies, it appears that crime left a stain the likes of which no washing machine could ever scrub away. My sources tell me that the two are no longer on speaking terms and that, despite many rosy public appearances together, the rest of the group has completely ostracized Zaya.

We can only hope that in the future she uses extra-strength detergent.

But let us return to the math at hand. As both a lead singer and a main dancer, Zaya is a natural fit for a solo act. But where does that leave poor, poor Bomb-POP and their adoring POP-splosions? It leaves them with a gaping talent void that I can only imagine will be filled with endless sobbing and pints of ice cream on the part of their unfortunate remaining members.

So, dear Readers, keep your eyes peeled for Bomb-POP's next comeback album, when I shall ask again: 12−1=??

The answer, I fear, is so much less than 11.

+ V +

CheeseburgerBlue14

GOD FINALLY . . . ! I never liked Zaya, she was always talking back to her unnies. Have some respect and then you won't get ostracized.

> **PJ_Day**
>
> she is such a good singer thooooo. you can't hate on "Back2Back."
>
> **CheeseburgerBlue14**
>
> Yeah, that song is pretty good. But it would be just as good without her IMO

StellaSays06

I feel so sad for little Zaya! She doesn't deserve to be treated like that :'(

K-POP_In_The_Shower

I'm a POP-splosion and I think whatever they decide together is the right decision.

_smilelikeyoumeanit

How can V break this news before Bomb-POP announces it???? This is such a personal decision and it needs to come from Zaya and her groupmates.

● **51 MORE COMMENTS>>**

Five

"ILEONA!" CHIMED ARIA.

It was morning. *Again.* Time to get out of bed and go hiking.

In the month and a half since I arrived, the rhythm of the academy had become mind-numbing—hike, study, dance, sing, sleep, repeat—the same six notes over and over and over. The only bright spots were my singing lessons with So-ri—and a few random run-ins with Joon, but who was counting? (I was; it was fourteen times in total.) I rarely ever left the building; my "accelerated training" schedule was just too packed. It didn't matter, though, I was too exhausted to ever leave anyway, and the only time I *wasn't* completely wiped was when I was sleeping. Then it was back up again in the morning to start at the top of the stanza: hike, study, dance, sing, sleep, repeat.

"Ileona!" said Aria again, her voice sounding about ten percent annoyed. "Come on, Alice, everyone else has been up for half an hour already." Aria stood over my bunk with crossed arms and her usual disappointed smile.

"Mmmph," I grumbled, rolling over to face the wall.

"OK . . . But Miss Jackie is on her way with some news, so you might want to start getting ready."

I rolled back and peeked over my sheets at the other girls. Mornings were usually pretty sleepy in our room, but not today. Yuri and Hayan were already up and dressed, and even Seol, who was usually the last out of bed, was fumbling around in her closet.

I rubbed the sleep out of my eyes and sat up. "Wait, we aren't going hiking?" Not that I wanted to; my thighs still ached from yesterday's workout.

"Mm-mmm," said Hayan, who was helping Yuri brush a big knot out of her hair. "No hiking."

"Miss Jackie say big room at five thirty," said Seol. She meant the main room in the girls' wing. I looked down at my phone—it was already 5:24. Shoot.

I sprang out of bed and ran over to my dresser, where I grabbed the first T-shirt and pair of jeans I could find.

"OK, well, if we don't head over now, we're going to be late . . . See you there," said Aria. She pushed open the door and the other girls followed her.

Seol was the last one to leave and hung back in the doorway watching me get ready. "Hurry, hurry," she said.

"I'm going as fast as I can," I assured her as I yanked on my jeans.

Seol peered over her shoulder, down the hall, and then back at me. She looked worried.

"It's OK; I'll be there in two minutes."

"OK . . . Bye-bye."

Seol let the door close, and I scrambled to pull on my T-shirt. I smoothed my tangled mess of hair into the neatest ponytail I could manage, then grabbed my phone and ran out the door.

When I got to the big room, the girls were already seated on the couch. Miss Jackie was standing in front of them waiting for me, her red lipstick glistening in the morning sun that streamed through the windows. As I approached the couch, her eyes scanned my sloppy hair and wrinkled tee, and I could tell she was docking me another point in her mental ledger. Unlike the other girls, I just never seemed to meet her impossibly high standards.

"Please sit," she said.

I sat down next to Seol at the end of the couch, and Miss Jackie started explaining something in Korean. I could only catch little pieces of what she was saying—"hair," "photograph," "day and night" stood out, but none of the words came together to make any kind of sense. At one point, Yuri kind of gasped and everyone grabbed one another's hands. Whatever Miss Jackie was saying had to be big, but I was forced to sit there in agony with my hands in my lap until she explained everything to me in English.

Finally, Miss Jackie turned to me. "Alice. I am pleased to announce that A-List's first concept will be a day/night look." She might as well have been speaking Korean, I had no idea what she was talking about. "The five of you will spend the morning in hair and makeup, and then you will have a photo shoot at the sound-stage this afternoon. The photos will be used for promotional materials and for A-List's debut album cover. You will also receive the sheet music for your first single."

Our first single! No wonder everyone was freaking out! If only Olivia were here so I could have someone to freak out with, too.

"Now, *please* get washed up and eat something; this is going to be an extremely long day. And when you are finished, head directly to the soundstage." Miss Jackie eyed my messy ponytail one last time, then whisked out of the room.

When we were sure she was gone, Seol dropped to her knees and threw her fists in the air. "AH-SSA!"

"Oh my god, our single!" I said to her, letting myself get swept up in her excitement. It was all coming together so fast. "I can't believe it's happening already!"

"Yah, day and night! So cool!" she exclaimed, grinning her face off. She got back up on her feet and jumped on me with a big hug.

"Oh!" I said, surprised.

"Daebakida. Congratulations!"

"You too, Seol!" I said, hugging her back. "This is so exciting!"

"Ye! Big, big day."

"Yeah, it is."

I expected the other girls to celebrate, too, but they were still sitting on the couch, speechless. Hayan and Yuri were embracing each other solemnly like someone had just died, and Yuri was even crying a little. Aria sat next to them with her fists pressed into the couch, staring at the floor with this funny expression. It was weird, the look was somewhere between laughing and crying, like she was trying to come to terms with everything Miss Jackie had just told us. It was kind of awkward, and I didn't really know how I was supposed to act, so I pulled away from Seol and went to find So-hyun. I could shower later—I didn't want to wait any longer to share the big news with someone I knew would be purely happy about it.

So-hyun was technically only supposed to show me around during my first few weeks on campus, but time kept passing and we kept hanging out, until one day we were just friends. Actually, she was turning out to be my best friend at the academy. She probably wouldn't have felt the same way about me if the other girls in her group lived on-campus, too, but that didn't really bother me; I was just so grateful to have someone else to hang out with that felt like a friend from home.

On the way to So-hyun's room, I texted Olivia:

ALICE

Shooting our album cover and getting our first single today!!

My phone buzzed from Olivia's response, but I had already reached So-hyun's room so I shoved it in my pocket and knocked on the door.

"Jamsimanyo!" said a sweet, singsong voice from behind So-hyun's door.

"It's me!" I called back.

"Oh, *you*," she grumbled, switching back to her normal voice. Her door cracked open and a half-asleep So-hyun poked her head out. "C'mon, man, I'm tryina sleep in here."

"You're still in bed?"

"We had an appearance on *Radio Star* last night. It was a long night. What do you want from me?" Sleepy So-hyun was apparently not to be messed with, but I was too excited to let her go back to bed.

"I've got big news for yooou," I sang, trying to entice her out of her room.

"News! Why didn't you say so? I'll be right out!" So-hyun slammed the door shut, leaving me in the hallway while she got dressed.

As I waited, I looked at a little plastic basket she had taped to her door. It was lavender and had these tiny daisies all over it, and it was full of folded-up notes from the other XOKiss girls. I think they felt bad that she was too young to live with them off campus, so they were always leaving cute little things for her, like stationary or snacks. It made me think of the Post-it that Seol had stuck to my bunk on my first night at the academy. It was still there next to the picture of Olivia and me. Out of all the girls in the group, I got along best with Seol. She was a little different from the others, and we kind of bonded over that, but I hadn't gotten any more notes from her since that first night.

After a minute or two, So-hyun still hadn't come back out, so I put my ear to the door and heard sheets rustling—she had gotten back into bed.

"So-hyun!" I yelled, twisting her locked doorknob back and forth. "Come on, it's almost six o'clock! Get outta bed and come to breakfast so I can tell you what Miss Jackie just told us!"

I waited another minute, then the door flew back open and So-hyun emerged, dressed in a cute rose-colored jumper and a white cardigan. "Fine," she said. "But I reserve the right to be grumpy as hell."

"No problem. All you need to do is listen." I was feeling giddy—about the single, about getting So-hyun out of bed—and I threw my arm around her neck as we headed toward the cafeteria.

"So what is this 'news' that you just *had* to tell me at this ungodly hour?" asked So-hyun.

"Guess who's shooting the cover for her first SINGLE today?" I said.

"Oh my god, WHAT?" she hollered, dropping the grumpy act and wrapping her arms around my head. "Congrats, girl! Seriously!"

"Thanfs," I said, my words getting muffled in her chest.

"Did you guys celebrate this morning?"

"Mm, not really; it was kind of weird, actually. I think the news kind of broke Aria."

So-hyun let go of my head so she could look at me sideways. "What do you mean?"

"I mean, Seol was really excited, but the other girls . . . they looked pretty shocked. Like Aria just sat there staring at her feet."

"Huh. Well, they *have* been waiting forever to debut. I bet they were just having a moment, you know? When the girls and I found out we were going to record our first single, we all bawled our eyes out."

"Yeah, you're probably right. I just didn't really know what I was supposed to do."

"Did you ask them if they were OK?"

"No," I admitted. "I don't know . . . We don't really have that kind of relationship."

"Well, after breakfast you should ask them how they're feeling."

"Yeah, maybe. I don't really think they want me asking about their innermost feelings though."

"I bet you'd be surprised."

The delicious smell of soup drifted from the kitchen as we walked into the cafeteria, an annoying reminder that I wouldn't be eating any. We stepped up to the food counter, where Joon and Soo-li, the solo artist who was allergic to strawberries (thank you, Olivia, for that incredibly useful information), were already in line.

"'Sup, So-hyun. Hey, Alice," Joon said, yawning.

"Hi, Oppa," said So-hyun. Olivia told me that you're supposed to call older Korean guy-friends Oppa, but I still didn't feel comfortable calling Joon that. I barely felt comfortable calling him anything at all. "Hey," I said instead, suddenly feeling extremely un-showered.

The three of them chatted in Korean while I kind of stood to the side, silently waiting in line next to them. It happened a lot, actually. Kids would just tune me out, and long stretches of time would pass when no one spoke in English. But it didn't bother me as much as I thought it would. It meant that I could just blend into the background and watch people, which was where I felt most comfortable anyway.

Eventually, So-hyun turned back to me and said in English, "Alice is doing her first photo shoot today."

"Oh, cool! That's a huge deal," said Joon.

"So exciting!" said Soo-li.

"Thanks," I said, beaming at them.

A woman behind the counter handed everyone a tray with a bowl of soup with a few side dishes except me—I got my standard plate of cabbage. We found an empty table in the back, and the four of us slid onto the benches across from one another. So-hyun checked to make sure Miss Jackie wasn't around, then snuck some pickled veggies onto my plate. "Sooooo, what's the concept?" she asked.

"Miss Jackie said it was a day/night look?" I said.

"Huh. That's a new one," said Joon. He looked at Soo-li and So-hyun, and they both shrugged. "So . . . what is it?" he asked.

"I don't know. It didn't really seem like a good time to ask questions."

"Yeah, it's pretty much never a good time with Miss Jackie," he said.

"Day/night sounds like something out of a magazine my mom would read," said So-hyun. In a posh-sounding British accent, she drawled, "The pah-fect maxi dress that seamlessly trahns-fohms from a day look into a night look."

"Or," I offered, "high school girl by day, assassin by night."

"Oh shit," she said, "that's actually pretty good."

"I bet you guys'll have to wear giant papier-mâché moons and suns on your heads," said Joon.

"Oh god, really? Would they honestly make us do that?"

Joon laughed, which made So-hyun roll her eyes, and I realized he was joking. "Ohhh. It was a joke. Duh, Alice," I said, shaking my head. Ugh, I can't believe I actually fell for that.

"Top10 would never make you look bad." Joon nudged my arm with his elbow to show me he was just playing around. "They always come through."

"I hope so," I said. I stuffed a big bite of noodles into my mouth to distract myself from the fact that Joon had just touched me.

"Have I ever showed you our first concept?" asked So-hyun.

"No, what was it?" I said.

"Here, lemme show you now."

So-hyun pulled out her phone, a gem-encrusted brick of sparkle and glitter with a case shaped like a bottle of Chanel perfume. It had a pearled strap so she could wear it like a purse. She swiped through her photos, then dropped her phone in my hands.

On the screen, the eight members of XOKiss stood on a white background striking these innocent-looking poses—blowing kisses, twirling ponytails, fingers pressed into dimples—all of them wearing identical tops and pleated skirts the color of Pepto-Bismol.

"It was a cheerleader concept?"

"Yuuup," she said.

Soo-li leaned over my shoulder and looked at the screen. "Wanjeon gwiyeowo!"

"Right?" said So-hyun. "She says we look cute. I mean, not to totally brag, but don't we just look so iconic?"

"*So* iconic," I said, laughing. I loved it when So-hyun just unabashedly complimented herself. It wasn't bragging; it was just So-hyun.

So-hyun zoomed in on Yeona, XOKiss' lead member who was also So-hyun's favorite even if she would never admit it, for the sake of group unity. Yeona was the only one who had dyed hair in the picture; it was a kind of deep cherry-red. "I loved Yeona's hair when it was red," said So-hyun. "We had such a freaking blast shooting this, too—oh my god, Alice, you're gonna have so much fun with your groupmates today."

I nodded, agreeing with her, but actually, I wasn't so sure. It was easy for So-hyun—she was so likable and outgoing, and she had everything in common with the other XOKiss girls. I was excited about the shoot, but it wasn't exactly because of my groupmates.

Joon leaned over me so he could get a better look at the screen, and he was so close I could smell his hair product. The scent must have been specifically formulated to make girls melt into the floor. "I remember when you guys shot that," he said. "You were like a flock of flamingos stalking around the academy."

"I'm sorry, but wasn't your first concept like Charlie Chaplin-themed or something?" said So-hyun, grabbing her phone back.

"Yeah, and I looked handsome as hell in that monocle."

"Mm, see," So-hyun said to me, pointing her spoon at Joon. "Big ego."

Joon jerked his chin up, flipping his bangs off his forehead, then flashed So-hyun a cocky smile full of perfectly white, perfectly straight teeth. It was Joon's signature move, and Olivia practically lost her mind over it. Now I understood why.

"What was your favorite concept?" I asked him.

"It was a dark concept. We were supposed to be these half-vampire, half-zombie creatures. But like, *cool* half-vampire, half-zombie creatures."

"What does that even look like?" I asked.

Joon took a big swig of tea and wiped his mouth with the back of his hand. "It was a lot of chains and torn black clothes—and a *ton* of fake blood. The problem with the fake blood was that it smelled like rotten eggs when it dried, and it got all crusted up in my hair. I couldn't get the smell out of my hair for a week, and I even had to toss my pillow."

So-hyun spat her soup back into her spoon. "Ugh, Oppa. Come on, we're all eating here."

"Sorry," said Joon, "that shit was nasty, though."

"Aside from the rotten-egg blood, it actually sounds pretty cool," I said.

"Yeah, aside from that I loved it. The best part, though," he continued, "was that all the BoMS wore glow-in-the-dark vampire teeth at our first comeback concert. It was this big surprise they planned for us, and it was so cool when the lights went down the first time and everyone smiled. The whole auditorium lit up with blue teeth."

"Wow, that sounds awesome," I said.

"It totally was," said Joon. "Instead of an ocean, they called it a Blue Smile."

Joon shook his head and kind of marveled at it for a second. "Sometimes I can't believe how creative our fandom is. The BoMS really are the best."

"Excuse you!" protested So-hyun, with a scandalized expression. "I would really beg to differ."

Joon put his palms up, pretending to back down. "OK, Queen

So-hyun, no one's fandom is as amazing as the HeartBeat. We all bow down to them."

"That's absolutely correct."

Exactly thirty minutes and one shower later, I met up with the other girls at the soundstage, which had been totally transformed since the auditions. People rushed around setting up the photo shoot: rolling out cloth backdrops, unfurling giant metallic reflectors, and taping all kinds of cords to the floor. It was like a scene out of *Downton Abbey*, when all the maids and butlers are scurrying around getting the estate ready for the arrival of the duchess of Saxlebury or whatever. The unbelievable part was that *we* were the duchesses of Saxlebury.

Lights popped and flared above our heads as we wove our way through all the equipment to the door where, just months earlier, Mr. Kim had made his one cameo entrance into my life. I hadn't gotten even a glimpse of him since. Miss Jackie was waiting for us on the other side, and she led us deep into an unfamiliar maze of hallways until we ended up in front of a turquoise door.

"This is our wardrobe department," Miss Jackie explained to me as she clasped the doorknob. "You will have your fitting here; then you will go to hair and makeup."

We stepped into a gigantic, warehouse-size room that had enough clothing to dress a small city. There was an endless row of garment racks running from one end of the room to the other, each one bulging with gaudy, glittering costumes. One of the racks near the door was overstuffed with ball gowns, and the racks next to it had all different kinds of rhinestoned suits. There was a whole shelf of old-fashioned hats, including a pile of electric-blue top hats stacked on top of one another like a layered cake. I wasn't really into playing dress-up when I was little—that was more Olivia's thing—but the costumes were so gorgeous that I wanted to dive into the racks and start trying everything on.

Miss Jackie led us to the middle of the room, where there were five garment racks set up for us, each one marked with our names. It only took a glance to get what Miss Jackie meant by a day/night concept: every piece of clothing, even down to the jewelry, was black and white.

Seol ran right up to her rack and started riffling through it, but the rest of us kind of hung back and took it all in.

"Daebak," whispered Hayan in Aria's ear.

Aria nodded once, her eyes glued to the rack with her name on it. Hayan, Yuri, and I watched as she stepped up to the hanging clothes and slowly ran her hand down a long black dress. When she was finished, she let out a long, heavy sigh, then turned toward us with a wobbly smile, wiping away a tear. Hayan and Yuri went to comfort her, Yuri touching her arm lightly and Hayan planting her hand on her shoulder, massaging it. Yuri whispered something softly that I couldn't hear, and the three of them stood there with their heads bowed, almost like they were praying.

I could hear So-hyun's voice in my mind telling me to ask them if they were OK, but it really didn't seem like they wanted to be interrupted, so I turned to my own wardrobe. I ran the tips of my fingers across the beautiful fabrics: a milky-white sheer blouse, an almost-iridescent ivory silk dress, the softest black leather jacket I had ever felt. Black and white was *so* much better than an assassin concept.

Miss Jackie let us inspect our costumes for only a moment, then she called something out in Korean, and about a dozen women wearing aprons full of safety pins and measuring tapes emerged from the back of the room.

"Ot beo-seo," said Miss Jackie. "Clothes off, girls."

"Here?" I wondered out loud. It was embarrassing enough that I had to get dressed in front of the other girls every day, but did I really have to get naked in front of all these strangers, too?

"Yes, *here*," replied Miss Jackie. It was still early, but Miss Jackie was already getting testy. I started peeling off my clothes, and before I even had both legs out of my pants, two of the stylists jammed a tube dress down over my head. They rolled it over my boobs, tugging at it to get it over my rib cage. I sucked in my stomach, but they gave up about halfway down my butt, leaving it all bunched up around my waist.

I peered down at the beautiful dress that was now all scrunched up around me. It was covered in sequins, one side was black and the other white, and there was a big satin ruffle running right down the middle. I looked like a smashed Oreo.

Miss Jackie noticed us struggling and walked over to me, her eyes locked critically onto my stomach where the dress bunched. She consulted with two of the stylists, their faces all frowns, while I stood there like a literal dummy.

"You should have no trouble fitting into this size," said Miss Jackie, tugging at my dress. "Your nutritionists have been keeping a very close watch on your calorie intake. Can you explain why we cannot seem to get you into this dress?"

"I don't know why it doesn't fit me . . . Maybe the nutritionists made a mistake?" I said, practically squeaking as I lied through my teeth. I knew exactly why the dress didn't fit; I had been eating half of So-hyun's breakfast, lunch, and dinner every day for the past six weeks.

Miss Jackie gave me a look like I had just told her the world's unfunniest joke. "Oh, I do not think there is a problem with your nutritionists. Perhaps, though, you have found a source of food outside your dietary regiment?" Her hand darted out, and she pinched my stomach between her thumb and index finger. She squeezed them together, hard, and a sharp pain hit me like a booster shot.

"I've—been trying some of the other kids' food—just to see what it tastes like!" I screeched, my breath caught in my throat from the pain. It was an extremely lame excuse. Miss Jackie and I both knew it. "I won't do it again. I promise."

"Yes, see that you do not. Or you will be eating your meals alone . . . in your room." She let go and snapped her fingers at the ladies-in-apron. Then she spoke to them in Korean, but the last part she said in English, just for me, "She needs something to suck up that stomach of hers."

One of the stylists brought out a pair of high-waisted spandex shorts and squeezed me into them, then they dressed me in a whole new outfit: a white blouse with billowy arms tucked into a black suede miniskirt. To cover up my stomach, they wrapped me in a half corset made of leather that laced up the front with tassels. The finishing touch was a pair of Balenciaga stilettos, one black and one white. I counted up all the labels—Fendi, Givenchy, Balenciaga, Dior—I had on more designers than the front page of Poshmark. The whole thing must have been worth more than my and Olivia's college funds put together.

When I was all zipped, laced, and buttoned up, Miss Jackie stepped back and considered me again. She tapped her finger against her chin and said, "Yes, this is the one. No need to try on anything else."

I turned to one of the full-length mirrors in the room so I could take a look at myself, and the first thing I noticed were all these new lines and curves I had never seen on myself before. I actually had cleavage—cleavage!—peeking out of the top of my blouse. My hips sloped down and out from beneath my corset, and the heels made my butt pop way out. A kind of embarrassing idea wormed into my brain—*I looked like a woman.*

As I stood there staring at this person I barely recognized, I could see the other girls behind me in the mirror, undressing and handing their outfits back the stylists so they could be altered before the photo shoot. I began to turn to follow them, but Miss Jackie came up behind me and held me in place with her hands on my shoulders. The hard tips of her fingernails pressed the sheer fabric of my blouse into my skin.

"Alice," she said, drawing out the *c* in my name so it came out like a hiss. "Meet Harmony."

"Meet . . . who?" I asked. I peered into the mirror, but we were alone.

"It is to be your stage name. Alice is the not the name of an idol, so instead your fans will know you as Harmony Choy."

"Harmony Choy," I repeated, trying it out. Sometimes Olivia and I would crack each other up inventing fake stage names, like Alisse or Madame Choy. Those names always made me laugh, but part of me seriously considered them. But Harmony? It was so meek and kind of corny; it didn't really seem to fit me at all.

"Can you tell me the definition of this word?" asked Miss Jackie.

I watched my mouth open then close in the mirror. I'd always just kind of *understood* what harmony was; I'd never really thought about its actual definition.

"Since you seem to be at a loss for words, I will tell you." Miss Jackie tightened her grip on my shoulders, and her fingernails made little moon-shaped indentations into my blouse. "Harmony is an agreeable girl, who places her fans and her duties above her own needs. She is always in accord with the members of her group, never so much as a step ahead nor behind. Her mood is tempered, serene, and she is always pleased to meet the expectations of her entertainment company, no matter the demand."

She paused to make sure I was listening, and I obediently nodded.

"Not only will this be the persona you present to the world," she added, "but Top10 hopes you can embody these qualities in your everyday life. Do you understand?"

I was staring at my legs in the mirror, but all I saw were two blurry sticks. Was this some sort of lecture for not sticking to my diet or did I do something else wrong? It was worrying to think that Miss Jackie saw me as some kind of troublemaker, even after all the weeks of hard work I'd been putting in. I didn't want to be in any more trouble than I already seemed to be, so if Top10 thought Harmony was a good stage name for me, then I would have to take it. "I understand," I said finally.

"Good," said Miss Jackie. She released her grip, letting her nails drag down my arms as she pulled away. "Now, please be on your way to hair and makeup."

She waved the stylists back over and they unbound me, leaving me standing alone and half-naked, back in my regular teenage body.

Two hours later, I was still in hair and makeup. The girls passed the time gossiping about people I didn't know and singing these Korean hand-clapping songs that sort of reminded me of "Miss Mary Mack." The stylists had cut and colored my hair, and now they were threading extensions into my scalp. As I sat there gritting my teeth, a low hum floated into the room, followed by the sound of flip-flops slapping in the hallway. It was So-ri.

"Guten Morgen!" my singing teacher called out above the drone of blow-dryers. She was carrying a jumble of papers under her arm, and as she worked her way down the row of chairs saying hello to everyone, she handed them each a few pages from the stack.

"Ah, la bonne étoile!" she crowed as she approached my chair. She raised a hand to my face and rested her open palm against my cheek. Her hand was as pillowy as a soft-boiled egg yolk. I tried to work up a smile but could only manage to grimace as the hairstylist dug his torture instruments into my scalp.

"Alice-yah, why so glum-faced? This is very great day for you."

"I know. I'm OK, really," I assured her, grimacing. I was still stewing over Miss Jackie's little lecture, and I guess my face gave me away.

"Hmm," she said, frowning. "Well, this will make you feel better." She snatched a few pieces of paper from under her arm and pressed them into my lap. I picked up the first page and read the title: *"2day/2nite" performed by A-List.*

"Whoa," I said under my breath.

I sight-read the first page as fast as I could, humming the melody as I went. The song started out fast-paced and poppy, then when the chorus dropped, it slowed way down and the melody got dark and mysterious. Most of the song was in Korean, except for the bridge and some of the chorus. I looked up at So-ri and grinned at her.

"Hǎo de! What I say? You feel better, right?"

"This looks so great, Seon-saeng-nim. I can't wait to sing it."

"You just wait, chica." Pushing hair supplies out of her way, she boosted herself up so she was sitting on the salon countertop, her legs dangling like a little kid's. She hollered something at the stylists, and they clicked off their blow-dryers.

"So!" said So-ri, addressing the room. "This is your new single, the song that introduces the whole world to your beautiful voices. At the Dream Concert, it happens like this. When you sing the verse, the lights go big and bright. But when the chorus come—*bam!*—all the lights go out and everything is dark except for secret lights that make your costume glow—what is the word? Ni . . . ni . . . neen?"

"Neon?" I guessed.

"Neon! Yes, your costumes glow neon!"

I thought about it for a second. "Ohhh! They'll be lit up by a black light!"

"Yes, like *that*," except she said it "like *dat*." "Will be very exciting surprise for your fans!"

The girls traded excited looks with one another in the mirror, and Seol shot me a thumbs-up from her salon chair on other side of the room. OK, I was wrong, this was *infinitely* better than a cheerleader concept.

Quieting us back down, So-ri continued. "And, I have special announcement for the new member." She reached over to me and patted me on the top of my head, to the annoyance of my hairdresser. "Alice will be the new main vocalist with Aria."

An "Oh!" escaped from my mouth. I tried to push it back in with both my hands, but it was too late; everyone's eyes darted from me to Aria to see how she would react. She brushed a strand of hair off her face like it was irritating her, but then she smiled politely and clapped for me, which cued the other girls to do the same. It was impossible to tell if she was annoyed or what—she was just so good at keeping her composure—but it was obvious she wasn't over-joyed about it.

So-ri tapped the sheet music in my lap with her small finger. "The bridge, the one in English. This is your solo, Alice."

If my heart had wings, it would have flown out of my chest, out of the academy, and into the sky. Harmony . . . Alice . . . Idiot McDumbface—they could call me whatever they wanted, I didn't care; I had a solo verse on our single and I was going to be a main singer!

So-ri tapped my sheet music again and said, "And here. Verse number three. This is solo for Aria."

Yuri squealed and reached out to grab Aria's hand. Now, a full smile broke out on Aria's face, and she nodded graciously while everyone clapped for her. I clapped, too, but I couldn't help noticing there was a lot more applause for her than for me.

"Mm-hmm," grunted So-ri. She pursed and un-pursed her lips like she was chewing on her tongue. "Two main singers . . . not so easy. The main singers have the most responsibility, but also the most fans, the most fame. Lots to share. You two think you can share?" she asked, looking from me to Aria and back to me again.

"Yes, Seon-saeng-nim," we both replied automatically. I didn't really know how we'd share the position, but now that I thought about it, it did kind of seem like a bad idea. Aria's whole life revolved around being the leader of A-List; it basically defined her. She was like the class president, valedictorian, and head of the cheerleading squad all rolled into one. The idea that someone like me—the kid who sat at the back of the class—could share the spotlight with her was kind of a cruel joke. Besides, there was no such thing as two class presidents.

"Good, good," said So-ri, nodding. "I think it is a good idea for you to do private singing class together, too."

And just like that, there went my heart. So-ri's office was the only place in the academy where I could work on the one thing I was good at without feeling judged. With Aria there, it was going to feel like every day was an audition.

"Sound good to you two?" asked So-ri.

Aria sat up straighter in her chair with a new, determined look on her face. She was trying not to show it, but something made me think she wasn't happy to share lessons with me, either. "Yes, Seon-saeng-nim," she agreed.

"Sure, sounds good to me," I said into my lap. Clearly, I didn't have Aria's acting skills.

So-ri clapped her hands, looking pleased with herself. "So that is that."

She stuck around, perched on the counter and chatting with us like a parrot until we were fully hair and makeup-ed. When we were done, and I had about five pounds of concealer on my face, they squeezed me back into my costume. As everyone headed to the set, I hung back in the wardrobe room so I could check myself out one last time.

I had been transformed into a perfect, plastic Barbie doll, except I looked more like Miko, Barbie's Asian friend. I scanned my reflection for any sign of Alice, but all I could see was Harmony.

As I stood there making sense of myself, the door opened and closed, then Aria appeared behind me in the mirror. It was staggering how gorgeous she was with her hair and makeup all done up. Her white halter dress hugged her body and shimmered as she moved like she was some kind of mermaid emerging from the ocean. Jet-black jewels hung around her neck, and a tiny black belt cinched at her equally tiny waist. She didn't need a corset to hide her stomach.

She smoothed down the front of her dress as if she were standing in the mirror all alone. We looked so different from each other. She had such high cheekbones and a swooping nose that ended in a smooth, round point. My face was flat and round, and the stylists had to cake on the highlighter to get any definition in my wide nose. My chin practically melted into my jaw, where Aria's was perfectly defined. She looked so elegant, so confident. She was like a newer, shinier version of herself, like Aria 2.0. I looked like a little girl playing dress-up in her mom's closet. I felt stupid comparing myself to her, but I couldn't help it. It made me feel pathetic.

"Congratulations on your solo and your new position," she said.

I flicked my eyes to my own reflection, hoping she hadn't caught me looking at her. "Thanks, you too—I mean, on the solo."

"Thank you." For a second, it looked like she was going to leave, but then she blurted, "You know, it took me a really long time to get that position. I had to do an internal audition for it before they even formed A-List."

"Oh, uh, I had no idea," I said. I could tell she wanted me to say something more, but I didn't really know what.

"It's just that you haven't been here even two months, and they're already promoting you."

"I'm sorry," I offered, "but, Aria, I was just as surprised as you were when So-ri announced it. I didn't ask for the position."

"I know . . . You're right." Aria closed her eyes and exhaled like she was resetting herself. "Well, we're in this together now. I can help you get up to speed with your parts so you're ready for our debut. There's less than three months left; that's not a lot of time and you have a lot of work to do."

"Um, thanks, but I think I'll be fine," I said, suddenly irritated. Maybe I didn't have a lot of training in dance or acting, but singing was the one thing I *did* know how to do. "I led my section in choir," I said, "I know what I'm supposed to do."

"Sure, but this is kind of different, don't you think?" Aria tilted her head and blinked her long, mascara-ed eyelashes at me. Maybe I was imagining it, but there was something kind of patronizing about it.

"I don't really see how it's different," I mumbled.

"Well, you probably had dozens of people in your choir. There's only five of us in A-List, so your voice really counts."

"Yeah, like I said, I'll be fine. I don't need any help."

We glared at each other through the mirror until Aria sort of scoffed like she was exasperated. "OK, fine. You don't need my help . . . We're supposed to be on the set in five; are you coming?"

"I'll just see you out there," I said.

"Great." Aria spun away from the mirror, and her hair twirled so close to my face that I could feel a little whoosh of air on my cheeks.

The photo shoot moved along in quarters of inches when it moved at all.

"Raise your chin a tiny bit," the photographer said through Miss Jackie. "Cheat your shoulders out one inch. Slide your foot to the left slightly . . . now, hold it!" There'd be a burst of flashes, then we'd change positions and do it all over again. They took a million solo shots of each of us—and just as many group shots. Aria and I were positioned next to each other in almost every one, but she was all smiles and grace, acting as if we never had our encounter in the wardrobe room.

By the time it was over, my toes were numb and my legs quaked from standing in stilettos for so long. We had skipped lunch and I was starving, but I couldn't wait any longer to tell Olivia about my big news so I snuck off to the third-floor studios to call her. I found an empty one and quietly locked myself in.

Sitting on the floor with one arm wrapped around my empty stomach, I pulled out my phone and realized I still hadn't read the texts Olivia had sent me earlier that morning. I scanned them as the phone rang:

6:12 a.m.

OLIVIA
Yaaayeee! Omgee I'm so happy for you!!!
What's the concept???
😄 😄 😄

3:40 p.m.

OLIVIA
Actually, I know you're busy but can you call me? They just announced some festival thing at school and I want to talk to you about it.
Do you think it would be weird if I went alone?

Olivia picked up on the third ring. "Hi!"

"Hey! How *are* you?" I held the phone tight to the side of my face, as if it somehow made me physically closer to her.

"Meh, I'm OK. Mom is being . . . Mom."

"Oh yeah? What's she doing?"

"You know, she's always just so distracted with work and stuff. She was supposed to take me shopping for new shoes after school today, but she canceled at the last minute."

"God. That's so *Mom* of her."

Olivia giggled, which made me smile. I could picture her lying on her bed on her stomach, her legs kicking around with the phone cradled in the crook of her neck.

"So, I have to tell you something really exciting," I said, my stomach starting to gurgle.

"*More* exciting news? Jeez!"

"I know; it's been kind of a big day."

"Yeah, tell me about it."

As I filled her in on my main-singer news, Olivia got so excited and loud I had to hold the phone a few inches from my ear. I could always count on her to have the exact right reaction to everything I told her.

"I *told* you that you were going to blow them away!"

"You're right; you totally did," I admitted, grinning.

"So, Al," she said, changing the subject, "what am I supposed to do about this festival thing?"

My stomach made a little burble of hunger, but I ignored it. "What is it again?"

"I don't know; it's some annual event they put on in the auditorium where each club has a booth, and there's food and games and stuff. It's in three weeks, and apparently everyone goes in groups, and I don't really have anyone to go with."

"What about that girl in your class that reads the same webtoons as you?" I said.

"Minji? She's probably already going with her friends."

"OK, why don't you ask if you can go with them?"

"Because! I can't just *invite* myself. That'd be so desperate."

My stomach groaned again, and it was so loud I wondered if she could hear it through the phone. "Well, is there anyone else you can ask?"

"Not really. Everyone kind of already has their own friend groups."

"Yeah, I know what you mean," I sympathized.

Olivia was silent for a second. "Do you think you could maybe come home that weekend and go with me?" she asked.

Of course I wanted to go home really bad, especially to help out Olivia, but there was no way in hell Miss Jackie would let me miss an entire weekend just for a school fundraiser.

"I don't think I can, Liv," I said. "Sorry."

"Yeah, I didn't think so." She sighed loudly into the phone, and her breath crackled in my ear.

"You know I would if I could."

"Yeah, I know," she said softly.

I didn't want to get off the phone with her, especially like this, but I was starting to feel light-headed. Plus, if I fainted in a locked room all by myself I might actually die.

"Hey, Liv? I think I have to go get some food. I haven't eaten since six this morning and I'm about to pass out."

"OK," she said.

"Sorry."

"It's okaaay," she said, sighing again.

"I promise I'll call you back tomorrow when things aren't so nuts, K?"

"K."

"OK, talk to you soon. Promise."

"Bye."

I hung up, then sprinted down to the cafeteria, my feet aching and my stomach complaining the whole way down.

[This page has been translated from Korean.]

03.11

CATEGORY: REVIEW

Top10 Entertainment Teases New Girl Group, A-List

Oh, Readers. Brace thyselves.

After months of wild and unverified speculation, today Top10 Entertainment revealed their plans for their new American trainee . . . It came in the form of a tragic PR stunt.

Around the ten o'clock hour this evening, Top10's PR team was deployed to high schools across Seoul, armed with stacks of photo cards. As students began to trickle out from their late-night study period, they were introduced to Top10's newest girl group—A-List.

The photo cards appear to be harmless enough. They feature the five members of A-List, leaning against a white backdrop in a yawn-inducing black-and-white concept, which Top10 cleverly rebranded as a day/night look. The concept treads ground that will be oh so familiar to long-standing K-pop fans: the girls are clad in mono-chromatic designer apparel, with vaguely mod hair and makeup. Long, bare legs abound . . . naturally.

But it doesn't stop there, Readers. Oh no, it does not.

What one thought was just a forgettable first impression was actually Top10 serving a bland appetizer before a "delicious" main course. On the front of each photo card is a rather cryptic directive that reads TURN OFF THE LIGHTS. You see, innocent Readers, when these photo cards are plunged into darkness, they glow in the dark. And when you do turn off the lights, make sure there are no parents present because the neon outlines of A-List's unclothed bodies pop off these photo cards like your mother's eyes will pop out of her head.

So please, shield your eyes, my dears, when you scroll down to the picture below, for the neon glow of A-List's stark-naked silhouettes may prove too much for the faint of heart (kisses to @jbom for procuring a photo card for me).

I wouldn't say this, um, *original* concept is slutty . . . but that's because I really don't have to.

Someone, please turn off the lights and put these girls to bed.

+ V +

I_Like_Him_More
She said "unverified speculation." V, get over yourself, that's like your whole thing.

Anonymous
So turn off the lights and A-List will take their clothes off? God, that is the definition of slutty.

Flowers_For_Me
I got one tonight! It's sosososo cool. I really was surprised when I turned the lights off the first time.

> **Taeyeon^_^**
> Ahhh, I want one! How can I get one, is it too late???

> **ParkBomIsLife**
> Top10 left a stack of them in front of Ewha Girls' High School! Hurry before they're all gone!!

> **Taeyeon^_^**
> Omg thank you so much!!

kdkkdkd
A-List, I didn't ask and I'm NOT curious

Minjun71
Ew, talk about attention-whores. Why do girl groups always feel like they have to do sexy concepts?

MisterNim
If the music is good then I don't really care what their concept is. We shouldn't judge until we actually hear them.

PeachPi
I don't know, I think they look kinda cool

Kwang-hee4Me
Another Top10 gimmick goes wrong

● **103 MORE COMMENTS>>**

Six

"ILEONA!"

Squinting, I lifted my head off my pillow and watched Aria rip
open our curtains.

"Ileona!" she repeated, this time shouting. She jiggled one of
Hayan's legs that was sticking out of her sheets, then made her way
over to my side of the room. I got up before she had a chance to do
the same to me, but instead she grabbed the post of our bunk bed
and shook it like she was strangling it to death. Seol sat up straight,
her hair sticking out like a half-blown dandelion, and shot me a
look like "What's *her* problem?"

Her mood only got worse during our morning hike, and by the
time we got back to the academy, the entire van was ready to escape
the Wrath of Aria.

When I got to the cafeteria, So-hyun was already eating with a
couple of her groupmates. I plunked down across from her, nearly
slamming my tray onto the table. "Hi," I grumbled, nodding to her
and the other girls.

"Wassup, girl?" said So-hyun between bites of rice. "You're
lookin' real salty this morning."

"Ugh, Aria is in the worst mood. I've never seen her like this before."

"Oh reaaaally." So-hyun lowered her eyes to her bowl and raised both eyebrows.

I put my chopsticks down and tried to make eye contact with her. "What—what is it?"

"It's nothing."

"No, come on; you know something. Just tell me."

So-hyun let out a long sigh and pushed her tray to the side. "Come here, I need to show you something." She waved me down to the end of the table away from the other girls and put her phone on the table. Its bejeweled case glittered under the cafeteria's fluorescent lights. "Look, I wasn't going to say anything, OK? But yeah, I *do* know why she's in a bad mood."

"Whoa. All right." I tucked my hair behind my ears and leaned in closer. I couldn't even begin to guess what she was about to say.

"K . . . so have you ever heard of the K-pop blogger V?"

"V? As in the letter?" I asked.

"Yup."

"Mmm, no." I had no idea who she was, but I'd bet Olivia did.

"Well, she posts on Naver Blog, this super popular Korean blogging platform, and she's like this really big deal," said So-hyun. "She's kind of an influencer, only she's totally anonymous because she never posts photos or videos of herself; she just writes. But she has a bazillion followers because she writes about"—So-hyun slid her elbows toward the center of the table—"*us.*"

"You mean idols?"

"Yeah, she has all this dirt on us. She knows where people live, who we're dating, when we're fighting with each other. And the worst part is: *it's all true.*"

"Oh god, that's so scary," I said.

"Hell *yes*, it's scary!"

"Is she, a mole or something? Like, is she one of us?" I asked.

"I don't think so, but she definitely works with sasaengs, otherwise I have no idea how she's gotten so much shit on us over the years."

That was a new one. "And a sasaeng is . . . ?"

"God, where do I ee-even begin?" So-hyun leaned way back in her seat like she had to rev up to explain it to me. "A sasaeng shouldn't even have the word *fan* associated with them. They're more like stalkers, so obsessed they'll do anything, even commit a crime, just to get close to you. Like, MSB has this one sasaeng fan who is totally off her rocker. This one time, she slept in the academy's garage and waited for them to come downstairs. Then she tried to cut off a piece of Min-gyu's hair with a pair of scissors."

"Jesus. That is so intense," I said. "Poor Min-gyu . . . Poor Joon!"

"I know. It's totally sad. I love the HeartBeat so much that I would do anything for them, like *an-y*-thing. But sasaengs? I just *can't* with them . . ."

"So what does this have to do with Aria's terrible mood?"

"Here," So-hyun said, reaching for her phone and opening up Naver Blog to a page that was a wall of black hangul text. "Lemme just read this to you."

As she read the post aloud, the whole cafeteria and everyone in it disintegrated; it was just me and the terrible words coming out of So-hyun's mouth. This random V person was talking shit about *me*.

"Wait, wait, wait," I said, stopping her midsentence. "The photo card does *what* when you turn the lights off?"

"Here." So-hyun slid her phone to me. "She posted a picture of it."

I took the phone in my hands, and at first I couldn't tell what I was looking at. The photo was taken in a dark room, and you could barely see the edges of the photo card. On the photo card itself were five glowing blobs. I zoomed in, and the outlines of our bodies came into focus, one of which was undeniably mine. Just as V had described, I looked completely naked.

"Oh my god," I uttered, cupping my hand over my mouth. It was like a neon car crash, too horrifying to look at yet I couldn't take my eyes off it.

So-hyun gently peeled my fingers from her phone, then tucked it out of sight. "Alice, honestly, it's not as bad as you think. You can't actually *see* anything."

"Thanks," I said slowly, still stunned. "But that's not really the point. No one told us they were going to do this. I feel so . . . violated." The thought of thousands of strangers looking at my naked body, even if things were pretty blurred out, made me wish I'd never even *had* a body. I wished that I was just a speck of dust that floated around, body-less and completely unnoticed. And, oh god, what if my parents saw it!

So-hyun reached across the table and touched my arm. "Girl, I know. Sucks when Top10 does shit like this."

"And this review is awful!" I moaned. "She thinks we're a total joke! How is it possible that I haven't even released a single song yet, and I'm already getting ripped apart online?" I yanked my hood down over my face, pulling it all the way down to my chin. "Mmmph!"

"If it makes you feel any better," she said, "a bunch of people in the comment section seemed to really like it."

"How many?" I said through my hood.

"Like five or six," So-hyun said hopefully.

"MMPHH!"

"Well, at least now you know why Aria was being so testy this morning."

"I guess so. But now *I'm* in a bad mood."

"Girl, don't freak out too much, OK? V has literally never once uttered a single nice word about an idol. Throwing shade is what she *does*. Tomorrow she'll find some other innocent victim to pick on, and everyone will forget all about this."

I let my hood spring back up off my face and looked down at my plate of cabbage. It made me want to puke. "Ugh, I'm not hungry anymore. I think I gotta take a walk."

"K. Tonight we're performing on this TV show *Inkigayo*, so I won't be around, but text me if you just wanna vent."

"Thanks, Soh." I sighed. Thank god for So-hyun. Without her, I wouldn't have had a clue about any of this. "And thanks for telling me about V."

"Yeah, duh! Believe me, it's gonna be so fine. I swear." She slid back down toward her groupmates, smiling, but it was the kind of smile you give when you don't really believe what you're saying.

I scraped my uneaten breakfast into a garbage can on the way out of the cafeteria, then dragged myself into the common area and slumped onto an empty couch. I only had about ten minutes until my Korean class started, but I let my body sink until my feet were splayed on the floor in front of me and my head was wedged into the crack between the seat and the backrest. Every time I blinked, the image of five naked, glow-in-the-dark bodies flashed behind my eyelids.

"Uh-oh," said a voice above me.

I craned my head, and I nearly fell off the couch when I saw who it was.

"Hmm," said Joon, concerned. He bent down closer, examining my face. "Oh, good. I thought you fainted again." He could barely contain his teeth from jailbreaking out of his mouth into a grin.

"Very funny," I muttered half-heartedly.

"Bad day, huh?" he said.

"Bad month is more like it."

"Come on, it's not *that* bad here," he said, flopping down on the couch next to me and dropping his backpack at his feet.

"How do you do it?" I asked.

"How do I do what?"

"How do you deal with critics?"

"Not very well," he admitted, throwing his feet up on the coffee table in front of us. "I try to ignore the reviews, but the guys always end up telling me about the worst ones anyway."

I scooched up a bit higher on the couch so I could see him better. "Wow, you don't read your reviews? I don't think I could do that."

"I don't know; reading negative shit about your art is just an act of masochism, I think."

"Hmm, yeah. I guess so."

"You know what I do instead, though?" he said.

"What?"

"I read fan comments. The BoMS know me way better than any critic does, so no matter what they say, positive or negative, I know I can trust it."

"Yeah, but doesn't it hurt way more when a fan says something negative about you?"

"Yeah," he said, scratching the back of his head. "Don't get me wrong, it can hurt. But it's just like any close relationship. I take it seriously because I know they're saying it out of love, and they want me to be the best version of myself."

"Huh, I never thought of it like a relationship. I always thought it was pretty one-sided, like I stan for an artist and they never think about me. At least not personally, anyway."

"No way, are you kidding me?" he said. He dropped his feet from the coffee table and planted them on the floor—apparently talking about his fandom really got Joon worked up. "I *live* for the BoMS. Without them, I'd have no reason to make music."

God. How was it possible for one boy to have all the things? He was gorgeous, charming, *and* caring! It seemed deeply unfair to all the other boys in the world.

"That sounds nice and all," I said, "but A-List doesn't have any fans yet. At least not more than five or six."

"Yeah, it takes a while to build up your fandom. Believe me, I know. But it'll happen for you guys. And once they're in, they've got your back, no matter what." Joon flicked his bleached bangs off his forehead, revealing two black eyebrows, his natural hair color. "Why, did you get a bad review or something?"

"Yeahhh." I sighed.

"Let me guess—did it say you looked slutty?"

I looked at him, startled. "Oh god, did you see the photo card, too?"

"Photo card? No, that's just what people *always* say about girl groups. It's messed."

Relieved, I relaxed back into my slump. "People are the worst," I grumbled.

"People *are* the worst," he said. "You know what some music reviewer wrote about us on Melon once?"

"What's Melon?" I asked.

"It's this music charting site; they have reviews and stuff. Anyway, the guy wrote—and I quote—'MSB's attempt at a dark concept was about as chilling as a baby lamb chasing a butterfly. If this was supposed to be MSB all grown-up, maybe they should head back to the playground.'"

"Oof, that's pretty brutal," I said.

"Yeah, that one stung." Joon leaned back and crossed his arms, and I tried not to notice the shadows his biceps made under his shirtsleeves. "I promised myself I wouldn't read any more reviews after that one."

"Were they talking about your half-zombie half-vampire concept?"

"Uh-huh. That album got a ton of bad reviews, but you know what? It was the most fun we'd ever had creating a concept."

"Really?"

"Hell yeah. We'd never done a dark concept before, so it really pushed us out of our comfort zone. The vocal style was totally different, too, like we experimented a lot with whispering and vocal fry. It was kind of scary at first because I didn't really know how to sing that way, but in the end I think it made me a better singer."

"I totally know what you mean," I said, excitedly tucking my hair behind my ears, "like when I first learned opera it was really hard, but once I learned how to manipulate my breathing correctly, I loved it because I had this whole new power behind my voice."

"Yeah, right? Plus, the music wasn't all bubbly and about falling in love like our earlier albums; it was way deeper and more emotional. I actually got to work through some of the difficult stuff I've been feeling lately . . ." Joon trailed off and stared out across the common area.

It was surprising; Joon was so confident and easygoing, and he had everything someone in our industry could want. What difficult stuff could he possibly be going through? "You mean you kind of processed some stuff through singing?" I said.

Joon turned back to me and shook his head slightly, almost like he was bringing himself back to reality. "Uh, yeah. You know how singing can bring stuff out of you, but then it also helps you work through it, too?"

"Totally, that's why I love it so much. It just taps into this part of you that's impossible to reach any other way."

"Yes, exactly." The corners of his eyes crinkled like he was seeing me, really seeing me for the first time, which was funny because I was feeling the same thing about him. It was cool hearing Joon talk so passionately about his art. It was pretty much the exact conversation I hoped I'd have at the academy.

"Anyway," he said, "my point is: maybe the critics didn't like the album, but it didn't matter because the guys and I really loved making it. Top10 let us experiment and it totally paid off."

"Sounds like you guys grew a lot," I said.

"Yeah. And no amount of criticism can take that away from us."

"That's really awesome, Joon. I should listen to the album tonight; I bet I'll hear it differently knowing that's how you feel about it."

"That's nice," he said, bumping his shoulder playfully into mine.

"You better toughen up, though, the reviews are going to get way worse once you actually debut."

"Pfff," I puffed. I rolled my head away from his, trying to look nonchalant about the fact that our shoulders were touching.

"Hey, I have something that might distract you from your bad review. I just got this." Joon reached down into his backpack and pulled out a sky-blue cube that looked like a cartoon version of a camera. "You know what an Instax is, yeah?"

"Yeah, of course."

"Wanna maybe take one together?"

"OK," I said, when what I really meant was "I would like nothing more in this whole wide world than to take a picture with you, Joon, thankyouverymuch."

Joon scrunched down lower on the couch so his face was right up next to mine. My breath caught in my throat as he hooked his arm around my neck so that he was kind of cradling my head in the pocket between his shoulder and elbow. I could smell his deodorant, something bright and fresh, which made me painfully aware that I didn't have any on myself. Why was I always running into this guy before I had taken a shower?

Joon held the camera up for a selfie, and I could see our faces in the tiny mirror next to the lens. I tried to smile, but I just ended up looking mildly freaked out.

"Um, can you at least *try* to look like you're having a good time?"

"Ha-ha-ha!" I giggled wildly. I was suddenly acting like a maniac who had just seen a boy for the first time in her life.

Joon repositioned himself, resting his temple on the top of my head. I could feel the soft wisps of his hair brush against my forehead, which wasn't helping matters *at all*. He tried to loosen me up by puckering his lips together and squeezing his eyes shut into a cornball kissy face. It was ridiculously unfair that he could be so relaxed about everything.

Mimicking him, I screwed my mouth up into my own kissy face. "Better?" I asked out of the side of my mouth.

"Niiiice."

Joon clicked the shutter on the camera and it flashed, then spit out a small, rectangular photo. He lifted his head from mine—sadly, *regrettably* even—and we watched as our faces slowly appeared on its glossy surface.

"Here," he said, handing me the photo. "You better hold on to this. If your music career doesn't take off, you can sell it for a ton of money."

I groaned and pushed him away from me with both hands, wondering if it looked as flirty as it felt. Joon bounced right back, flashing me his patented cheesy smile. "All right, back to work," he said, standing up and throwing his backpack over his shoulder. "Gotta keep those critics employed, am I right?"

"Yeah, totally," I said, nodding, unable to knock what felt like a seriously over-the-top grin off my face.

"Later, Alice."

"Later," I called after him.

I watched after him longer than I probably should have, then exhaled and realized I had been barely breathing since the moment he showed up. Who knew if Miss Jackie would have qualified that as fraternizing with a boy, but jeez, it sure felt like it was.

I held the photo up close to my face so I could examine every single thing about it. We looked like two idiots whose lips were trying to find each other's in the dark—but one of those idiots was me, and the other was Joon Kwon. *Of MSB.* And our faces were so . . . *close.* Olivia was going to die. No, Olivia was going to die, then come back to life, then immediately die a second time.

I pulled out my phone, snapped a picture of it, and posted it to my Finsta, tagging Olivia right in the middle of Joon's pursed lips. I watched it upload, then tucked my phone back into the kangaroo pouch of my hoodie. A minute hadn't even gone by when my phone buzzed with a new text.

OLIVIA
ASHKLJFJAJALLLHGH
OMFREEEAKINGGOODDD
I'M DED
☻☻☻☻☻☻☻

ALICE
lolll

OLIVIA
HOWWHATWHYHOW?????

I grinned at the screen, then looked down at our picture in my hand. Joon was right; I didn't feel bad at all anymore.

The sound of Aria's voice inside So-ri's office gave me that twisty feeling in my stomach, like right before you get a shot at the doctor's.

"Alice-yah, iriwa!" exclaimed So-ri when I turned into her office for my voice lesson. Aria and I smiled stiffly at each other from across the tiny room. At least she seemed to be in a better mood than she was this morning.

"Chicas, today I want to know you as a duo," said So-ri. "So! We begin." She scooted behind her little electric piano and brushed off an empty bag of fish jerky. We started with lip trills to warm up, and Aria and I stood there next to each other, lips buzzing up and down the scale like a pair of singing bees.

When So-ri felt like we had warmed up enough, she plucked two wrinkled pieces of sheet music off her desk and handed them to us. "I want to start with something little bit different. Aria, you know this. Alice, this is new for you."

I looked down at the sheet music and saw that the lyrics were in English, but I didn't recognize them and there was no song title. It was a melancholy song in the saddest of the keys: D minor. With anything else, I would have been anxious about the fact that Aria had a leg up on me since she knew the song, but I was pretty confident in my sight-reading and the song seemed slow and simple.

"Sing this," So-ri said to me, tapping her stubby finger on the top staff. "And you," she said to Aria, "sing the harmony. I will not direct too much; this is only to get comfortable together." She plopped back down at the piano and dropped her hands down onto the keys, playing the first chords.

It sounded like a Celtic folk song—melancholy and ancient. It sort of reminded me of Simon and Garfunkel or the Crosby, Stills, Nash & Young stuff my dad played when I was growing up. I always thought the two- and four-part harmonies in some of those songs were so pretty.

Then it was our turn to sing.

"There was a house not so far from my ooown . . . Not a one lived there; t'was nobody's hooome."

Right from the start, Aria and I had trouble finding each other in the music. So-ri had us start and stop a couple times just to play us our opening notes, and when we finally got going we sounded shaky, like two people dancing together who didn't know who was supposed to be leading. It was almost like we were singing two completely different songs.

"A mother, a child, and a broken heaaart . . . Once did dwell until the three did paaart."

"Watch your intonation, Aria!" shouted So-ri over her piano. "Jaw is too tense, Alice! Wider, please!"

Once we really got going, it was immediately clear Aria had amazing control over her breath. It was actually really impressive. My old teacher always used to describe my voice as soulful, but Aria's was different; it sounded pure and crisp, like jumping into a crystal-clear pool on a really sweaty day. Together, our singing styles made a kind of hauntingly beautiful sound.

"More support!" yelled So-ri, pointing to my stomach with her right hand while continuing to play with her left.

"In the years of their absence, a deep quiet blooomed. The home 'came a house . . . 'came four empty rooooms."

By the second chorus, we'd stopped accidentally singing each other's notes and we started to sound confident in our own parts. I couldn't help peeking up at Aria, and when I raised my head from my sheet music, she was already looking over at me. We made eye contact for a half of a half of a millisecond, just long enough that I could tell she was feeling it, too.

"Now no place for mother or chiiiild . . . The house grows broken and the yard grows wiiild."

"Very nice, very nice!" trilled So-ri.

We came out of the bridge strong, and it occurred to me that I'd never actually performed with someone as advanced as Aria. When

I was in choir, I used to have to sort of hold my section up when we sang. Not because the other kids were bad or anything, but because I had a lot more training than they did and my voice is pretty powerful. With Aria, though, I didn't have to worry about what she was doing, and I could focus more on pushing my own signing forward.

"Home is a trouble . . . A place to forget . . . Home is a heart . . . Forever in debt."

"Buonissimo, molto buonissimo!" cried So-ri when we were finished. "I have a feeling you two girls could make magic together." Aria and I smiled at each other, hers without its usual tinge of disappointment.

"You enjoy that?" So-ri asked us.

"Yeah," I admitted.

"Yes," said Aria. "I love the way we sound together." I smiled down at my shoes; what a relief it was to hear her say out loud what I felt inside.

"Good thing I make you both main singers, huh?" teased So-ri. She winked at us and I laughed, long enough to make it seem like her joke was no big deal, but short enough so it didn't sound like I was trying to rub my main-singer status in Aria's face. "So! Now we make things little bit more challenging. I want to do an exercise to fix something I notice just now. We will do *U*'s. Come in close so I can see your mouths better."

Aria and I moved in closer to So-ri's piano and began repeating *U*'s up the scale to the tune of So-ri's piano.

"Youu-You-You-YOU-you-you-Youuu," we sang, over and over.

"STOP!" cried So-ri when we got to the F major scale. She threw up her hands in the air like the piano keys had suddenly caught fire. "Right there. Alice, again please."

Why was she singling me out? I sounded totally fine. I breathed out to clear my throat and began again. "Youu-You-You-YOU-you-you-Youuu."

"Hear that?" So-ri asked, cocking her head at us.

I didn't know what I was supposed to be hearing, but Aria immediately nodded. "Yes," she said, "at the top, she's going flat."

My hand zoomed up and self-consciously touched my throat. "I'm not going flat. I'm hitting the notes."

"No, I can hear it," Aria insisted. "When you try to hit the B, you're flat."

"I really don't hear that."

"Aria is right; you are going flat," corrected So-ri.

"Oh," I said, frowning. This was exactly why I didn't want to do my private lessons with Aria. How was I supposed to learn if she was constantly pointing out all my mistakes?

"I think this is bad habit you get from trying to sound like Top 40 radio," said So-ri. She was teasing again, but this time it didn't seem all that funny. "This is what I want to fix," she said. She hoisted herself up from the bench and reached out to touch my neck. "See, when you move out of your chest voice, you begin to sing from the back of your throat and you lose your range. You call it abduction, when your vocal folds go wide."

"Yeah, I know what abduction is," I said. Chord closure was beginner-level stuff; it was something I learned years ago. It was mortifying that she was spelling it out for me like this in front of Aria.

"OK, so you know," said So-ri. "Then I want you to reverse it." So-ri traced her finger horizontally along my neck starting from the middle of my throat. "Imagine bringing your chords *together* to get you there. Picture them going down, together, *then* up. You can do that?"

"Yes, I can do that," I said, determined to get it right this time.

"Good. We do short vowels now."

So-ri resumed her position over the piano, and I started in again. "You-You-You-YOU-you-you-Youuu," I sang in almost pizzicato fashion.

"I can still hear it," said Aria.

I frowned again, not directly at her but in her general direction.

"Mm, yes," agreed So-ri. "Try bending forward to pull in more air from your belly. Now again." She sang out "YOUU" to give me the starting note.

Leaning over my feet, I tried focusing on breathing from my stomach, but I could see Aria examining my posture out of the corner of my eye. "Youu-You-You-YOU-you-you-Youuu."

"Mm, that is not it," said So-ri.

"No, it isn't," said Aria, agreeing. "You still sound a little off on the high notes." Why did it suddenly feel like I had two instructors instead of one?

"I can do it," I insisted. "Let me do it again." My fists were balled up so tight I could feel my fingernails pressing into my palms.

"I know you can," said So-ri, almost smiling.

"Youu-You-You-YOU-you-you-YOUU."

"Very close! But you are too tense—relax!" she said.

I closed my eyes so I couldn't see Aria in my peripheral vision. Shaking out my hands, I visualized my vocal chords coming together, lifting the sound out of me, instead of forcing it out with the muscles on the side of my neck. I curled my back into a C shape and let it out.

"Youu-You-You-YOU-you-you-YOUUUU!" It was like something had freed up in the back of my throat, and there was a sudden clarity in my voice. It felt amazing. I opened my eyes and So-ri was laughing, her wrinkled face all squinched up like a baby's.

"Alice, such a gorgeous sound you make when you focus!" she said, clearly delighted with my quick progress. "Feels different, yes?"

"Yeah." I grinned. "It feels like it's sitting in a totally different place in my throat now."

"Good, good! One more time now so Aria can hear your power."

I sang it again, demonstrating for Aria, who looked everywhere but directly at me.

"You hear that amazing power she have behind her voice, Aria? Sounds like me when I still had a voice," she said with a chuckle.

"Mm-hmm," Aria said tightly.

"When you pay attention to your body," said So-ri, talking directly to me now, "you unlock the energy inside you." She made her point by rapping on my sternum a couple times. "This power is inside you—I see it. We just need to bring it out."

"Thank you," I said proudly.

So-ri nodded, but she was still considering me with pursed lips. "Also . . . You say you know what abduction is. OK. But sometime you need to remind yourself of the basics. No one is so good that they do not need to keep learning. You understand?"

"I understand," I said, the pride in my voice gone. I knew I had gotten a little impatient when I couldn't hit the notes, but I didn't realize it was so obvious.

We spent the rest of the class working on projection, and I was able to keep my chords throughout most of it. We did *A*'s and *Ah*'s and ended with *Ooh*'s, and it felt like by the end of class we had done all the vowels twice through.

"I want to talk. Sit, sit," said So-ri when we were done. She dusted off two beat-up-looking stools, and the three of us made a little circle next to So-ri's piano. "I want you to think about the first song you sing together today. What made it work?" She blinked at us, and when we didn't answer, she said, "Alice, what you think?"

"Um, well, I think we were able to get pretty in sync," I answered.

"You mean with timing?" said So-ri, purposefully misunderstanding so I would say more.

"No . . ." I said, shaking my head slowly. "More like we were feeding off each other. Like I knew where she was going and she knew where I was going, and we were going there together . . . It was equal, I guess."

"Good. Aria, what about you?" asked So-ri.

"Sure, I felt that." Aria's voice sounded vaguely sharp, like she had slipped back into her bad mood from earlier, though I didn't really get why.

"Why you think you feel that way?" prodded So-ri.

"I don't know," she said, crossing and uncrossing her long legs. "I think it's because we're both very advanced and we both know what we're doing . . . and I don't have to lead so much when I sing with Alice." Aria turned her head to the side like it almost hurt her to admit it.

"Maybe you are better singers when you sing together?" So-ri asked.

I wouldn't go *that* far, but I nodded. "Maybe."

"Yeah, maybe," echoed Aria.

So-ri leaned back with her arms crossed and smacked her lips. "Is good to be on the same page with each other when you sing together. But that needs to happen before you come to class. I am giving you two some homework," she said. "One: do the vocal exercises we practice today at least half hour every day. And two: I want you two to find something you both like and do it together."

God, we already saw each other almost every minute of every day. It was hard to imagine finding even *more* time to spend together. What we were going to do, start taking showers at the same time, too?

"What's something you both like to do?" asked So-ri. Aria jiggled her foot up and down, and I studied the lines on my palm. I actually had no idea what Aria and I had in common.

"Aria, what do you like to do for fun?" said So-ri.

I turned to Aria, curious to know the answer. As far as I could tell, the only thing she did for fun was tell everyone what time to go to bed and when to wake up. I couldn't even remember if I'd ever heard Aria laugh.

"Well . . . I like writing poetry . . . but that might be a little hard for two people." She thought about it for a second, licking her lips. "Maybe we could ride bikes? There's a pretty trail along the Han River we could do together."

"Alice?" said So-ri, looking at me.

Between all the hiking and the hours-long dance classes, the idea of adding one more physical activity to my plate made me want to faint all over again. "I'm not really a big biker," I said, "sorry."

"Alice, what do you like to do?" asked So-ri.

"Ummm," I said, stalling. It had to be something that didn't require any skill—and preferably something we could do without having to actually talk to each other. "We could watch old movies together? I like stuff with Greta Garbo and Katharine Hepburn."

Aria thought about it. "Yeah, OK, I could do that."

"Good girls," said So-ri. "How about you do that one time a week to start, OK?"

"OK," said Aria.

"Sure," I said. I guess one movie a week with Aria wouldn't kill me.

On the way to our next class, Aria asked me about my favorite movies and told me some of hers. She was trying to figure out something for us to watch together, but she seemed distracted and distant. Even though she was totally composed on the outside, I could tell there was a whole storm whipping up inside.

The other girls were stretching along the mirrors when we got to the dance studio, and Mr. Moon was in the corner of the room cueing up some music on the stereo. As he reached over to fiddle with the volume, his arms bulged out of his cut-off T-shirt so much that it was almost obscene.

Hayan waved us over to the wooden barre where she had a leg propped up, stretching out her hamstring. "Today, we learn the new routine for '2day/2nite,'" she announced.

Seol, who was bent over in a wide-legged downward dog, lifted her head, revealing a way-too-big grin. "Hayan and Mr. Muscleman make it together . . ."

Yuri brought her hands to her mouth and giggled.

Hayan rolled her eyes and switched her legs on the barre in one fluid motion. "Yes, some steps I create with the choreographers."

Aria stepped up to the barre right next to Hayan and began stretching out her back. "Hayan showed us some of the steps last night when you were studying with So-hyun," she said. It was a little passive-aggressive dart aimed directly at me, but I just tried to ignore it.

"It's so, so good," fawned Yuri. "I love it!"

"That's cool you got to have some input on our choreography, Hayan," I said. "I didn't know trainees had any say in the group's creative direction. I'd love to collaborate on some of our music one day."

"Me-ee too!" called Seol from her downward dog. "I want to write verses for A-List. Maybe we can write together, Alice."

I smiled at Seol's upside-down head. "Yeah, that would be cool."

BOOM-BAP! BA-BOOM-BOOM-BAP!

A hard beat blared from the speakers overhead. "Here we go! Everybody up, front and center!" instructed Mr. Moon in Korean.

Mercifully, I hadn't thrown up since our first dance class. When it came to group lessons, I had graduated from puking beginner to intermediate queasy, meaning I could pretty much keep up, but sometimes I still moved like a marionette doll whose strings were all tangled.

BOOM-BAP! BA-BOOM-BOOM-BAP!

I was able to get all the way through the leg lifts, hops, and jumps of our warm-up without tripping over myself, and then Mr. Moon flicked his remote at the speakers.

BOOM-BAP! BA-BOOM-BOOM—

The beat dropped to silence, meaning it was time to learn our new routine. Yuri skipped over to the mirror at the front of the class and propped her phone up against it.

"You're recording us?" I asked.

"Yes!" chirped Yuri. "So we can watch the routine, euhh . . . for review."

It made sense. I recorded myself all the time in my voice lessons so I could check my technique and hear myself from a different angle. But still, it wasn't like I was dying to have my desperate flailing recorded for all eternity on someone else's phone. It was embarrassing enough that I had to watch myself in the studio mirrors. "OK . . . um, thanks."

Yuri bobbed her head once. "You welcome!"

Mr. Moon had Hayan come forward so she could demonstrate the first couple counts. She took a few steps forward and settled her body into position. "Five-six-seven-eight!" counted Mr. Moon, and she snapped into motion. Hayan was definitely the most serious and reserved one in the group, but whenever she danced she got this kind of freeness about her, like the only time she was truly happy was when she was dancing. She sauntered forward a few steps, swishing her hips. Then, lifting her knee and pointing her toe to the ground, she made an X with her arms. She threw her arms back, snapped her head to the side, her hair whipping across her face, then sort of gyrated her hip around her leg. That was it. It didn't seem that hard, actually. Mr. Moon had her do it again, in slow motion, while everyone followed along.

"On my count!" said Mr. Moon in Korean. "Everyone!"

He started calling out the beats, but for some reason I couldn't replicate what Hayan had shown us. Somewhere in the pathway between my brain and my limbs, there must have been a short circuit; my arms and legs just refused to cooperate. It was like I was inside that freaky dream where someone's chasing you, so you try to run, but your legs drag like they're moving through molasses.

Mr. Moon strutted over to me, still calling out the beats. "Let's go again!" he directed when we were done. He watched me like a hawk as we moved through the combination a few more times, but

I only got worse and worse until I just gave up. Mr. Moon rubbed the stubble on his square chin like he was trying to decide what to do with me. Finally, he called out to the others to take a seat on the floor. Now it was just Hayan and me, standing at the front of the room for all to see.

"Watch me," said Hayan. She showed me the hip-gyration part again but did it much slower than before. She ticked off the beat each time she moved her hips to the left or the right. "Boom. Boom. Boom-boom-BOOM. See?"

"Uh-huh," I said, trying to swallow what felt like hot, dry sand in my throat.

"OK, you try."

I stuck out my foot and moved my hips left and right, but unlike Hayan, who could pop her hips to the beat, mine just kind of sloshed around uncontrollably.

"Mmm," said Hayan critically. She tugged on her ponytail, tightening the elastic around it. "I show you one more time."

This time, as Hayan danced out the steps, Mr. Moon put his hands around my waist and moved me in time with her. His hands were so huge that his fingers almost met in the middle of my stomach. Of course I was supposed to be paying attention to the timing, but all I could think about were the camera and the six eyes of the other girls, glued to my waist as our hunky instructor moved me to the rhythm of Hayan's dancing.

"One more time," he said, and he and Hayan stepped back to watch me.

I repeated the move, but everyone could see I still wasn't getting it. This wasn't like my voice lessons, where I could just will myself to be better in a matter of minutes.

"Again, but turn your head on the downbeat," instructed Hayan.

I did it all over, making sure to turn my head at the right time, but now my hips were off.

"Left hip moves first," she said. "One more time."

Wrong again.

Suddenly, Aria called out from the floor, "No, no—your left side."

"I *know!*" I snapped.

Hayan flipped her ponytail off her shoulder and glared at me. Her stare was a hundred miles long; it went right through me and kept on going all the way to the ocean.

"Sorry," I muttered, reigning my annoyance back in. "I got it. Left side first." I wished I hadn't lashed out like that, but I couldn't control my frustration, just like I couldn't control my arms and legs. I felt like an idiot that I couldn't do this one small move—we were only on the first freaking combination! And why did everyone have to sit there and watch me anyway? Couldn't they go work on something else while I figured this out? The pressure to get this right was so high that I felt like I was a balloon about to pop.

"OK, ready?" asked Hayan.

"Yep," I said, gritting my teeth. I was going to get this down even if it killed me.

"Five-six-seven-eight!"

I marched forward and threw my foot out, making an X with my arms, then whipped my head to the side, but I was already getting offbeat, so when I got to the gyrating part, I just stopped and stomped my foot hard into the ground. "Ughh!"

Hayan put her hand on my shoulder, trying to calm me down. "It's OK. It is very hard, I know."

"I just can't do it!"

"Yes, you *can*. Try again, one more time."

"How many times do I have to do this?" I demanded, shrugging her hand off.

Hayan planted her fists on her hips—I had clearly crossed a line. "Until you do it right."

"I'm not *going* to get it right. This is pointless!" I argued. Sweat was pouring off me so I stripped off my sweater, balled it up, and threw it across the floor.

"OK, OK!" interjected Mr. Moon, clapping his massive hands. He waved Aria over, dictating something.

"He says he wants to work with you one-on-one while the rest of us work with Hayan," she said.

"Great," I muttered, turning away from her. In a way, it was a relief, but the fact that I was so bad that I needed special help really stung.

Aria touched my back tentatively. "I think it's a good idea, Alice. You could use the extra attention." Her voice was soft, but she still had that kindergarten-teacher tone, like she knew this was for my own good even if I didn't.

"It's OK," I said, shifting my weight so she wasn't touching me anymore. "You don't need to explain it to me; I know I need help."

"Good," she said, her voice hardening, "you do."

It was a lot easier to get the steps down when the girls weren't watching. Mr. Moon was really patient and took things slow with me until we got through about half the routine. I was even able to join the rest of the group for the last part of class, which made me feel a lot better. I only wished that's how every class could go, that I could just show up already knowing the steps so I didn't have to learn it all from scratch in front of them.

With class finally over, everyone packed up their stuff and migrated toward the door. Aria called out to me. "Alice?" she said.

"Yeah?" I said, picking up my crumpled sweater from the floor.

"Let's watch Yuri's video together so we can figure out what went wrong with that first combination." She was always doing that, saying "*let's* do this" or "why don't *we* do that," instead of just saying what she really meant, that she wanted *me* to do it.

I exhaled, touching my hand to the bridge of my nose. I was completely wiped, but mostly I didn't want to have to witness myself jiggle around off tempo like some kind of broken windup toy. "We've been working on this routine for hours. I'm starving and I need a break. Can we just watch it later?"

"Don't you want to get this right?"

"Of course I do. But do we have to do it this minute? I only have, like, forty minutes until my next class, and I still need to eat dinner."

"Well, why don't we just watch it while we eat?" she suggested.

"What, in the cafeteria?"

"No, we can eat really quick, then come back here and watch it so we can get some more practice in."

God, she never let up! Didn't Aria ever get tired or need a break? She was like one of those perpetual-motion machines; she just kept going and going and going! I looked to the other girls, desperate for backup, and thankfully Hayan came to my rescue. "Aria," she said, pulling on the back of Aria's arm, "we can watch later. Let's eat dinner now."

Aria glanced down at Hayan's hand almost as if it had brought her back to her senses. Hayan was pretty much the only one in the group who could reason with Aria, and I was always grateful when she did it. "Oh, sure . . . Yes, let's just eat dinner. We can always just watch it before bed."

"Come on," said Hayan, tugging on her arm. Hayan pulled her over to the door and held it open so we could all pass through.

On the way out, I caught her attention and silently mouthed *thank you*.

With the faintest smile, Hayan bowed her head at me, then gently pushed me out the door.

It was one of those days that felt like it would never end, and by the time I left my last class—a late-night world history lesson—it was ten p.m. The last thing I wanted to do was watch a video with Aria while she pointed out all my previous failures. It was a one in a million chance, but maybe she had forgotten about it by now.

When I got to our room, I hung back in the doorway like I was checking the temperature of a pool before I jumped in. Aria and Yuri were sitting on Aria's bed with their legs tucked up underneath them. Aria had a sheet mask on and was smoothing one onto Yuri's face. Hayan had a sheet mask on, too, and she kept her face tilted toward the ceiling so it wouldn't slip off as she blocked out some choreo. Whenever Olivia bought sheet masks, I always teased her, saying that she looked like Michael Myers from the movie *Halloween*, her face creepily white and expressionless.

"You want to do sheet mask?" Seol asked. She was sitting at the table in front of a little stand-up mirror, struggling to correctly line up the nose hole on her own sheet mask. "Here," she said, momentarily giving up, "I have one extra." She handed me a little foil packet with a picture of a honeycomb on it. It read: INNISFREE MY REAL SQUEEZE MASK.

"Thanks," I said, quickly taking it from her, "I'll put it on in the bathroom." Seol nodded and turned back to her mirror, and I gathered up my towel and the plastic caddy with my shower stuff in it and headed off to the girls' bathroom.

I dragged out getting ready for bed long as I could, taking a shower and shaving my legs again—though I had done both already that morning. I even flossed my teeth, which I never did except for the one week a year when my dentist guilt-tripped me into it. The directions on the package said to wear the mask for up to twenty minutes for best results, but I added an extra five minutes just to be sure.

All my dawdling worked. The lights were off when I got back to the room, and I breathed a small sigh of relief. Sliding into bed as quietly as I could, I first tucked Joon's Instax up next to So-ri's business card and the picture of Olivia and me, then took out my phone.

ALICE
Hey, are you awake still?

OLIVIA
Yeah, I'm up!
Can you talk?? I WANT TO KNOW ABOUT JOOOON.

ALICE
No, sorry, I'm in my room and everyone is asleep :(

Almost as if she were reading my texts, Aria's voice called out from the dark. "Alice, can you please turn down the light on your phone? We're all trying to sleep."

"Sorry," I mumbled. I turned the brightness on my phone all the way down and pulled my sheet over my head for extra coverage.

OLIVIA

k

So how did it happen, what did he say to you, what
was he wearing?? Tell me every single detail!!!

I typed out my entire encounter with Joon in as much detail as
I could remember, especially the part where he put his arm around
my neck. As expected, Olivia freaked.

OLIVIA
OMG, he tooootallly likes you!!!!!!!!

ALICE
Nooo. He's just being nice.

OLIVIA
Yeah right. I've never had a boy work so hard to make
me feel better.

ALICE
That's just because boys your age don't know how to
have an intelligent conversation.

OLIVIA
LMAO

So do you like HIM??

ALICE
I mean . . . kinda?

Yes, yes, I liked him SO much.

ALICE
It's more than that, though. I like the way he thinks

about music. I've never really met someone who feels the same way I do about singing.

OLIVIA
That's so awesome, Al.

ALICE
Yeah

So what's up at home, anything new?

"Alice?" interrupted Aria.

"Yeah?" I said, peeking over my sheets.

"You know we have to get up in almost five hours; shouldn't you go to sleep?"

"I'm just texting with my sister; I'll be done in a few minutes."

"OK . . . I know you think you're being really quiet, but I can hear you moving around."

"I'll try to be more quiet," I said.

"Thank you." Aria turned over in bed and huffed a little as she pulled her sheets up to her neck.

OLIVIA
Actually Dad finally figured out his visa and he got a job!

ALICE
Oh, thank god! What a relief!

OLIVIA
I know right?

ALICE
What's the job??

He's working for some startup that sells pet supplies
or something.
But last night we went out to hot pot to celebrate.
It was this cool place that had a huge toppings bar.
They had over thirty kinds of toppings you could
choose from.

Something in my heart twitched. Mom's and Dad's and Olivia's lives were all moving along just like before I left. Thinking about them at some fun restaurant celebrating together was a little too much. I bet Dad even did his funny thing where he said "Cheers, m'dears!" when they all clinked their glasses together. Except there were only two of his dears there; his third dear was suffocating under a sheet so she didn't wake up her bossy roommate.

ALICE
That's cool

OLIVIA
Yeah we gotta go there again when you come home.
When ARE you coming home anyway????

ALICE
I don't know. Probably not for a long time.
They're really ramping up my training.

"Mghmm!" Aria suddenly cleared her throat and stuffed her pillow over her head.

ALICE
Hey, sorry, I think I have to go.

OLIVIA
Already?? :((((

ALICE
Yeah :(

OLIVIA
But we barely got to talk

ALICE
I know, it's just that I think Aria is going to kill me if I keep texting with you.

OLIVIA
Can't you just tell her to chill out?

ALICE
lol, yeah right. Then she'd REALLY kill me.

OLIVIA
OK, fine, but I really need to talk to you, can you call me tomorrow please?

ALICE
I'll try

OLIVIA
Can you just do it?

ALICE
I said I'll try. I have like an 18-hour day tomorrow.

OLIVIA
You know, you're just like Mom sometimes. You're such a workaholic.

ALICE
Liv, it's not like that. I'm literally training for the biggest

moment of my life right now. I'm sorry if I happen to be a little busy at the moment.

OLIVIA
Yeah, that's called WORK.

ALICE
All right fine I'll call you. I have to go to bed now OK? Good night.

OLIVIA
Night.

[This page has been translated from Korean.]

03.20

CATEGORY: SCOOP

Soo-Li Plus Hee-Tae Equals Two

It's Saturday, and everyone knows what that means. It's the day that Soo-li traipses down to Cofioca, orders herself a black winter melon milk tea with pearls, and posts yet another photo of it on Instagram.

Soo-li, please. For the sake of everyone's sanity, we all know you're an idol and that idols get their caffeine hits at Cofioca, but we get it. Enough. STOP.

However.

Unlike every other Saturday of the year, Soo-li's post today contained something new . . . if you looked hard enough.

Just beyond the black-as-a-rotting-tooth milk tea, past the globules of boba pearls, you will spy at the bottom of the frame a glinting metal spoon. (Because apparently plastic straws just won't do when it comes to stirring Soo-li's beverages.)

"So what?" you say. "Who cares?" you say. Well, dear Readers, *you* care, because in the reflection of that lustrous spoon is the lustrous head of one Park Hee-tae, the lead actor from *Royal Sun*.

I would never claim that the twenty-four-year-old Top10 idol and the thirty-eight-year-old K-drama star were dating without substantive proof. But if you'll allow me to do some math, as I am wont to do, I'd like to add it up for you. The post was tagged in Cheongdam-dong, where Hee-tae currently owns an apartment. If you zoom in, you can see that the two are sitting on the white leather couch in his bedroom (we've seen this couch before in two separate posts, one from July, 2019, and another from August, 2020). The two appear to be unchaperoned, for no Top10 minder would ever allow this picture to be taken. So here they sit—Soo-li and Hee-tae—alone, on the couch, in Hee-tae's bedroom no less. Two plus two equals four every time you add it up, my Dears. Or in this case, Soo-li plus Hee-tae adds up to a caffeine-induced scandal.

And, Readers, you can thank the gods someone polished that little silver spoon.

+ V +

💬 COMMENTS ═══════════════

WHEN21
OH SHIIIIIIIIIII . . . . . .

so_LIVE
Bow down to V for her detective skills!

Aegyoona
STAHP.

PinkVelvet
Did she just . . . ??!

bobobobobobo
This is so shameful. Clearly we weren't meant to see this.
You're not saying it but you're insinuating it and that's just
as bad.

> **baekhyun babygirl**
> Ugh, yes, disgusting, V!!! You're the one who needs to
> stop. No more Scoop posts!!

> **Anonymous**
> Seriously, this blog would be so much less gross
> without the Scoop posts

> **devil_wings**
> You dare question V? V IS scoop posts.

uh_oh_17
Soo-li was born gagging on a silver spoon.

SMTownie
I CANNOT right now. What?? He is old enough to be her
father . . . !

U^ ɪ ^U

Omg Soo-li is going to be in so much trouble. Top10 is going to FREAK when they see this.

Anie9

My poor little Soo-li. This is going to be so bad for her.
。˚˚('O`)˚˚。

 242 MORE COMMENTS>>

Seven

"ONE MORE TIME FROM THE TOP!"

Aria, Yuri, Seol, and Hayan broke from the poses they were holding and sighed all at once. Mr. Moon wasn't happy, and everyone knew it was my fault.

A dark sweat spot had formed on my sports bra, right in the middle of my boobs. I'd been watching it spread in the studio mirrors all afternoon. If I gave it every inch of my body and soul, I could get through most of our Dream Concert set now, but it didn't matter how many times we went over it (three hours every single day, to be exact); I still couldn't hit my mark at the end of "2day/2nite."

This was how it was *supposed* to work: right after Aria's solo, I would swap places with her at the front of the stage so I could take my solo, the bridge. Then the third chorus would drop, the black lights would turn on, and we'd all dance back to center stage. We'd do this move where we threw up peace signs each time we sang "2day" and "2nite," then we'd tap them to our chests and throw them in the air again. Then, when the crash cymbal rang for the last time, I was *supposed* to have my right arm propped up on Aria's shoulder, and Hayan was *supposed* to be leaning her back against me.

The problem was: I could never seem to make it back to center stage in time. It wasn't like I had a problem with timing—I knew *when* I was supposed to hit my mark; it was just that no matter what I did, no matter how hard I tried to force my legs to get there, I was always late. My legs were cursed—they just did whatever they wanted whenever they wanted. So what usually happened was that Hayan ended up stumbling backward into nothing, and the whole thing would end in a clumsy mess. All because of me.

"Here. Your mark here," said Hayan, pointing to the spot on the floor where I was supposed to have ended up.

"I'm trying," I panted.

"Alice, you need to start stepping back to center on the four. You never hit your mark on time because you always start too late," instructed Aria.

"I *know*, Aria. I said I was trying."

"All right," she said, swiping at the beads of sweat on her forehead, "you don't need to get so snippy about it. I'm just trying to help."

"I'm not snippy, I'm just tired." Tired of Aria always acting like she was the only adult in the room.

"No more talking! Let's dance, girls!" Mr. Moon commanded in Korean. Exactly like my dancing, my Korean was getting better but only if it was spoken s-l-o-w-l-y.

Hayan blew a strand of hair out of her face, and she and Aria tromped away from me, trading this conspiratorial look. They tried to hide it, but I knew what they were thinking; anytime we'd have to rework something or Mr. Moon wasn't satisfied with us, the four of them would trade the same look, like "Alice screwed it up for us again." They didn't have to be so secretive about it; it was obvious I was the one thing holding the group back from nailing our routine. Whenever they did it, I wanted to scream, "Everyone knows I'm terrible; just admit it already!"

As we took up our starting positions for the thousandth time, there was a knock on the door. Mr. Moon walked over and opened the door to a trainee who bowed, then whispered something behind her hand. Mr. Moon nodded, then announced that class was canceled and we were all supposed to go to the cafeteria for a school-wide meeting. The girls shot each other a different look now, a puzzled one. Yuri started anxiously twisting her ponytail around her fingers like she was worried, but it was hard to tell because Yuri always looked a little worried.

We grabbed our stuff and filed out of the rehearsal studio into the hall, where it was total chaos. Teachers and students streamed out of classrooms all at once, and everyone seemed to be talking about the surprise meeting. By the time we made it down to the cafeteria, the room was totally packed. I broke off from the girls, crossing my arms over my chest to cover up my massive sweat spot while I squeezed through the crowd looking for So-hyun.

I found her huddled in the back of the room with all seven of her groupmates. They sat in a clump with their heads together, whispering about the meeting, like a flock of butterflies that had all landed on the same flower.

"What's going on?" I asked, crouching down next to her table.

So-hyun nudged the girls down the bench to make some room for me. "No freaking clue. Yeona thinks there's some sort of shake-up inside the Top10 leadership. It's happened before."

"What, like they're replacing Mr. Kim or something?" I asked So-hyun.

"God no! Never. But maybe one or two of the executive producers or something."

A man in a gray suit strode up to the front of the cafeteria and flapped his arms to get us to quiet down, but nobody paid him any attention. Suddenly, there was a commotion near the cafeteria doors. We craned our necks to see what was happening but couldn't see anything, so So-hyun jumped up onto the bench to get a better view.

Standing on her tiptoes, So-hyun peered toward the door. Suddenly her eyes got so big I swear her eyebrows almost flew off her forehead. "It's Mr. Kim!" she hissed down at us as she frantically crouched back into her seat.

The commotion got closer and closer, until Mr. Kim materialized, typing away on his phone, surrounded by an entourage of managers and producers. As the group made its way through the crowd, they were followed by a wave of silence. By the time he made it to the front of the room, the only sound in the cafeteria was the clacking of Mr. Kim's texting. He sidled up to the man in the gray suit, still typing, and grunted at him. The gray suit nodded and cleared his throat, then launched into a serious-sounding lecture.

He was talking so fast that I couldn't keep up, but he sounded really angry and kept wagging his finger at us like we were in some kind of trouble. The longer he spoke, the more worried So-hyun looked, which was scary because So-hyun never looked worried. I didn't even know she was even capable of being worried.

Finally, I just couldn't take it anymore. "What the hell is going on?" I whispered into So-hyun's ear.

"It's complicated," she whispered back.

"Just gimme the SparkNotes."

"The *what?*" she whisper-yelled.

"Just give me the gist of it."

"Oh."

So-hyun wrapped her arm around my neck so she could put her mouth right up to my ear. "Did you see V's post this morning?"

"No." I hadn't wanted to look at her blog since she tore us to pieces.

"Well, she caught one of us on a date and now Mr. Kim is *pissed*."

"Oh shit . . . who was it?"

"You know Soo-li?"

She meant the girl with the strawberry allergy.

"Well, you won't be seeing her around campus for a while. She's being pulled from all her public appearances . . ."

"Wait, what? Just for going on a date?" I asked.

"OK, so the guy she got caught with is Hee-tae!" She paused, waiting for me to react, but I had no idea who she was talking about. "Right, so Hee-tae is this really famous actor. He's, like, fifteen years older than Soo-li. Dating is one thing, but dating a gross older guy *and* keeping it a secret from Top10? That's, like, the mark of death."

"Shit," I said again. Now I got it. This was bad, like contract-ending, career-exterminating bad, and way worse than what V had done to us.

"And . . . wait, hold on." So-hyun lifted her head so she could hear better, when a big groan rose up from the cafeteria.

"Oh my GAWD," she moaned, dropping her head onto my shoulder limply.

"What? Tell me!" I shook her impatiently until she lifted her head.

"They're taking away our phones," she whined.

"No way; are you *serious?*"

"Yah, girl. Serious as a heart attack. When one of us gets in trouble, we all get punished."

Olivia. How was I supposed to talk to Olivia if I didn't have a phone, and my laptop had every parental control known to man on it? She was already so annoyed at me for never having time to talk; how was she going to deal when I couldn't talk to her *at all?*

So-hyun slipped her phone out of her sleeve and stroked it softly as if it were a Persian cat. She kissed it, then slid it out of its sparkly case. "They can take my phone, but they are *not* taking my Chanel phone case."

I looked down at my own phone case, a cheap plastic sleeve the color of an under-ripe lime. This was so ridiculous. We weren't allowed to have phones at my school back home, but this was totally different; we actually lived here! It had to be against the law or something. Rubbing my thumb over the screen, I decided to call Olivia right after the meeting, before Top10 took it away. But So-hyun nudged me with her elbow and jutted her chin toward the end of the table—a teacher carrying a small box was taking all of her groupmate's phones.

"They're taking them right *now?*" I nearly gasped, clutching my phone to my chest.

"Yuuuup."

This was really happening. I had to text Olivia now.

Alice
Top10 is taking my phone awa

But that's as far as I got. The teacher stretched her arm past So-hyun and snatched my phone out of my hands before I could even hit send. She took So-hyun's, too, and dropped them into the box with the others like she was tossing cans of beans into a shopping basket.

"Farewell, dear friend," said So-hyun, saluting the box as the teacher moved on to the next table.

It was like watching my right arm float away in the teacher's box.

"Everyone, quiet down!" exclaimed the man at the front of the room, flapping his arms again for quiet. He said a few more words, then he edged out of the way, making room for Mr. Kim.

Mr. Kim stood there finishing up a text, then looked up at the room, irritated, as if we had all suddenly appeared in front of him with the sole purpose of interrupting his screen time. He burped into his hand, then muttered something I couldn't understand. The whole room groaned a second time, but Mr. Kim had already walked off, his head buried in his phone again.

So-hyun threw herself onto the table. "Oh my freaking *gawd*."

"What—what!" I cried. I was practically ripping my hair out. It was excruciating getting information like this.

"We're on lockdown this week," she mumbled into the table. "No one can leave campus unless it's for official business."

"Oh. Well, that doesn't really change anything for me," I said dryly. "It's not like I ever get to leave this place anyway."

"Fine for *you*, but I have places to be . . . boys to check out . . . longingly . . . from a distance."

I patted the back of So-hyun's head sympathetically. "I know, I know. You poor little perv."

So-hyun sighed dramatically, then picked herself up with a new, mischievous expression. "OK, I know what we have to do."

Leaning across the table, she waved her groupmates into another huddle. She whispered something that made everyone smile and nod, then she stood up grabbed me by the hand. "Come on, let's get the eff outta here."

She pushed us through all the other people trying to leave the cafeteria until we came up behind Joon and some of his group-mates. She whispered in his ear and he shot So-hyun a thumbs-up, then leaned over and mumbled something to the guy next to him.

"What was *that* about? And where are we going?" I asked, scur-rying after So-hyun's bobbing ponytail toward the girls' wing.

"We're going to my room for supplies. I am *not* getting locked in this godforsaken place on a"—she held up her hands, pinching her fingers together—"*Fri-day night*—without a drink in me."

When we got back to So-hyun's room, she slammed the door and locked it, then got down on her hands and knees in front of her closet. Pushing aside the hanging clothes like they were a pair of curtains, she revealed a mini-fridge that she was definitely not supposed to have. She rooted around in the fridge and emerged triumphantly with three extra-large bottles of beer called Cass. "Jja-jaaan!"

This was the moment I was supposed to tell So-hyun that I'd never had alcohol before (besides random sips from my mom's wineglass, which definitely didn't count). She probably would've gone out of her way to make it seem like it wasn't a big deal, but then it would have *become* a big deal. So instead I just said, "Sweet."

So-hyun pulled out a rose-gold Louis Vuitton bag and stuffed the bottles inside, along with a stack of metal cups that looked like they had been stolen from the cafeteria. It was weird seeing her pack up alcohol like it was no big deal.

"All right, let's go!" said So-hyun, lugging the bag up onto her shoulder.

We walked out into the hall and ran right into Aria, Yuri, Hayan, and Seol. Yuri looked upset, probably about losing her phone, and everyone kind of had their arms around her shoulders, consoling her.

"Alice?" said Aria. She had broken off from the group to come talk to me. "Hi, So-hyun," she said politely.

"Hi, Aria," So-hyun said, smiling.

"I just wanted to ask, Alice, if you want to watch a movie later? I was thinking we could try *Woman of the Year*." When I hesitated, she added, "Maybe it'll cheer us up about the lockdown." She gave a little half smile like she was trying to commiserate, but it seemed pretty forced.

"Tonight?" I said, stalling. I looked back at So-hyun with her giant bag full of beer, on her way to have who knows how much fun with Joon and all their groupmates. I made eye contact with her, silently pleading with her to give me an excuse not to hang out with Aria, but she didn't bite.

"Um, I don't think I can tonight. Sorry," I mumbled.

Aria eyed So-hyun, who was shifting her heavy bag from one shoulder to the other. "Actually, do you think I could talk to you alone for a second?" she asked.

So-hyun smiled graciously and pushed me toward Aria. "Just meet me at the elevator when you're done, K?"

"Sure."

Aria led me down the hall, to an empty corner of the common

room, in front of a bookshelf full of used books and old magazines. "Where are you and So-hyun going right now?" she asked.

"Um, we're going to go hang out with some people," I said, trying to keep it as vague as possible.

Aria raised an eyebrow. "Are you sure that's a very good idea when we have so much homework to do?"

Homework on a Friday? Was she being serious? "We've been going over our routine nonstop all week. I think it's OK to take a break. I mean, it's Friday night . . ."

"I'm not just talking about our routine," she said. "I'm talking about the homework So-ri gave us, too, remember? That's why I asked if you wanted to watch a movie. And don't you have a history exam on Monday?"

"I have all weekend to study for that," I said. Why was she worrying about my history exam, anyway? My schoolwork had nothing to do with her or A-List.

"But don't you think it's a little irresponsible to leave everything till the last minute all the time?" she pressed.

I never knew how to deal with Aria when she lectured me like this. It was annoying but also made me feel bad about myself, like she thought I was some kind of hoodlum. I reached out to the bookshelf and fidgeted with the spine of a book, rocking it in and out of its slot on the shelf. "I really don't think this qualifies as last minute."

"Alice, please," she said, pushing the book out of my hand and back into its place. "This isn't like your old school back in America. I know it was probably fine if you slacked off there, but it's not like that here; you have to keep on top of things."

Did she think I was some kind of delinquent or something back home? I tipped the book back toward me and pulled it off the shelf so she couldn't take it away from me again. "I didn't slack off back home, Aria. And I'm definitely not slacking off here, either."

"Come on," she said, frowning at the book in my hands, "that's not what I meant."

"Well, that's kind of what it sounded like."

"I'm just trying to explain to you that your actions have bigger consequences here at the academy." She put her hands on her hips, her elbows jutting out like she was some kind of peeved hall monitor. Aria was probably the only nineteen-year-old in the world who used terms like *actions* and *consequences* when it came to school. "I'm supposed to be the leader of this group, and as the leader, I need to make sure everyone is keeping up with their work."

"Look," I said, flipping the pages of the book with my thumb, "I'm not behind in my homework, I'm going to study for my test later this weekend, and we can watch a movie any other day. You know . . . you really don't need to worry about me so much."

"I'm not worried about you; I—"

"So-hyun is waiting for me," I said, cutting her off, "so I really have to go." This conversation was going around and around in circles, and I just wanted out.

Aria dropped her hands from her hips, relenting. "Fine. But can you promise that we'll watch a movie tomorrow?"

"Yes, whenever you want," I said, relieved to be done with our little talk. I shoved the book into the bookshelf, not even bothering to put it back in the right spot. "All right . . . see you later."

"Bye," she said.

As I sped out of the room, I glanced at her. She was putting the book back where it belonged, because of course she was.

When I got to the elevator, So-hyun was leaning against the wall, drawing a face on her hand with a purple glitter pen. "So . . . you wanna explain what that was all about?"

"I'd rather not," I said.

But she wasn't going to let me off the hook so easily. "What's the deal, anyway? Why don't you ever want to be around your groupmates?"

"It's just that . . . I don't fit into the group. It makes everyone's lives better if I just avoid them. I don't have to be constantly reminded of how perfect they are, and they don't have to be constantly reminded of how I ruin everything."

"Girl, whaaat? You don't ruin everything; how can you possibly think that? Your voice is like the most angelic thing that's ever graced my ears."

"That's nice, but you're a little biased being my friend and all, don't you think?"

"Come on, everyone at the academy knows that. Your groupmates know that, too. What makes you think you don't fit in?"

"I dunno; I can just tell . . . Also—" I said, stopping short.

"What?"

"Well, lately things have been getting pretty tense between Aria and me. Something's definitely changed."

"Whadya mean?" she asked.

"It's hard to explain . . . It's like, we used to be civil to each other, nice even, but now I can feel her really losing her patience with me. And to be honest, I'm getting pretty fed up with her, too."

"Have you tried talking about it with her?"

"No! God. I could never talk to her about that."

So-hyun hoisted her bag up higher on her shoulder. "Yeah, well, being in a group full of big personalities can be pretty rough. We've had our issues, too."

I was so surprised. "No way; you guys are like sisters."

"Yeah, and sisters don't get along half the time. You know that."

"True," I admitted, feeling a twinge of guilt about Olivia. I probably should have been trying to find a way to call her.

So-hyun hit the down button on the wall next to the elevator with her free elbow. "I've actually learned that the scariest way is the best way sometimes; you just have to be honest and get it all out in the open—otherwise you're just going to get more and more pissed at each other."

"Or you can simply bury your feelings deep down inside and never let the other person know how you feel about them." I was only half kidding.

So-hyun shot me a sideways look. "You know, you can't avoid her forever. One day you're going to actually have to hang out with her."

"Not if I have you around," I joked.

"Right," she said dryly.

The elevator doors dinged open and we took it down to the first floor. She explained to me that she liked to hang out in the wardrobe room because all the clothes muffled any noise, and no one ever went down there anyway.

The marble lobby was empty except for a guard who was scrolling through his phone, looking bored as hell. We slipped past him and tiptoed our way to the soundstage, and I couldn't help feeling like we were two cat burglars breaking into a bank. When we got to the pitch-black soundstage, a light flared up in So-hyun's hand. I looked down and was shocked to see it was a screen.

"What is *that*?" I whispered, grabbing her wrist and yanking her hand up to my face so I could get a better look. Sure enough, she was holding a phone. "I thought you turned your phone over in the cafeteria!"

"Um, *puh-lease* don't tell me you thought I gave Top10 my only phone." So-hyun jerked her hand back and aimed the phone's flashlight right at my face.

I shielded my eyes and shook my head at her. "You're a freaking genius, you know that?"

"What can I say," she said, shrugging, "I'm amazing."

We picked our way across the stage, stepping over all the wires and cords on the ground, then through the maze of makeup and fitting rooms, until we made it all the way to the wardrobe room. Sitting on the floor among the racks of clothes were Joon and all of his and So-hyun's groupmates.

"NAWATTA!" hollered So-hyun, pocketing her phone and triumphantly drawing two bottles of beer out of her bag.

"EOHHH!" everyone yelled back at her.

"Scoot over!" said So-hyun, and they made space for us on the floor. I sat down next to Joon and pulled my knees up to my chest to hide my gross sweat stain. Why did it not occur to me to change my clothes before we came down here?

Joon had a few green bottles of crystal-clear alcohol and a mountain of snack bags sitting next to him.

"Oppa finally coming through for us," said So-hyun, nodding at his stash of snacks.

"I'll take that as a thank you," he said. He threw a bag of chips at her, then tore the rest open, pushing them into the middle of the circle.

"Woori halabeoji malgo-neun geu-geo ah-moo-do ahn meok-eo!"

said the guy sitting across from me. Everyone laughed and I blinked at So-hyun for a translation.

"See those white tubey things?" she said. "They're called ssal-ro-pung. He said no one eats those except his grandfather."

"I really like them!" exclaimed Joon defensively. "Here," he said, tossing me a bag, "you're an unbiased observer. What do you think?"

I reached into the bag and pulled out one of the crackers. It was light and airy and looked like a dehydrated corn on the cob. I crunched into it and chewed thoughtfully behind my hand. I expected it to taste like a Rice Krispies Treat, but it didn't really taste like anything. It was sort of like eating Styrofoam. "I think I might hate this," I admitted finally.

Joon howled and dropped backward into a garment rack. Everyone else lost it and threw crackers at him while he played dead on the floor.

"Sorry!" I said sheepishly, which made everyone crack up again.

So-hyun rolled her eyes and twisted the cap off one of her bottles. She poured beer into each of the glasses and passed them out one by one.

I anxiously watched a full glass travel around the circle toward me, and when Joon handed it to me, I tried to take it as nonchalantly as possible, like I'd held a glass of beer so many times in my life that I'd lost track. Nervously, I tipped it up to my mouth. It smelled sweet and sour at the same time.

"Wait! Not yet!" yelled out So-hyun.

Mortified, I realized she was talking to me. I half dropped, half shoved my glass in between my crossed legs, making it slosh out all over my socks and sneakers. We hadn't even started drinking yet, and I was already doing it wrong.

"You ever had somaek?" asked So-hyun, mercifully ignoring the pool of beer forming around my ankles.

I shook my head.

"It's beer with a shot of soju in it. Don't worry; it'll get you niiiice and drunk." Except that's exactly what I *was* worried about.

Joon passed around one of his green bottles, and each person poured a little into their beer. When he held the bottle up for me, I froze. I didn't want to pour too much soju in my cup because I didn't want to get super-drunk, but I didn't want to pour too little or I'd look like a total lightweight. When I didn't take the bottle from him, Joon scooched toward me and in a low voice said, "I can show you how much, if you want?"

"Um, OK, thanks," I said gratefully.

He dropped a small amount of soju in my glass, and when he was done, he handed the bottle to me and smiled. I quickly passed it off to So-hyun as if I were going to get wasted just from holding it. So-hyun lifted her full glass, toasting the group. "All right, my babies . . . Geon-bae!"

"Geon-bae!" we all said. Everyone took a big swig from their cups, and I did, too, drinking until So-hyun put her glass down. The somaek was sweeter than I expected and had the faintest taste of rice. Actually, it was pretty good and a lot better than the wine my mom liked to drink.

And then, all of a sudden, I felt . . . fine. It was sort of like when you're swimming and you open your eyes underwater the first time and realize it's no big deal. So-hyun raised her glass at me and I raised mine back, then took another sweet sip.

We sank into drinking and talking and laughing, and after a couple of hours, and a couple more glasses of somaek, I had completely forgotten about my anxiety (and my wet socks). I leaned back into the floor, untucking my knees and letting my body spread out. Everything felt like it was tumbling out of me—stories, jokes, laughter, even some really bad Korean that made me and everyone else laugh even harder. I couldn't stop it; I didn't *want* to stop it. It felt so good to let it all come out.

Eventually, So-hyun put on the latest XOKiss album. She and all her groupmates got up in the middle of the room and did some of their choreo, while the rest of us cheered them on from the floor. Even though they were just messing around, they were still perfectly in sync. You could tell they'd been performing together for years, and yet they still had so much fun dancing together. And at the center of them all was So-hyun. She was the golden child that all the other girls fawned over. Somehow, it didn't seem to matter that she was so much younger than the rest of them; they actually seemed to love that about her.

When their single came on, we all started singing. It'd been playing nonstop around campus and on the radio, so everyone knew all the lyrics. The sound was incredible. All the costumes insulated the room just like a recording studio, so even though there were almost twenty of us, we sounded crisp and fine-tuned. A couple of the guys started improvising and playing around with harmonies. Their voices bobbed and wove around ours like dolphins threading in and out of waves. It'd been forever since I sang with so many people at once, but this was so much more exhilarating than chorus—I was literally surrounded by professional singers. My heart was beating ferociously like I was on the verge of that epic heartbreak feeling. But it wasn't just from the singing, it was from singing with people like me.

At some point, it occurred to us that we were in a room full of costumes, and so everyone started taking off their clothes and dressing up. Joon took out his Instax, snapping pictures of everyone as they modeled their ridiculous getups. So-hyun and Yeona tried on these shiny gold robes with matching boxing gloves and punched at Joon's camera, while I sat on the floor, happy to be watching safely in my own clothes.

"C'mon, Alice, dressing up is mandatory!" yelled So-hyun over the music.

"Ummmm, good, thankyewverrymush," I slurred. It was getting difficult to actually articulate the things I was saying. I had to think really hard just to separate out each word. "Thank-you-very-much," I said, trying again.

"No way," said Joon, swaying as he bent down over me, "you are *not* getting out of this."

He was wearing a snakeskin jacket and pants with zebra stripes. He looked like he had just robbed a zoo.

"I *would* get dressed up . . . I just haven't seen anything I like," I said. I crossed my arms clumsily to make my point.

"Jeez, *some*one has high standards. It's not like you're sitting in a warehouse full of designer apparel or anything . . ." he said, waving at all the clothes around us.

"Pfffft, *fine*," I relented.

Struggling to stand up, I tried to grab onto some dresses hanging next to me, but they gave too much and I lurched toward Joon. He grabbed at my elbow, trying to hold me up, but overshot, and we both fell through the dresses, ending up in a lump on the floor beneath the garment rack.

"You gotta stop fainting on me!" he cackled.

"I didn't faint!" I cried, giggling hysterically.

"Close enough!"

"You have a skirt on your head," I said, still giggling.

Joon pulled it off his head and picked a couple hangers off of my legs. "Come on," he said, pulling me to my feet. "I think I saw a clown wig that would look amazing on you."

I followed Joon, stumbling through the bulging racks, until we made it to the very back of the room. We stopped in front of a rack of flamboyant fur and leather jackets. The music and the other kids were muffled by all the thick coats, and I became extremely aware of how alone we were.

Joon ran his hand down the sleeve of a silvery-gray fur coat. "How's this?"

I shook my head. "Fur's not really my thing."

"I'll keep that in mind," he said, moving on to the next garment rack. "Man . . . I can't believe what happened to Soo-li."

"I know. I didn't realize what a huge deal it was to get caught dating."

"Yeah, dude, Top10 isn't playing around. Why do you think I go on dates in my car at the Leeum parking garage down the street?"

"Ew, I didn't know that was your thing," I said, wrinkling my nose up. It didn't sound like a very nice date.

"Hah, yeah, it's weird I guess. But tinted windows are the best."

"When you put it that way, it sounds kinda . . . naughty." We both busted up laughing again. *Naughty?* Where the hell did that word come from? I must have been really drunk.

"Nah, it's not like that. Well, I mean, *some*times it's like that . . ." He held up a neon-pink feather boa that must have been six feet long. I shook my head again, and he draped it back on the rack.

"It's just that car dates are one of the only ways you can really talk, you know? It's the only time when you're really alone with each other, and no one is breathing down your neck, watching you."

Maybe it was because I was drunk, and words were practically falling out of my mouth, or maybe it was because it felt like Joon had brought me back here for a specific reason, but I was suddenly feeling extremely confident. "No one is watching us right now . . ." I suggested.

Joon got quiet. Then he spun around and looked at me seriously, his million-gigawatt grin long gone.

"Hey . . . did you have a boyfriend back in the US?"

"Uh, *no*," I said. He was standing so close to me that I could see the little constellation of freckles on his bare neck.

Joon raked his hand through his bangs and turned his head to the side, like he was trying to make up his mind about something.

"I did," he said quietly.

"You *did?*" I said way too loud. I could tell I had a totally shocked look on my face.

Joon's whole body winced. "Yeah . . . Sorry, I just thought I could tell you, you know, because you're from the States." He was talking really fast now, like he couldn't wait to get out of the conversation. "It's not really something you can admit here, especially doing what we do . . . Shit, I shouldn't have said anything." Joon started to push past me, his perfect face blotchy and upset, and I knew I really screwed up. I honest to god thought he was going to kiss me, and instead he just told me the biggest secret of his life. Suddenly, I felt completely sober, and I knew I had get past my shock and humiliation and fix this.

I put my hands on Joon's shoulders and stopped him. "Wait, no,

I'm sorry. I was just surprised. You can talk to me about it." Gently, I said, "So, you're gay?"

"Not gay, not really," he said, studying his hands. "I've dated girls, too . . . I guess I like both."

"That's cool," I said. "So . . . what was he like?"

"My boyfriend? Um, he was nice. Hot. Made really good nachos . . . I don't know—this is weird!" Joon groaned then covered his face with his fists.

"It's not weird," I reassured him, pulling his fists down from his face. I just wanted to keep him talking. "How did you guys first meet?"

"We met at school—he was in my chemistry class. He had a boyfriend before we dated, so when they broke up I knew it would be safe to, you know . . ." Joon stopped and looked up at the ceiling.

"Make a move . . . ?"

"Yes!" He buried his face into the crook of his arm, groaning again.

"It's OK!" I said, tugging on his sleeve. It was unexpected to see him all embarrassed; he was usually so confident. It was like a whole new Joon—a Joon who I cared about a lot. "Are you guys still together?"

"No. We broke up when I moved back to Seoul. I just . . . I just really miss him. And I wanted to talk about him with someone."

"I'm sorry, Joon. That really sucks. But I bet he misses you, too."

"Yeah, I don't think so. I look at his Snap sometimes, and he has a new boyfriend."

"Oh my god, you should *not* be looking at his Snapchat!" I scolded.

"I know; it's stupid," he said. "I'm dumb."

"No, I'm just teasing. It's natural. I would totally look at my ex's Instagram . . . if I even had one . . ."

Joon's grin reappeared, and he tossed his bangs off his eyebrows. "Don't tell anyone, OK? No one else knows."

I pretended to lock my lips with a little key. "I won't tell a soul, I promise."

"Thanks."

Joon straightened up and reached his hand into the clothes hanging behind me. When he pulled his hand back, he was holding a red leather jacket with giant metal spikes on the shoulders. "This has your name written all over it."

"Oh, hell yes," I said.

He held the jacket open for me while I worked my arms into the way-too-big sleeves. It was really heavy, like I was wearing an entire cow. As Joon adjusted the jacket around my shoulders, I got this really warm feeling in my chest, not like the one I got when I first met him, when I couldn't get over how hot he was, but a different one, like we had just gotten a little closer. Like we were becoming real friends.

Joon lifted his Instax camera from around his neck and held it up to his eye. "Say tinted windows!"

"Tinted windows!"

THE FIX

[This page has been translated from Korean.]

04.08

CATEGORY: RANT

A Little Note About Scoop Posts

OK, Readers, it's time to get something straight.

Please, take a seat, turn off that video you're watching, and close the door. Because I'm only going to say this once.

In the days following my post about Soo-li and Hee-tae, Top10 canceled all of Soo-li's scheduled appearances and shut down her social media accounts. Many of her top fan sites are also down due to furious Hee-tae fans over-whelming their servers. #SilverSpoon-li has been trending on Twitter, and anti-fans are running wild with new accu-sations, some even too sordid to grace the pages of this blog.

To those who have decided that I am somehow to blame for this unfortunate turn of events, I recommend looking inward before vilifying me. *I* did not cancel Soo-li's appearances;

her producers did. *I* did not delete her Instagram; her entertainment company did. *I* did not swarm her fan sites; Heetae's fanbase did.

And one more thing, my dear Readers, *I* did not create a society in which a woman can be canceled for being in an older man's apartment, while the man is allowed to go on with his merry little life—*you* did.

Yes, the world of K-pop has a disease, but I am not the cancer. I am the doctor shining her light on a tumor eating the industry from the inside out. The more we expose the truth about these idols we claim to love, the more we can accept that they are merely human and the less perfect their entertainment companies will expect them to be. So to those who are calling for me to discontinue Scoop posts, I impolitely decline.

And to anyone else who takes issue with my content, I want to direct your attention to a small button on the top of your screen, the one with the X. You're welcome to exit at any time and find another platform for all your K-pop news. There are literally thousands of them.

+ V +

Firefly
MIC DROPPPPP

ItzyBitzy00
Ummmmmmmmmmm, for real tho? None of this would have happened if you didn't blog about it.

2NE1Minutes
ㅋㅋ V is so right, she just tells it like it is and then you all lose your minds.

Anonymous
How's the weather up there on top of your high horse, V?

> **+ V +**
> Extremely pleasant and guilt-free.

Aegyoona
Oh, thank GAWD. I LIVE for Scoop posts.

squishy_cat
So true, why wasn't Hee-tae canceled? Did you guys see him on Weekly Idol?? They teased him about Soo-li and that was basically it.

> **Guragrrrl**
> Yeah that was messed. I feel bad for Soo-li.

PinkBellaBarbie
Wow, I see a conspicuous lack of apology. ㅎㅎ

HoneyB
Wahhhhh. Soo-li!!!

2ALife
V, you are a walking, talking hypocrite.

zelu-b0t

Srsly, it's amazing someone so heartless can still pump blood up to her brain.

+ V +

Some of us seem to have forgotten that these idols are professionals. They have been trained to deal with both positive and negative critiques alike.

ItzyBitzy00

"Critiques" ㅋㅋㅋㅋ

 **99 MORE COMMENTS>>**

Eight

"STAND UP AND DO IT AGAIN," SAID MISS JACKIE,
who was pacing in front of us in the dance studio, just a few inches
from our bowed heads. "Harmony"—yes, she called me that now—
"I want to see ninety degrees, exactly."

One of the many side effects of Soo-li's disappearance was that
Miss Jackie had ramped up our humble lessons. When we debuted
at the Dream Concert in just T minus forty-six days, every group
on that stage would be considered our senior, and I'd have to bow
down to them when we were all in public.

"Lower . . ." said Miss Jackie testily. "LOWER, until you can see
the caps of those chicken-bone knees!"

I couldn't help it, but there it was. A tiny giggle came out of me,
and now it was sitting in the middle of the studio. *Chicken-bone
knees* was such a ridiculous phrase; it was like something an old
grandma would say in a creaky voice about someone she thought
was too skinny—"You need more meat on your bones; look at those
chicken-bone knees!"

A finger jabbed me in the back of my lowered head. "Do you
think this is a joke?" spat Miss Jackie.

Shit.

I kept my nose pointed to the ground. "No, Miss Jackie."

The tips of Miss Jackie's suede heels appeared on the floor under my head.

"Let me ask you something, Harmony. Who do you think this class is for?"

"For our seniors," I answered.

"Incorrect," barked Miss Jackie. She loved singling me out in class and making me look like a moron in front of the other girls, especially when I didn't have the right answers, which was basically always. "This class is for *you*," she said, drilling her sharp fingernail deeper into my hair. "Not your seniors, not the other girls who have spent their entire life bowing, but *you* and you alone. Do you know *why?*"

Her fingernail was starting to hurt, and I searched frantically for another answer. "Because . . . I don't know how to bow?"

"*Because* the last girl who failed to bow correctly to her sunbaes became so riddled with scandal that no one paid any attention to her singing and dancing. Everyone in this room seems to understand the importance of respect except *you*. And yet here they are"—her stockinged legs turned toward the other girls, who were still folded in half next to me—"faithfully by your side, learning what they already know, hiking every morning with you, practicing choreography over and over again with you—all for *you*—so you can perform together, as a unit. Do you understand?"

"Yes, Miss Jackie," I said through gritted teeth. The irony of it was that she was blaming everything on me when *she* was the one making us do it.

"Good." She pulled her finger from my scalp, and I let out a giant breath. "Now . . . Say you are sorry."

"What . . . ?" I involuntarily raised my head, and Miss Jackie slowly pushed it back down with her finger.

"Tell the girls that you are sorry for wasting their time," she instructed.

"But I . . ."

Miss Jackie cut me off. "Or would you like to wake everyone up an hour early tomorrow for a few extra miles of hiking, hmm?"

Someone whimpered, and it sounded like Yuri. I looked to my left and saw four upside-down pairs of eyes looking right at me. Hayan blinked hard at me like she wanted me to just obey already.

"Sorry," I muttered. It literally hurt to say it, and not because all the blood was rushing to my head.

"No—jwe-song-hamnida—in Korean." *Tap-tap* went Miss Jackie's fingernail into my scalp. "Apologize to the other girls in Korean for wasting their time."

This was so embarrassing I could have literally keeled over and died. There was no reason to make me say it in Korean; Miss Jackie just wanted to humiliate me in front of everyone. The blood in my head was pounding now, and an angry tear squeezed out of my eye and down the side of my nose.

"*Joe-song-ham-ni-da,*" Miss Jackie pronounced slowly, digging her nail deeper into my scalp with each syllable. "Say it."

"Joe-song . . ." I started. But I couldn't do it. It was like my whole body was fighting against giving her the satisfaction.

Miss Jackie bent over me, and her mouth hovered right above my ear. "*Finish it.*"

The hot tear was clinging to the tip of my nose now, then gravity took over and it dropped smack onto the toe of Miss Jackie's suede shoe, creating a tiny, dark splatter. *"No . . ."* I whispered. The word came from far away, like I was hearing someone else say it.

"No?" she said, enraged. "Is that *all* you have to say for yourself?"

Apparently, it *was* all I had to say because I just hung there, speechless.

"It appears that your talent has gone to your head," she said. "You seem to think that the rules do not apply to you. *Very well.*" Miss Jackie stood up abruptly and walked to the door. With her back to us, she said, "Class is dismissed. I will see you tomorrow morning at four a.m. for your morning hike." The girls shot up out of their bows, their mouths hanging open.

Before she was out the door, she added, "And you can expect the same for the remainder of the month."

The door clicked shut and we all stared at it in shock.

Aria was the first to break the spell, and she whipped around to face me. "What is *wrong* with you?" she yelled. The question exploded out of her like she'd been holding it in for months.

"Nothing's wrong with me!" I said, struggling to control my voice from slipping into a high-pitched whine. "It's not my fault Miss Jackie is such a bitch."

"Miss Jackie might be a bitch, but you could've just said you were sorry." Aria jabbed her finger at me like she was scolding a toddler.

"I *did* say I was sorry," I argued.

"But you didn't say it the right way," she said.

"Well, sometimes it feels like I don't do *anything* the right way!" I could feel the angry tears in my eyes.

"Come on, Alice, that's ridiculous." Aria was using her patronizing mother-knows-best voice.

"Oh, right," I said. "I forgot, you couldn't possibly know how that feels because you never do anything wrong."

Aria lifted her perfect chin high in the air so she was looking down at me. Even when she was pissed, she looked flawless. "That's because *I* follow the rules. And I try to at least make an effort."

"How can you even say that?" I demanded. I wanted to tear my hair out and my scalp along with it. "I'm killing myself trying to follow all the academy's rules. And I put in the effort—I've never worked so hard in my entire life!"

"I'm not talking about your effort in class. I'm talking about your effort with *us*." Aria was yelling now, and Yuri tried to put her hand on her shoulder to calm her down, but Aria just batted her away. "You've gone out of your way to completely avoid us since the day you got here!"

Of course she was right; I *was* trying to avoid her a lot of the time, but what she didn't get was how hard she made it for me to *want* to be around her. "What more do you want from me? We spend every single day together! We talk all the time!"

"Yeah, about choreography and breath work. Not about things that actual friends talk about."

"Well, it's not exactly like we are friends," I said, even though I knew I sounded childish.

"You know that's why Top10 has us dorm together, right? And why So-ri gave us that homework assignment?" said Aria. "So we can become friends? You haven't even *tried* to watch a movie with me! We're groupmates—we're supposed to be like sisters."

"Well, you guys already had a whole sister thing going on before I showed up," I said, the angry tears now flowing. "You made it pretty clear from day one that I didn't have what it takes to be part of A-List."

"I told you," Aria said, exhaling to try to calm her voice. "I didn't mean that and I apologized. Are you going to hold that over my head forever?"

"It wasn't just that one time. You're constantly reminding me that I'm not good enough."

Aria squinted at me. "When do I ever do that?"

"I don't know, how about in every dance class we've ever had together? Or when I don't wake up at the right time or go to bed at the right time, or when I don't *breathe* correctly!"

Aria shoved her hair out of her face. "I'm just trying to help you, Alice. That's literally my job, to help you. You shouldn't take it so personally." She looked down at her nails like she was trying to decide if she should say out loud what she was thinking. Finally, her mind made up, she lifted her eyes full of fire. "Honestly, it's been exhausting trying to fit you into this group. I know So-ri thinks you're some kind of musical genius, but I don't know why she or Top10 ever thought you could work with us."

I shrank back into myself, wheezing. It was like she had squeezed every last ounce of oxygen out of me, all at once. This was exactly what I always feared she thought about me, and now I knew it was irrefutably true.

The fire in Aria's eyes flamed out as soon as she saw me cower away from her. For a second, it looked like she was going to take it all back, but then her jaw tensed and she crossed her arms, saying nothing.

Hayan, Seol, and Yuri kind of hovered between us, unsure what to say or do. I could tell I was about to fall apart completely, and I didn't want Aria to see how badly she had hurt me. I turned around and walked over to the window and pretended to look at the street. It was drizzling outside, and through my anger and tears, all I could see was a fuzzy gray soup.

"So that's it then? Conversation's over? You're just going to walk away like you always do?"

I didn't say anything. I knew if I did, I would start sobbing.

"Great," said Aria sarcastically. I heard her open and close the door behind me, and I could tell there was only one person left in the studio with me. Seol walked up and patted me lightly on the shoulder. I ignored her. And when I finally looked up, she was gone, too.

I waited until their footsteps disappeared, then I crumpled to the floor, sobbing. I pulled my knees in tight and heaved into them. It wasn't fair; it just *wasn't*. That Miss Jackie wanted to teach me some cruel lesson about unity when it was Aria who left *me* out, and then somehow I got blamed for it all.

I let myself cry until the knees of my leggings were a soggy mess. Once I got my breathing under control, I wiped my face with the back of my hands, pulled myself together, and headed to So-hyun's room, hiding my tearstained face from anyone I walked past.

"Hey!" she said, throwing the door open. "Whoa, what's going on?"

"I'm sorry," I mumbled, "but can I please borrow your phone? I really need to talk to my sister."

"Oh my god, of course!" So-hyun rummaged through her purse

and pulled out her backup phone. "Are you sure there isn't anything I can do? Do you want to talk about it?"

"Not right now. I just want to talk to Olivia. I'll be back soon, OK?"

"OK, girl. I'll be here if you need anything."

"Thanks," I whispered gratefully. So-hyun gave me a quick hug around the neck, then I headed to the third floor with her phone hidden in my sleeve.

I ducked into the first empty studio I could find and sank into the floor with the phone in my lap. I typed Olivia's number, one of the only phone numbers I had memorized, and hit send.

ALICE
Hey it's me Alice

I listened to the nothingness of the soundproof studio as I watched the screen, waiting for the little thought bubbles to appear from Olivia's typing. A few minutes passed, and when I didn't get a response, I tried again.

ALICE
Sorry, I'm texting you from someone else's phone
because Top10 took mine away from me a while ago

Another agonizing minute went by, then a message popped up.

OLIVIA
U haven't texted me in forever
U just disappeared

ALICE

I know, I'm really sorry. Like I said, I didn't have a phone or anything

OLIVIA

Well, a lot happened since we last texted and I really needed to talk to you. I went to that festival thing by myself and I couldn't find anyone to hang out with. I just had to sit in a corner alone all afternoon until Dad picked me up, and no one talked to me, not even once. Everyone in my class saw me by myself and now they all think I'm such a loser.

Shit, I had totally forgotten about the festival.

ALICE

I'm so sorry, that sounds awful. But I'm sure no one thinks you're a loser.

OLIVIA

It was so embarrassing. I could barely walk into class on Monday.
I don't want to back to that school ever again.

ALICE

Liv, I really think you're blowing it out of proportion. You're new there, people know you don't have a ton of friends yet.

OLIVIA

How do you know? You're not here.

ALICE

I just know, OK?

Hey, can you actually talk on the phone right now?

Something really bad just happened . . . . . .

Olivia stopped typing for a minute, then finally responded.

OLIVIA

Not really

I'm pretty busy rn.

I sat up from the wall, not quite believing what I was reading.

ALICE

Please don't be mad at me right now, OK? I really

need to talk to you.

Can I please just tell you what just happened?

OLIVIA

I gotta go

Text you later or something

"Text you later or something"? What the hell? I did that thing where you reread the texts and dissect all the commas, periods, and exclamation marks (or lack thereof) to make sure you're not missing anything, even though you know deep down you read it right the first time. And of course, I did read it right the first time. Olivia was ghosting me.

I locked So-hyun's phone and scowled at myself in the black screen. Then I squeezed my fist around it until a sharp pain shot across my knuckles. Before I knew what I was doing, I launched the phone across the room. It spun in the air and hit the foam padding in the wall across from me, then bounced harmlessly across the floor as if it couldn't care less about how hard I threw it. Even the goddamn phone didn't care how I felt.

Furious, I unleashed a scream, the kind that's so loud it burns your throat on its way out. But just like the phone, it fell dead in the echoless studio.

Nine

EVER SINCE WE WERE LITTLE KIDS, WHEN MOTHER'S
Day rolled around, Olivia and I always complained to Mom and Dad
about the fact that there's a day for mothers and a day for fathers,
but there's no day for kids. And every time, Dad would always tell
us the same thing: "That's because every *other* day of the year is for
children." We always hated that answer, but as we got older it kind
of became a tradition to joke about it. So when I found out that
Korea has a national Children's Day, I almost couldn't believe it.
And now it was my first day off from the academy.

"There she is!" called Dad when I emerged from the subway
station.

"Hey, guys!" I said. "See, Dad, I told you—Children's Day!"

"Ha, you did! I guess you were right all along."

Mom and Dad and Olivia were waiting for me at the top of the
stairs at Dong-Incheon station. It was one of the only holidays
when Top10 would give us time off from our lessons, and for some
reason, Mom and Dad had wanted to meet in this small town, way
outside the city.

I walked up to them, and Dad wrapped his arms around me, pulling me in for a hug. "Good to see ya, kiddo."

"We missed you, sweetheart," said Mom, joining the hug.

"I missed you, too," I said, sighing. I had almost forgotten about their good Mom and Dad smell, and I wanted to memorize it so I could bring it back to the academy with me.

Mom kissed me on the forehead, then held me out by my shoulders so she could get a good look at me. "Wow, Alice, you look so different! Look at your arms," she said, squeezing my bicep, "you have muscles!"

"And your hair is so long!" said Dad, smoothing my hair down with his open palm. "Wow, it grew *really* fast."

"Dad, they're extensions!" I laughed.

"Oh, I knew that." He shot me a dad wink, which meant he definitely did *not* know that.

When Miss Jackie first told me I could go home for Children's Day, my heart sprang up about five inches in my chest, but it dropped right back down again when I thought about how Olivia blew me off the last time we texted. And sure enough, now she was acting weird. Normally, she would have screamed when she saw me. She would have run down the subway stairs and jumped on me, too. But now she was off by herself, sitting on top of a brick wall, kicking her feet up and down.

"Hey, Liv," I called out to her cautiously.

"Hey," she said. She kept her head down and worked the heel of her shoe between two bricks.

OK, so she still wasn't talking to me. This was going to be such a fun day off.

"Come down off of there and give your sister a hug," ordered Mom.

Olivia reluctantly jumped off the wall and came over. I wanted to throw my arms around her to prove that everything was OK between us, but instead I let her give me this half-hearted side hug.

"So why'd you guys want to meet all the way out here?" I asked, turning to Mom and Dad.

"Ask Mom," said Dad.

"A woman at work told me about this place that's famous for its spicy fried chicken. I thought it'd be fun for us to get some and eat it in the park—sound good?" said Mom.

"Uh, yeah, that sounds *amazing*," I said. The words *fried chicken* sounded impossibly good. I hadn't eaten anything that wasn't green and mushy in months, let alone fried meat.

It was actually warm outside, one of the first days of the year that was too hot for a jacket. We walked a few blocks in the sunshine talking about Dad's new job, past a bunch of other families who were celebrating the holiday, too, and turned into a covered street with a crowded market inside. There were all kinds of stalls selling fruits and vegetables, with big tubs full of different kinds of cabbage and scallions—and these string beans that were longer than my whole arm. There was a woman sitting on the ground with baskets of raw fish, and she had a little fan blowing on them to keep the flies away. Another guy was selling fried potatoes out of a metal cart. He cut them into one superlong spiral and sold them on a stick.

"I think that's us," said Mom, pointing to a long line at the back of the market.

"Sheesh, look at that line. This must be some good frickin' chicken," joked Dad.

"As long as it's not cold cabbage, I don't care how long the line is," I said. I could smell the simmering oil all the way from where we were standing, and it was making my mouth water.

We threaded our way to the back of the market and got in line. At the front of the line, a woman used giant wooden spatulas to toss fried chicken in a wok.

"I'm going to wait over here," mumbled Olivia. She trudged over to an empty bench and slumped down on it.

"What's up with her?" I asked Mom and Dad.

"Oh, you know, just being a moody teenager," said Dad as he cleaned his glasses on the hem of his shirt.

"Dad, *I'm* still a teenager," I said.

"I know, but she's brand-new at it. She's really giving it her all."

I rolled my eyes and looked at Mom. "Do *you* know what's going on with her?"

"I'm not sure; she's been pretty quiet for the past few weeks," she said.

"That's weird," I said, "usually you can't get her to stop talking."

"True," she said, smiling. "But you know what I think it is, honey? I really think she's been having a hard time with you being away."

"You think it's something to do with me?" I said, taken aback.

"I do," she said, brushing the hair out of my face, "and I think you should talk to her about it."

"I mean, I'd love to talk to her if she'd even say two words to me."

"Why don't you go over there and catch up with her, and Dad and I'll stay in line and get lunch?" said Mom.

"OK." I sighed.

I got out of line and walked over to the bench where Olivia was busy scrolling through Snapchat.

"Cool if I sit?" I asked.

"You can do whatever you want," she said.

Well, this was going to be pleasant.

"So what's up?" I asked.

"Nothing," she said, not even bothering to look up from her phone.

"Nothing at all?"

"Yeah . . . nothing."

"Have things gotten better at school?"

"I guess."

"Why do you guess?"

"I dunno; it just has." She still had her head bent over her phone, and her thumb was scrolling nonstop.

I slung my arm over the back of the bench, deciding to try a different tactic. "Hey, do you read V?"

"Uh-huh," she said.

"Can you believe she did that to Soo-li? You know, I haven't seen her around the academy once since that all went down."

"Nope."

It was like trying to have a conversation with Siri. No, it was like trying to have a conversation with Siri if your phone was broken and she was pissed at you. It was excruciating.

"Olivia," I said, impatiently tugging at her wrist. "I haven't seen you in five months; can you actually talk to me?"

"I *am* talking to you," she snapped.

"Well, can you, like, put down your phone? You haven't even made eye contact with me since I got here."

Olivia exhaled loudly and locked her phone. "*Fine.* What do you wanna talk about?"

I sighed and closed my eyes, trying to will the frustration out of my voice. "Well, Mom said you've been having kind of a hard time the past few weeks."

"Why are you talking to *Mom* about me?" she demanded.

"I wasn't talking to Mom about you; she just mentioned it literally four minutes ago."

"Well, Mom doesn't know what she's talking about!" Olivia picked up her phone and flipped it back and forth in her hands.

"So . . . *are* you having a hard time right now?"

"No! God, I'm *fine*! You can't just disappear, then come back all of a sudden and ask me all these stupid questions!" Olivia unlocked her phone and angrily started scrolling again.

"OK, OK, *sorry*. I won't ask you any more questions!"

God, why was everyone always yelling at me? Was literally every person in South Korea mad at me right now? It was so petty, but what I really wanted to say was "You're lucky to even *have* a sister who asks you questions." I mean, what did Olivia think was going to happen when I went to the Star Academy? How could she be mad at me for "disappearing" when she was the one who convinced me to move into the Star Academy in the first place?

We sat on the bench silently while a family with two little kids in a stroller walked by. The little boy was holding a balloon shaped like a cartoon chipmunk, and I had the sudden urge to grab it out of his hands and squeeze it until it popped.

Olivia kept scrolling and I kept my mouth shut, until finally Mom and Dad came over with a giant bucket of fried chicken.

"Here you go, hon," said Mom, handing me a pair of long, wooden chopsticks and some napkins.

"Thanks," I mumbled.

I fished a piece of chicken out of the bucket, but when I bit into it I was so mad I could barely even taste it.

"I have big, big surprise for yooou!" sang So-ri when Aria and I walked into her office for our lesson. "Ven conmigo." She grabbed us both by the hand and pulled us over to her desk, and as soon as she let go of our arms, we shifted a couple inches away from each other.

The tension with Aria had only gotten worse since our big blowup. Apparently, getting everything out in the open did *not* always make things better, despite what So-hyun had said. There was a real chill between us now, like we lived on a freezing tundra and Aria was its ice queen.

"Look at this," said So-ri. Brushing aside a couple empty bags of chips and a stack of sheet music, she revealed a small white-plastic baton. It looked kind of like a Wii remote. "Jja-jaaaan!" she said.

"What is it?" I asked.

Aria gasped and covered her mouth with her hands, whispering to herself, "It's our light stick!"

"Whoaaa," I said under my breath. I really wasn't in the mood for surprises after my ruined trip with my family the day before, but this was extremely exciting.

Aria had this expression of complete awe. She picked up the light stick and cradled it delicately in her hands like she was holding a fragile baby bird. The top was a translucent 3-D pyramid, and inside the pyramid was a black letter A. Two shiny black stripes spiraled down the white handle, crisscrossing over a button with the words A-LIST embossed on it.

"Go! Turn it on!" urged So-ri.

Aria pressed the button with her thumb, and a soft-white light pulsed from inside the pyramid.

"Our color is white!" she said with quiet excitement.

"Yes. Diamond white," said So-ri. "So pretty, yes?"

"It's beautiful," said Aria.

"Yeah, it's really cool, Seon-saeng-nim," I said.

"Someday you will perform for a whole arena full of these light sticks!"

"A white ocean," Aria said as she clicked the light stick off and delicately placed it on the desk. I picked it back up and was surprised to find that it was heavier than I expected. The weight of it—and seeing *A-List* stamped on the button—made everything seem so real. Back in January, when Aria first talked about a light-stick ocean, it seemed so far away, like something that would happen to some person who wasn't me. But now the Dream Concert was almost here, and there might actually be people in the stands waving light sticks just like this one—they'd be waving them for *us*.

"So," said So-ri as she tore open a bag of multicolored corn puffs and popped one in her mouth, "today we do '2day/2nite.' Let's warm up, please."

After we got our warm-ups out of the way, we started in on our single, and right away something was off.

"Turn off the lights . . . And turn today into tonight . . . Turn off the lights."

"OK, OK, stop!" said So-ri after only a few verses in. Her hand disappeared into her bag of puffs and crinkled around until she found one. "First verse, please."

"Nae-ga ileo nasseul ttae neon salajyeosseo."

It wasn't the Korean that was throwing me. Singing somehow made speaking other languages easier; like when I sang Italian opera, it was just a string of beautiful notes and syllables. The problem was that I was supposed to be singing the harmony, but I kept slipping into Aria's part. I couldn't help it; she was just singing so aggressively that I couldn't find my notes.

"Alice, what happen?" asked So-ri. "You are straining your voice now."

"It's just that I'm trying really hard to stay in my part," I explained.

"Yes, but you do not find your notes by forcing. This is not the power I teach you. You practice your exercises?"

"Yeah, I've been practicing every day," I said for Aria's benefit just as much as So-ri's.

"Your vocal folds, you press them together too hard now."

"I'm trying really hard not to," I said, gripping my throat with both hands. "Can we just try again?"

"Yes, OK."

"Nae-ga ileo nasseul ttae neon salajyeosseo."

Again, I fell right back into the melody. My voice merged with Aria's, note for note, and this time I could feel the strain in the back of my throat; it sounded taut, almost raspy. Even though I was singing loud enough to match Aria, there was zero power behind it. I sounded terrible, and that meant *we* sounded terrible.

So-ri stopped playing again, clicking her tongue at me, and I could tell by the way Aria flipped her hair away from her face that she was getting annoyed with all the starting and stopping.

"Where your head, Alice?" demanded So-ri.

"I don't know . . . sorry," I said. "I guess I've just been a little preoccupied this week. I can focus, I promise."

So-ri clapped her hands together, creating a little cloud of puff dust. "Both of you do jumping jack, twenty-five. Vámonos."

Aria glared at me, and we both started jumping up and down, our arms just barely missing the overstuffed bookshelves next to us. So-ri liked to do this when we were getting in our heads too much, and the weird thing was: it usually worked.

When we were done with jumping jacks, we stood back in front of her piano.

"Ready?" asked So-ri.

"Yes," said Aria.

"Ready," I said.

"Nae-ga ileo nasseul ttae neon salajyeosseo."

I was still struggling, but now there was something off about Aria, too. Her voice was all over the place like she was getting worked up. It sort of had that warbled sound that happens when you're about to cry but you're trying not to.

"Turn off the lights . . . And turn today into—"

Aria stopped abruptly and threw her hands in the air. "I can't do this if she's not going to listen to me when we sing together!"

"I *am* listening to her!" I insisted. "It's impossible not to! You're completely overpowering me right now. There's absolutely no room for my voice!"

"You think this is *my* fault?" said Aria. "You're the one who can't stick to the part you were assigned!"

"Enough!" said So-ri, banging on the piano keys. She pulled her legs from the pedals and turned to face us. "Someone want to say what is going on, hmm?" she said, crunching a big puff between her front teeth.

"I don't know," I mumbled.

"Me neither," said Aria.

"How homework going? You watching movies together?" So-ri asked.

Aria tapped her foot on the floor, and I balled up my fists into the pockets on my sweatshirt. Neither of us looked at So-ri. We hadn't watched a single movie together, but I wasn't going to be the one to admit it.

"Hmm, seems like no," said So-ri, frowning. "This is not good. Only three weeks until you debut your single at the Dream Concert, and you two cannot even sing your own parts."

"I'm singing my part just fine," said Aria under her breath.

So-ri pinched her lips together but decided to ignore her comment. "What happen when the other girls sing with you, hmm? You supposed to be leading."

I brought my thumbnail up to my mouth, saying nothing, and Aria just kept tapping her foot.

So-ri rolled her bag of puffs up tight and wrapped a rubber band around it, her face puckered and stern. "No more songs today, only exercises. We do *euh*'s. Right now."

Aria and I both let out frustrated sighs. So-ri was making us do exercises instead of working on our single to punish us for not doing our homework. She turned back to the keyboard, and we began working our way up the scales. I was fine at first. My vocal folds closed like I wanted them to in my lower range, but as we started getting up into the higher registers, my voice started coming out harsh, like when someone talks too loudly into a microphone.

"Right now too much closure, Alice. You need to find the balance of release *and* closure," instructed So-ri.

"I *know*," I said. There was a sting in my sinuses, and when I briefly squeezed my eyes shut, I was surprised to find that tears came out.

So-ri stopped playing midscale. "Alice, why you crying?"

"I . . . This is j-just s-so hard!" I stammered.

"Yes?" she said, a frown forming around the edges of her mouth.

"It's just that singing is the one thing I'm actually good at, and I can't even get this stupid chord-closure exercise right."

"No one said this would be easy; do you ever hear me say that? No—in your first lesson, I say it would be very difficult."

"But this isn't even fun anymore. There's just so much pressure on me right now!"

"I put this pressure on you because I know you can handle it," countered So-ri. "So, you ready to stop crying and keep going?"

So-ri was right. She did tell me this was going to be hard, and avoiding the problem wasn't going to make things any easier. I sniffed back my tears a few times and nodded, determined not to cry any more. "Yes, I'm ready," I said. "And I'm not going to give up."

"I know you won't, Alice," said So-ri. Her voice was still sharp, but at least she sounded like she believed in me. "Now, we do it again."

We did it again, and again, and again, for the rest of the lesson. It never got any easier, but I didn't complain anymore, at least not out loud. When we were finished, So-ri silently turned away from her piano and gathered up all the sheet music on her stand. I wanted to stay back and talk with her—I don't know why, maybe to make sure I was still on her good side or something—but I decided against it.

On her way out, Aria slung her backpack over her shoulder, lifting her long, glossy hair out from underneath it. She had one foot out the door, and at the last second, she turned to me. "Good job today," she kind of mumbled over her shoulder.

I raised my eyebrows in surprise, but before I could respond, she walked out the door.

Ten

"GIRLS!" MISS JACKIE BARKED, SNAPPING HER
fingers above her head. The whole cafeteria gawked at her as she
made a beeline toward the table where Aria, Yuri, Hayan, and Seol
were eating lunch. When she got to their table, she fired off a com-
mand, but all I could hear was "Mr. Kim" and "Now!" I watched
from across the room as they bolted up from their seats and started
making their way toward the exit, leaving their spoons and chopsticks sticking out of their bowls like a bunch of darts in a dartboard.

"Go! Go!" said So-hyun, pushing me off the bench with both
hands.

"OK, I'm going!" I wiped my mouth with the back of my hand
and chased after them, still swallowing my last bite.

I had no idea what was going on, but one thing I did know was
that a surprise meeting with Mr. Kim meant one of two things:
either you were about to get the best news of your life—or the
worst. It was like getting called to the principal's office, only if the
principal had the power to destroy all your hopes and dreams in
one fell swoop.

We hustled upstairs, and when we came out onto the fifth floor, I couldn't help but stop and stare. My mom always made jokes about getting "the corner office" one day, as if the pinnacle of her career was having two walls worth of windows, but now I understood what she was talking about. Mr. Kim's office was ginormous, taking up more than half of the fifth floor. Encased entirely in blue-green glass, it was filled with dark leather furniture, expensive-looking art, and Korean antiques in little glass cases, like in a museum. It was like looking into an aquarium full of rare tropical fish, and at the center of it all, sitting at an enormous glass desk, was the great white shark himself, Mr. Kim.

"Inside now!" hissed Miss Jackie as she hurried us into the office.

Mr. Kim lazed in his leather-and-chrome chair with one foot draped over an armrest. As usual, his eyes were glued to the screen of his Samsung and he barely noticed us assemble into the room. Two of Mr. Kim's entourage hovered next to his chair, and hanging in the windows above them were the ethereal faces of Top10's most successful idols.

I parked myself behind Seol and hunched down into my hoodie, hoping to stay out of Mr. Kim's line of sight. Miss Jackie clicked the door closed behind us, then walked to the front of Mr. Kim's desk, yanking the hood off my head on her way.

The producer standing to the left of Mr. Kim rubbed his hands together and started speaking, just slow enough so that I could understand most of what he was saying. "Girls, you are extremely fortunate! Late last night, 6IXA canceled their appearance on *M Countdown*. Mmm, something about a dehydrated dancer." He waved his hand in the air as if shooing away a gnat. "And this morning, we got the call . . ."

He paused for dramatic effect, and the girls grabbed on to one another in anticipation. For a second, no one breathed and the only sound in the room was the *pik-pok* of Mr. Kim's texting.

"*M Countdown* would like to invite *you* to appear on the show today in their place!"

"HEOL!" cried Seol. The girls fell all over one another, screaming and jumping up and down like a pack of wild hyenas.

Noticing I wasn't exactly jumping up and down myself, Miss Jackie eyed me suspiciously. "Harmony, is there a problem?" she asked over all the screaming.

"Oh, um, I guess I don't know what *M Countdown* is?"

Miss Jackie pursed her lips at the girls, and they immediately quieted down. "*M Countdown* is a live music show that features performances by only the most relevant K-pop idols. It broadcasts in countries all across Asia. It is quite an honor for them to extend an appearance to a group that has yet to debut."

A little thrill started to bloom inside of me. All those early mornings, all those agonizing hours of hiking and dance lessons, all those months of struggling with Aria, it was going to pay off . . . *today*. I was going to get to sing in front of a real, live audience—me!—on television, in a matter of hours. No offense, 6IXA, but amen for you.

"*Ahem*," interrupted the producer. "Just one small caveat—it's nothing really . . ." he said, waving his hand again. "There won't be a musical number tonight, only a quick interview."

Sweat prickled across the palms of my hands and zoomed up into my armpits. An *interview*? I could barely construct a sentence in Korean, and now I was going to have to speak in front of all of Asia?

"Also," said the agent, "you'll be sharing the stage with MSB to lend you a little, mmm, star power."

Yuri gasped and the girls went back to jumping up and down all over again. I peered up at the towering group portrait of MSB that was hanging just to the left of Mr. Kim's head, and Joon's airbrushed face stared back down at me. It was the version of him that the rest of world knew and loved, the idol, the prince of Top10 Entertainment. I could barely connect his image to the Joon I knew in real life.

"Girls! Please settle down," said the agent with a patronizing chuckle. "This is an extremely important day for A-List. You have much work to do before the show. All your regular lessons are canceled. After lunch, you'll go straight to hair and makeup to begin preparing for your appearance. Now, go! Represent Top10 well!"

"Kamsahamnidaaa!" chimed Aria as the girls bowed excitedly. I quickly bowed behind them, then leaped to the door, ready to flee to freedom.

"Harmony! Stay for a moment, please," called Miss Jackie.

Everyone stopped short in a jumble behind me, looking back at Miss Jackie in confusion. She shooed the others out with her hand, smiling mysteriously. "Just Harmony, please."

I gripped the doorknob, not quite ready to let go of my escape hatch, as the others passed through the doorway. On her way out, Seol punched me softly on the arm and I tried to muster a smile for her. Aria was the last to leave and she hovered in the doorway like maybe they forgot to ask her to stay, too, but when Miss Jackie cleared her throat, she flung her hair over her shoulder and left.

"Please, sit," Miss Jackie said, gesturing to an overstuffed chair in front of Mr. Kim's desk. Grudgingly, I turned around and dropped into it.

"Harmony, since this is A-List's first public appearance, we would like you to help the group shine." I glanced up at the producers next to Mr. Kim, and they looked down at me like I was a puppy chasing its own tail, cute but pitiful.

"Me? But Aria is our group leader . . ."

Miss Jackie raised an open palm to silence me. "Mr. Kim has a brilliant idea," she said, nodding toward Mr. Kim, who didn't seem the least bit interested. "Today you will share the stage with Joon, who, just like you, is MSB's American ambassador. It is important that our ambassadors distinguish themselves, as they will lead their groups when the time comes to debut in America. As such, Mr. Kim would like you to make a splash. He would like you to have . . . a personal exchange with Joon on camera today."

I glanced back up at airbrushed Joon, but he just stared back at me mutely. "I'm sorry," I said as delicately as I could manage, "but I don't understand?"

"We'd like the two of you to interact onstage," explained Miss Jackie impatiently, her eyes narrowing.

This was just as mystifying, but it was clear the question-and-answer portion of the meeting was over.

"Yes, Miss Jackie," I said, even though I had no idea what I saying yes *to*.

"Good."

A throat-clearing noise sputtered out of Mr. Kim. His thumbs stopped their texting and hovered over his phone. In slow, halting English, he spoke: "I will not be . . . disappointed."

Everyone in the room froze, stunned by his interruption. Almost imperceptibly, his eyes behind his orange-tinted glasses raised to meet mine. I shrunk back into the chair, fighting the urge to flip my hood back up on my head.

After the longest ten seconds of my life, Mr. Kim resumed his texting, and the entire room exhaled.

"Now back to the cafeteria to finish your lunch," said Miss Jackie. "But do not overindulge; you do not want to be bloated for the cameras." With a flick of her manicured fingernails, she dismissed me. I gave a quick bow, then fled from the room.

My feet tore down the stairs, my head full of buzzing bees. I was getting OK at understanding Korean, but speaking it myself was totally different. I could handle basic questions just fine, but I was pretty sure the host of *M Countdown* wasn't going to ask me "Where is the bathroom?" on live television. And what the hell was a "personal exchange" anyway? Hopefully, Joon would be able to explain it to me because I had exactly zero idea what any of it meant.

But when I got back to the cafeteria, Joon was nowhere in sight.

"Yaasss, girl! *M Countdown!*" So-hyun exclaimed in her megaphone-loud voice when she saw me. Obviously, she had heard the news. She jumped out of her seat and grabbed me low around the hips, picking me up in a big bear hug. She might have been tiny, but she had the strength of a freaking honey badger.

"OK, OK, OK!" I laughed, squeezing out of her arms.

I flopped down onto the bench, but she continued to march around in a small circle, chanting *"M Countdown, M Countdown."* I used the opportunity to take a giant bite off her plate. She was eating dessert, a big, fluffy stack of brick toast oozing with honey and topped with chocolate chips, strawberries, and a cloud of whipped cream. I wasn't supposed to eat off her plate anymore, but the circumstances called for drastic measures.

"I guess someone leaked the news," I said, my mouth full of mochi and whipped cream.

"Duh! Did you guys freak?"

"*Duh.* I mean, everyone else did. They practically lost their minds."

"Girl, I cannot *believe* you're going on *M Countdown* today! Damn, you're only five months into your training. That's like . . . *unheard* of."

"Yeah, well, don't get too jealous; we don't even get to sing," I said, frowning into her plate of brick toast.

"Oh, what? That sucks for reals," she said, disappointed for me. "So what is it, like an interview or something?"

"Yeah, just an interview. Also, can you explain something to me?" I stuffed another bite of toast into my mouth—I was officially stress eating.

"What?" she said.

"Mr. Kim wants me to have a 'personal exchange' with Joon onstage," I said, using air quotes to emphasize *personal exchange.* "Got any idea as to what the hell that means?"

"Ha! He wants you to *flirt!*" exclaimed So-hyun, shoving me hard in the shoulder.

"*What?*" I was about to tip a strawberry into my mouth, but I fumbled and it rolled down my sweatshirt, leaving a bright-red trail right down the center. After everything Joon told me the other night, about his secret and how he still missed his ex-boyfriend, the last thing I wanted to do was flirt with him *on camera.*

"OK, maybe 'flirt' is too strong a word. It's more like he wants to create some *intrigue* between you and Joon." So-hyun wiggled her fingers when she said *intrigue.* "Just don't go overboard," she warned. "There's a ridiculously fine line between flirting and ending your career. I'm sure you'll be fine though."

"Easy for you to say," I grumbled, daubing at the fruity carnage on my shirt with a napkin. "You actually enjoy flirting in public."

"Truer words have never been spoken," said So-hyun solemnly. She snatched back her fork and pushed my cold cabbage back in front of me.

"Why would Mr. Kim ask me to do this, though? What for?"

"It's easy publicity," explained So-hyun matter-of-factly. "You create a little TV moment with Joon, his fandom gets riled up, and suddenly everybody is talking about A-List."

"But I thought we weren't supposed to 'fraternize with boys.' Isn't that why Soo-li got in so much trouble?"

So-hyun shushed me with her hands so I would lower my voice. "That was totally different. He was old enough to be her father, and Mr. Kim didn't give his blessing."

I guess it made sense. It was like right out of a cheesy rom-com— if you took a nobody like me and put them next to a somebody like Joon, suddenly the nobody would become a somebody, too. Or at least people would ask, "Hey, who's that awkward girl flirting with Joon?" The only problem was: this wasn't a cheesy rom-com, this was terrifyingly real. If I screwed it up, I could not only blow up my life's dream, I could also blow up my friendship with Joon.

"OK," I said, "but I don't even like Joon like that." Anymore . . .

"It doesn't matter if you actually *like* him or not. You just fake it."

I dragged my fork across my cold cabbage in a zigzag pattern. "OK. But why *me*?"

"Mr. Kim probably wants to show off his shiny new American," answered So-hyun.

I pretended to tip a cowboy hat on my head. "Pleased to oblige, pardner."

"Yee-haw," added So-hyun dryly.

"Well, then what?" I asked.

"What 'what'?"

"What do I do? Teach me the ways, O Jedi Master."

"Oh, thank you, Jesus, Mary, and Joseph, I thought you'd never ask," she said.

So-hyun came over to my side of the table and straddled the bench so we could face each other. "All right, when Joon makes a joke or something, cover your mouth with your hands, then point at him and say something stupid but innocent, like, 'Oh, Oppa! You're so funny!'" She was using her girly-girl stage voice now, high-pitched and sugary sweet, and somehow she managed to look devious and innocent all at once. "Then giggle, like, A LOT." She bent forward, scrunching her tiny shoulders up to her ears and laughed into her hands. "Hee-hee-HEE!"

"Get a room!" shouted someone from the table next to us.

"See! It works!" said So-hyun excitedly, returning to her natural voice.

I made a show of rolling my eyes, and she came at me with her two fingers, poking me in the belly.

"Ah! Ah, stop! Everyone's looking at us!" I cried, edging away from her. "As impressive as that *was*, there's no way I'll ever pull it off like you," I added. "I'm gonna look so dumb out there."

"Girl, come *on*. We all look like raging dummies onstage once in a while. That's what being a celebrity is all about. The secret is not to care so much. You *do* want to be famous one day, right?" So-hyun shook her head at me, then started back in on her brick toast.

I turned back to my cold pile of cabbage; it had been boiled so long it was almost translucent. Of course I wanted to be famous one day; that's *all* I wanted.

OK, I would fake it.

I stuffed a huge forkful of green mush into my mouth and swallowed, hard.

THE FIX

[This page has been translated from Korean.]

05.13

CATEGORY: RUMOR MILL

An *M Countdown* Upset

The sun has barely peeked her head over Seoul, but already there's gossip stirring. Keen-eyed night owls would have noticed late last night that 6IXA canceled their *M Countdown* appearance. SST Entertainment made the announcement on the 7EVEN fanclub page, explaining that K-luv collapsed from exhaustion during rehearsals (much love to @BamBamBias from the 7EVEN fanclub page for notifying me).

Fragile baby K-luv.

This debacle should serve as a warning to all entertainment companies: idols are expected to work hard in order to remain competitive, but no one should work so hard that their bodies break. K-luv, we hope you recuperate speedily. Pray.

However, in a move that could only be described as controversial, *M Countdown* has invited A-List, the yet-to-debut-but-already-infamous girl group, to take the stage in 6IXA's place. Can anyone recall the last time a rookie girl group replaced a senior boy band on *M Countdown*? I grieve for those poor 7EVENs in attendance. At the very least, they can rest their tearful eyes on MSB's gorgeous visages, who are also taking the stage today.

My prediction is this: Top10 will direct A-List to do something scandalous. Something netizens will eat up like a forkless baby left to a birthday cake. And best believe, you'll read about it here first.

+ V +

💬 COMMENTS ══════════════════════════════

exo_Baby 17
~~~~PRAAAAAYYYYY~~~~

....

Mm (ง ᵕ)ว mama
Daebak! Can't wait to see A-List perform finally! I loved their day/night concept ^_^

> **FireT**
> it was ok. it was basically just a black and white concept. AOA did it better.

> **Krystal**
> YASSSS. Day/Night concept was so epiiiiic.

+ V +

Yes, vvv curious to see A-Lists's appearance. Their concept was gimmicky, but looks are only skin-deep . . .

rose&thorn

If you really cared so much about idols you wouldn't spread rumors about them.

bobobobobobo

This is why I don't read V much anymore

+ V +

The information you get *for free* on my blog is not "rumors." All information is verified. You need to check your facts like I do, @rose&thorn.

Kwang-hee4Me

@rose&thorn Don't read V or you'll get read ㅋ ㅋ ㅋ ㅋ ㅋ ㅋ ㅋ ㅋ ㅋ ㅋ ㅋ

<3-pop

NOOOOOOO!! I've been waiting since April for this appearance. How will I get my K-luv fix now??? (ㅠ_ㅠ) (ㅠ_ㅠ)(ㅠ_ㅠ)

 **130 MORE COMMENTS>>**

Eleven

MISS JACKIE HERDED US, MADE-UP AND COSTUMED,
into the elevator and down to the garage, where a black van with
tinted windows was waiting for us. I grinned to myself thinking
about how I had called Joon's tinted windows naughty. Hopefully,
it'd be easy to find him when we got to the show.

The driver got out and rolled back the sliding door for us, and
sitting right there like a jolly garden gnome was So-ri. "Hola, chicas!" she said between bites of squid jerky.

"You're coming?" I asked.

"For moral support. I want to see my girls in their first public
appearance," she said. I slid in next to her and she squeezed my
hand, leaving a dusting of fishy salt.

Aside from So-ri's humming, the ride on the way to Sangam was
dead quiet. Everyone seemed on edge. Yuri kept nervously tapping
her high heels together, while Aria stared straight ahead, practically
boring a hole into the seat in front of her.

I would have subjected myself to a hundred hours of humble
lessons with Miss Jackie for one minute on the phone with Olivia.
I was going to appear on international television—live!—and my

sister had no idea. Or maybe she did. Maybe she was rushing home from school right now so she could make a giant bowl of popcorn and watch it with Mom and Dad. I could almost see her pushing them down onto the couch, explaining what a big deal the show was. But there was no way for me to know; we hadn't talked since Children's Day.

I watched the cityscape change out the window as we left Gangnam and headed toward Sangam, the area of Seoul where all the big broadcasting companies are. The Paris Baguette and Lotteria storefronts disappeared and were replaced by sleek glass towers the color of the sky. I'd never been to this area of the city. It was supposed to be the heart of the entertainment industry in Seoul, but it looked more like the boring financial district in San Francisco.

As we headed along the Han River, pedestrians squinted at our tinted windows, trying to see who was on the other side. If they thought there might be celebrities inside our van, after tonight, they'd be right.

The van started to slow as we turned down a busy street that funneled us into a gigantic plaza. We came to an abrupt stop, smack in the middle of the plaza where hundreds of teenage girls were lined up outside the *M Countdown* studios. They were armed with MSB swag, handwritten signs, and cameras, some with zoom lenses the size of my thigh.

"Look," said So-ri simply, pointing out the window, "fans."

"Yeah, but not ours," I said. Just as I said it, though, there was some movement in the crowd.

Seol scooted over to get a better look and pressed her face up against the window. "Hey, they're coming over here!" she said excitedly in Korean. Sure enough, the girls in line had started streaming over to us, curious to see who was inside our van. They circled in closer as the driver popped out of the van to come around and open the door for us. I almost lost him in the crowd, there were just so many people.

"Remember," said Miss Jackie, "your first steps outside this van are just as important as your performance onstage. These girls may not know A-List yet, but they certainly will after tonight. They deserve your respect and attention. They want to see grace, love, humility, and most of all, *magic*." Then the door flew open, and the buzz of the crowd burst into the van.

Aria, Hayan, Yuri, and Seol swept past me and stepped into the sea of fans. Bowing gracefully, Aria introduced us to the crowd, and then a million hands reached out for handshakes and autographs.

Before I could get out of my seat, So-ri tapped me on the shoulder. Pushing a thin black pen into my hand, she whispered, "Just enjoy." I smiled warmly at her, then gripped the pen and launched myself into the crowd.

"What's your group's name?" someone called to my left. She was speaking in Korean, but I understood her pretty well.

"We're A-List!" I beamed. I'd never actually said it out loud before, but now that I had, I felt so proud.

"A-List! I know you!" she exclaimed, her eyes growing bigger. "I really love your day/night concept. I even have your photo card in one of my binders!"

She knew who we were! A total stranger knew who we were! I took a mental picture of her—green sweater, black bangs, pink cheeks, extremely friendly smile. She was maybe twelve or thirteen, around the same age as Olivia, and she was still in her school uniform. This was the very beginning of my public life as a singer, and I wanted to hold on to her and this moment forever.

"What's your name?" she asked.

"I'm Harmony Choy; what's your name?"

"Kim Ji-woo," she replied. "Can you sign my binder?"

"Yes, I would love to!"

As I signed her binder, I started to understand what Joon always said about his fans—that it was a two-way street. Ji-woo was the one asking for something, but I was the one who felt like I was getting a gift. It dawned on me that I had no dream without fans. Without them, I would just be a girl who liked to sing.

I lifted my pen from her binder and scanned what I had just written. It read: *Thank you, Ji-woo, for supporting A-List. I will never forget you. All my love, Harmony Choy.*

"Ten minutes!" announced a woman wearing a headset.

We were gathered in a greenroom inside the *M Countdown* studios, and it was just like the backstage area I'd imagined when I fantasized about being famous. There was a cushy velvet couch and plush armchairs—and big mirrors with director's chairs in front of them for hair and makeup touchups. A person with a walkie-talkie stood right outside our door with the sole purpose of getting us anything we asked for, whenever we asked for it. But there was nothing we could possibly need; the room was stocked with all kinds of Korean treats—black sesame mochi, grape and lychee jellies, mounds of mini chocolate pies, and three different flavors of Lotte cream cakes. Even if I were allowed to eat any of it, I wouldn't have been able to; the glow from our autograph session had worn off, and now I was starting to feel really anxious.

A screen hung above the snack table broadcasting a live feed of the stage, where MSB stepped to the beat of the pounding bass.

"HEY, YOU GIRL! NEOMAN-I NAUI SESANG!"

The audience chanted back at MSB in a single voice so deafening it almost drowned out the music. I had hoped I'd get a second to talk to Joon before we went onstage together, but I never got the chance; we were taken to our greenroom as soon as we walked into the building, and Miss Jackie never let us out again.

"OK, A-List. Gather up." It was Aria, standing in the middle of the room and beckoning us toward her. The other girls huddled around her, and So-ri shooed me toward them.

"So, as your team leader, I've been thinking a lot lately," she began, her hands clasped together in front of her as if she were praying. "This is it—the moment we've been waiting for our whole lives. I know we've had our issues, and we struggled through a lot to get here." Aria's gold-flecked eyes darted up at me, and I didn't have to look around the circle to know that everyone else was looking at me, too. "But let's put that behind us, OK? Let's walk out there tonight as sisters—because when we're on that stage, all we'll have is one another."

I wanted to believe her, that she and I could somehow pull together and act like sisters, but after everything we'd said to each other, it was really hard to imagine.

"So, here's what I've been thinking. What's one thing that every girl group needs before showtime?" A little smile hovered around Aria's lips as she looked around the circle at us, but no one knew what she was getting at.

"A drink?" joked Seol. We all laughed, but it was over quickly; we all wanted to know what the big surprise was.

Aria's lips opened into a full-on grin. "No-oo, we need a pre-show ritual!"

Crickets.

"Just follow me," she said, laughing. I hadn't seen Aria in such a relaxed mood since—well, since ever. She held up her hands, putting her index fingers and thumbs together in the shape of an A, and we mimicked her. "OK, say it out loud—AAA . . ."

Hayan, Yuri, Seol, and I all repeated after her; then she put her A into the middle of the circle. We did the same, and when our hands all touched, she sang out, ". . . LIST!"

"A-LIST!" hollered Seol, then she tapped her fingers on her chest and threw out two peace signs in air—she was doing the choreo from our routine.

The giggle started with Yuri, then Seol caught it, and then we were all laughing together. It was the kind of group laugh that was less because something was funny, and more because it was such a relief to be laughing together. I never would have imagined it, but the handshake, or ritual or whatever Aria called it, had actually kind of worked.

I watched everyone lose themselves in the moment, and I noticed that Aria had an actual, ear-to-ear smile, not the rigid one she usually wore. And that's when I realized what was going on with her: she was *happy*.

"A-List, you're up!" The woman with the headset was back and she waved us urgently out the door. She ushered us down a dimly lit hallway, the audience getting louder and louder as we approached them. We turned a sharp corner and she stopped us, just at the edge of the stage. MSB's set was over, and now Joon and the rest of his group were joking around with the hosts while the crowd ate it up.

There were so many of them, two hundred of the most die-hard K-pop fans in the known universe, decked out from head to toe in bright-blue MSB swag. This was our first (and maybe only) chance to show them that we were worth cheering for, too.

Before I knew it, the hosts were announcing us in Korean. ". . . TOP10'S NEWEST GIRL GROUP—A-LIST! A-LIST, COME ON OUT!"

Aria, back to business now, strode confidently onto the stage and we followed. But just before I crossed from the shadows into the spotlight, Miss Jackie snagged me by the wrist. She narrowed her eyes at me, a little reminder to do what I was told. She didn't have to worry about me, though; I was way more terrified of Mr. Kim than the idea of botching the Korean language in front of tens of thousands of people; I'd be a good girl and flirt.

The stage lights were burning hot and so blinding that I couldn't see the audience two feet in front of me. It was like looking out into a big black void. Just like we practiced in our humble lessons, we bowed ninety degrees (exactly!) toward MSB as they shifted over to make room for us onstage. I ended up right next to Joon and tried to catch his eye, hoping I could trigger some sort of mind meld with him, but he didn't seem to notice.

"Hi, hello! Welcome to the show! Can I get everyone's names?" said one of the hosts in Korean. Once we had each bowed and announced our names, the hosts plunged into the interview, most of which was directed at Aria. She bantered with them about our day/night concept and our upcoming debut at the Dream Concert, chatting up the hosts as if she'd done this a million times before.

I was more than happy to let her take the lead so I could just blend into the background. But as I stood there under the hot stage lights, I became hyperaware of all the cameras pointed at us. I tried to control my expression—smiling, looking interested but not *too* interested—but everything I tried felt all wrong. A vein behind my right eye started to twitch, and I could feel my jaw cramping from all the smiling. All I wanted to do was reach up and wipe off the makeup melting onto my upper lip, and I prayed the cameras weren't zoomed in enough to see it.

"So what do you like most about living in Seoul?" asked one of the hosts. There was a moment where no one said anything, then it hit me that he was speaking English. The girls and MSB had all swiveled their heads in my direction, and the hosts were peering at me, waiting for an answer. I was so focused on how I looked that I had completely lost track of the conversation, and now, horribly, it was my turn to talk.

I wish I could say that I had some grand plan for what I did next, but really it was more like all the cameras, and lights, and hundreds of eyes, all gawking at me, flipped on some ancient boy-flirting switch that had been buried inside me for the past seventeen years. It was like what Dad taught me about driving on the highway—when you merge from the on-ramp into traffic, you have to step on the gas and trust (and pray) that you'll catch up to everyone else.

Now I was pushing the gas pedal all the way down to the floor. I felt my hands lift to my mouth and my shoulders scrunch up, and the cutesiest squeak of a voice came out of me. "Well, the best part has been meeting new people, like my friend Joon here." Then something bubbled up from my chest, into to my throat, and out of my mouth—*Oh god, here it comes*—"Hee-hee-HEE!" Horrified, but too far along to stop myself, I watched as my index finger poked Joon right in his ribs.

The audience gasped an extended "Oh-waaah!" I squinted, trying to make out the faces in the crowd, but I couldn't see anything beyond the edge of the stage. Was it a good oh-waaah or a bad oh-waaah? *Oh god, what did I do?*

A look of surprise flashed in Joon's eyes, but it happened so fast it must have been imperceptible to everyone but me. Within a millisecond, his face relaxed and the class-clown twinkle in his eye had returned. He looked into the audience with a crooked smirk and leaned back, crossing his arms lazily across his chest. Then he said something in Korean that went completely over my head. The audience burst into squeals, and his bandmates slapped him on the back, laughing.

"Kamsahamnidaaa, MSB and A-List!" said the hosts. An applause sign lit up, and the crowd erupted into cheers and clapping. We all threw up some peace signs and finger hearts, then the cameras lowered, the house lights came up, and we were offstage just as fast as we got on it.

For a minute, we were all sardined together on the side of the stage. I tried to squeeze past Yuri and Hayan so I could reach Joon, but Miss Jackie intercepted me and whisked us toward the exit. As we sped away from the stage, I whispered to Seol, asking her how she thought it went, but she just patted me on the back with this crumpled smile.

Just outside the exit, a huge crowd had formed. Some were holding handmade signs that said things like I <3 MSB or CHINJEOL IS MY

ULTIMATE BIAS. I pulled the pen that So-ri gave me out of my pocket, ready to sign more autographs, but when we stepped into the night air, the crowd didn't make a move.

Hundreds of faces gaped at us as we walked past them toward the van, but aside from a few whispers, no one in the crowd said a word. Feeling suddenly exposed, I clutched at my stomach as we awkwardly climbed into the van in silence.

When the doors slammed shut and the van headed out of the courtyard, I waited for Aria to come at me, to point out all the things I did wrong, just like she always did. But she didn't; she did something way worse. She broke into tears.

She buried her face into her hands, her glossy hair shivering as she wept. Aria crying was even scarier than Aria was the rest of the time, and every time she heaved out a sob, it was like an accusation hurled right at me for ruining the biggest night of her life.

Hayan tried to comfort her by putting her arm around her shoulders, but Aria pushed her away. Crossing her arms and legs shut, Hayan scowled at me like it was my fault that Aria had rejected her.

Then there was a small moan in the very back of the van, and I craned my neck to see who it was coming from. It was Yuri—now she was crying, too. And just like that, the whole van was in tears.

"I'm sorry!" I cried, half pleading and half defending myself. "I didn't mean to . . . I was supposed to . . ." but I wasn't even sure what I did wrong exactly; it was all just so confusing. It didn't matter what I did; even if I did what I was told, I still couldn't get it right. I wanted to explain that I was only obeying Mr. Kim, but I was afraid to say anything about it with Miss Jackie in the van.

No one responded, and I couldn't stand to look at everyone's makeup-stained faces, so I tucked my arms and legs up, trying to make myself as small as possible. Pressing the side of my face against the cold window, I tried to drown out all the sobbing with the sound of wheels against pavement.

When we got back to the academy, I veered off from everyone without saying a word. I just wanted to crawl into the smallest hole in the world and never come out again for a thousand years. As I headed up to the third floor, So-hyun careened around a corner, her ponytail bouncing crazily on top of her head.

"Giiiirl!" she said breathlessly, bending over to catch her breath. "V posted a review of your appearance!"

"Already?" My heartbeat was banging away inside my eardrums.

Bent over and panting, she wagged her phone above her head. "Come on, I'll read it to you."

I grabbed So-hyun's wrist, and we ducked into an empty recording booth, turning the lights off so no one would see us. Before she unlocked her screen, So-hyun put her hands on my shoulders and looked at me solemnly. "I just want to warn you: it's not good."

I nodded and tucked my hair behind my ears. I felt sick, but I needed to know what V was saying about me. I needed to know the way you desperately need to come up for air after holding your breath underwater for way too long.

We sat shoulder to shoulder, our heads bowed over the screen, and So-hyun began to read aloud.

THE FIX

[This page has been translated from Korean.]

05.13

CATEGORY: SCOOP

Joon of MSB & Harmony of A-List Dating??

Buckle up, Buttercups, this one isn't going to be pretty.

If you caught today's broadcast of *M Countdown*—let's be honest, if you're reading this blog you *absolutely* caught today's *M Countdown*—then like me, you witnessed a slow-motion car crash on live television.

At first blush, the ever-outrageous rookie group, A-List, began their brief appearance on solid footing. Aria (which is definitely not her real name), A-List's leader, was enigmatic, gracious, and perfectly prepared. She's clearly received excellent training from her benevolent overlords at Top10 Entertainment.

It was when our inquisitive hosts turned their attention to the group's American-born member, Harmony, that things began to derail. Tae-min asked Harmony what she liked most about living in Seoul. Her favorite thing about our mother country, dear Readers? None other than MSB's own English-speaking member and fandom favorite, Joon. And please note, Readers, the word *Oppa* did not deign to grace her rookie lips. She did, however, employ an abomination of a giggle. She also—*gasp*—TOUCHED him. Color me repulsed. This girl needs to humble herself quick if she's going to remain on any Korean stage.

Of course, the ever-charismatic Joon, looking a little caught off guard, deflected her flirtation by replying "Who doesn't love me? I'm everyone's favorite!"

My Loves, I can already hear the gears turning in your charming heads. How, you may ask, does this tiny TV travesty warrant the consequential title of this blog post, "Joon of MSB & Harmony of A-List Dating"?? Well, approximately one hour after the broadcast of *M Countdown*, one of your fellow readers DMed me the picture below. No, your eyes do not deceive you. That is your cherished Joon with his arm hooked around the neck of a lip-puckered Harmony.

Match made in heaven? Well, you be the judge.

+ V +

So-hyun scrolled down, and there it was, my selfie with Joon. I cringed so hard I thought I was going to implode. My stupid duck-face lips and pinched-up eyes were on blast, on V's blog, for all the world to see.

"And then there's just a bunch of comments." So-hyun sighed, dropping the phone into her lap.

"I want to hear them," I croaked.

"Girl, are you sure? There are a lot . . ."

"Yeah, I'm sure." Hearing the fan comments was more important than hearing from V.

So-hyun patted me on the back and continued:

● COMMENTS ════════════════════════════════════

ayoomi111
There's no way that they're dating. V's right, Joon totally deflected.

> **MissLee**
> Joon only deflected because he was trained to and he's really good at his job.

Guest
Zoom in to the lower-left corner of the pic and you can see how he cradles her shoulder with his right hand. That is WAY too intimate for friends :(

@_@
waahhh, say it isn't sooooo :((((

JoonOpparJoon
Can you believe this b*tchhhhh? They haven't even debuted yet and Harmony already thinks she's good enough for Joon. She has princess syndrome.

NooniNo

More like D-List

> **Kwanghee21**
>
> D-List!!! ㅋㅋㅋㅋㅋㅋㅋㅋㅋㅋㅋㅋㅋ
>
> **kAnA**
>
> Welcome to the birth of your first Anti-fans A-List . . .
> ㅋㅋㅋㅋㅋ
>
> **SNSD 41**
>
> Omg, yes! Antis are called D-Listers now!!!!!!!!
>
> **+ V +**
>
> Dearest Readers, please keep the derogatory comments to a minimum. Remember, we're fans first.
>
> **Guest**
>
> You're kidding, right?
>
> **Chipwhich**
>
> hahahhah good joke, V

NoodleGirl

Harmony deserves to be taught a lesson. You can't just waltz onto the K-pop scene and assume you're good enough to date senior members from your company.

> **MIckieB**
>
> f$&k A-List . . . . . .
>
> **JoonOpparJoon**
>
> @NoodleGirl Def. What should we do??
>
> **NoodleGirl**
>
> Let's bomb the A-List's social media so they have to take it offline.
>
> **Oona <3**
>
> No something BIGGER than that.
>
> **k.rnd**
>
> yah, they deserve way worse than that

JoonOpparJoon

I just started a D-List gallery. Sorry, V, you can't stop the D-Listers!

(✿♥‿♥) aj

Yaaaaaaasssss

HaniBanani

Everyone to the gallery!

TaeyonBoo2

This is so goood.

....

Hallyu_VIP

What the actual f&#%$ V?? Someone obviously had to do something shady to get this photo. Why are you working with sasaengs and why do you keep insisting that you care about idols? If you really cared about them you'd STOP POSTING PERSONAL INFORMATION.

> **Matchastar**
>
> @Hallyu_VIP I came here to say this! V is only encouraging sasaengs to snoop more.

> **+ V +**
>
> I merely post the truth, it's not on my head if you can't handle it. Please, Readers, do NOT kill the messenger.

Stormy9

grrrrr ㅅ_ㅅ

Hallyu VIP

Sasaeng = violating idols. This post = violating idols. V = sasaeng. Do the math.

Chipwhich

srsly???? You have no principles!!!

NoodleGirl

I think maybe it's time for V to learn a lesson, too . . .

Stormy9

def

oRANGElAVENDER

Does anyone else feel like this is getting out of hand?? We can't just let the antis do whatever they want to A-List. It's people like them that give fandoms a bad name.

> **OkGirl**
> ^^^THIS

Azzie

Bad, bad rookies1!!! No one is allowed to touch Joon except me!

"There are five hundred and thirty-nine more comments," said So-hyun. "And it only gets worse." She pushed the phone away from us as if it was responsible for the mess I was in.

"Holy shit," I said, practically wheezing.

"Yeah," said So-hyun, her eyes wide. "Holy shit."

"I don't get it, how the hell did she get her hands on that photo?" I asked.

"Do you still have the photo?"

"Yeah, it's in my room."

"Hmm . . . Did you post it somewhere?"

"Yeah," I admitted, "but only on my private account."

"How 'private' is your private account?" she asked skeptically.

"*Really* private. I only have like twenty followers, and they're all people from back home."

"And I assume Joon was smart enough not to have posted it anywhere."

She wasn't trying to be mean, but it still stung. "Yeah . . . He never took a photo of it."

"Shit," said So-hyun.

"What?"

So-hyun rocked back against the wall and breathed out a sharp sigh. "Sounds like someone got herself hacked."

I let out a long groan and pushed the heels of my palms into my eyes. "You're saying someone hacked into my Finsta and sent the selfie to V?"

"Yup, I'd bet you a million dollars that's what happened."

I let my head fall back against the wall and screwed up my eyes, trying hard not to cry in front of So-hyun. Hundreds of little foam fingers stuck out at me from the soundproof ceiling, like they were all pointing right at me. I couldn't help it—two hot tears seeped out.

So-hyun cupped my knee with her hand and jiggled it back and forth. "Don't cry; please don't cry. All your makeup is going to run, and you'll look like the queen of the dead," she pleaded.

"I messed up so bad, Soh," I cried. Tears streamed down my cheeks and started to pool in the crevices of my ears.

"It's OK, it's OK," So-hyun said quietly. She linked her arm with mine and put her head on my shoulder. I smeared my tears across my cheeks with the back of my fist and looked down at her blurry head. I didn't need to guess what was going happen; I had already seen it play out once before. Top10 was going to disappear me like they did to Soo-li when she posted the milk tea selfie. So what was the point of the past five months? I was so freaking close to debuting; just one week, one tiny blip of a week in the history of my life, and I would have been on that Dream Concert stage.

Then something way more horrible occurred to me. Mr. Kim wouldn't just punish me, he'd probably punish Seol, Hayan, Yuri, and Aria, too. If it got really bad, he might even cancel A-List all together. I clamped my eyes shut as another wave of tears came over me. I couldn't let that happen to them—even Aria didn't deserve that—it wasn't their fault I had screwed everything up.

"I've never really seen a backlash like this before," So-hyun whispered to herself. She had the phone back in her hands and was scrolling endlessly through the comments.

"What will the antis do?" I asked.

"I don't know . . ." she said, biting her lip. "It might be no big deal." But So-hyun didn't look at all convinced.

There was nothing I could do but wait and see.

Twelve

THERE'S THIS ONE "WOULD YOU RATHER!" QUESTION that everybody asks, and it goes "Would you rather have the power to be invisible or the power to fly?" I always pick flying, every single time. Sure, if you were invisible, you could sneak backstage at concerts and spy on people and steal stuff without getting caught, but how could anyone pass up flying? It's *flying*. If I could fly, I would just take off and go to Tokyo, or Rio de Janeiro, or I'd just go home. Anywhere that was far, far away from the academy.

The problem was: I ended up with the wrong superpower. From the moment I got back to our room after So-hyun read me V's post, it was like I was invisible; the girls were going out of their way to completely ignore me. If I had a super-villain name, it would be something like Black Death or The Plague, because that's how hard they were avoiding me. Aria didn't even bother waking me up the next morning, and by the time I got out of bed, everyone had already gotten ready and left.

I knew I'd be in deep trouble if I was late for the van, so I grabbed a pair of leggings and started pulling them on, when there was a sharp knock on the door. Hopping on one foot, I looked up and found Miss Jackie's dark silhouette in the doorway.

"Harmony, please finish dressing and meet me at Mr. Kim's office. I want you there in ten minutes. Do you hear me?"

I swallowed, barely getting out a "Yes, Miss Jackie."

"And do not dawdle," she added. She snapped the door shut as I scrambled to pull my leggings the rest of the way up.

So it was true; they were going to make me disappear, too. First Soo-li, now Harmony Choy. I never should have let myself believe I was actually going to become a famous singer. Of course it was all going to blow up in my face.

As I climbed up to Mr. Kim's office, my legs started to shake with every step. I was getting panicked. The question was: Were they going to cancel A-List or just replace me with some other trainee? It would hurt so much if someone else took my spot at the Dream Concert. I could almost feel it, like it was an actual, physical stab of pain.

"Please, come in," said Miss Jackie when I got to the fourth floor.

The other girls weren't with her, so I knew immediately they were only going to let me go. Miss Jackie would probably tear my contract into a million pieces, and Aria, Hayan, Yuri, and Seol would throw a parade and use it as confetti.

My whole body was trembling now, and Miss Jackie practically had to carry me into Mr. Kim's glass chamber. He was sitting at his desk all alone, his usual entourage of producers nowhere to be seen. I guess so that there wouldn't be any witnesses present when they did whatever they were about to do to me. He wasn't texting like usual, either. He just watched me over his half-moon glasses as I sat down in front of him. There was something all messed up about his face, though; his lips were pulled back and I could see his teeth, including a big silver molar. He was smiling.

"Harmony Choy. The new rookie," he said slowly, leaning an elbow into his desk. "You made Top10 extremely happy."

I gaped at him and then up at Miss Jackie. What the hell was going on?

Mr. Kim waved his hand at Miss Jackie like he wanted her to take over the conversation, and he leaned back in his leather chair with his hands resting on his round stomach.

"Yes, Harmony," said Miss Jackie, sounding like she almost didn't believe what she was about to say, "as a result of your stunt at *M Countdown*, A-List is now trending on nearly every social media platform. It appears as if the whole world of K-pop is talking about you and Joon."

"And that's . . . a *good* thing?" I asked.

"Very good!" grunted Mr. Kim. I swear, he was almost winking at me.

Miss Jackie folded her hands together and continued. "In the future, if you are asked about Joon, all you are to say is that you were feeling anxious about your debut so your Oppa took the photo to make you feel better. Do you understand?"

If only she knew how right she was. "Yeah, I understand. So . . ." I asked cautiously, "I'm not being canceled?"

"Canceled!" sputtered Mr. Kim. "Not canceled. Rewarded!" Mr. Kim rearranged himself in his chair and sort of chuckled, but it sounded like he didn't have a lot of practice at it.

"But . . . why? When Soo-li was caught—" I stopped midsentence when Mr. Kim's lip curled at Soo-li's name.

"Soo-li was a different matter entirely," sniffed Miss Jackie. "She violated rule number one—she was fraternizing with a man without Mr. Kim's express permission. That was not the narrative we created for her, and we have no tolerance for that kind of blatant disregard for the rules. But *that* is none of your concern. As Mr. Kim was saying, he would like to give you the day off. We will give you a pass to leave campus for the afternoon," said Miss Jackie.

"Oh, wow, thank you!" I said. I could barely believe this was actually happening.

Mr. Kim beamed down at me like some kind of benevolent dictator, like he had just handed me the keys to the kingdom. And honestly, that's exactly how it felt.

I nearly flew down the stairs back to my room, ticking off all the things I needed to do. I'd have to borrow So-hyun's phone so I could make sure everyone knew I was coming home, I'd have to make sure I had my T-money card so I could get on the subway, and I'd probably need a sweater, too, even though it was getting pretty warm outside. I didn't even care if Olivia talked to me this time; I just couldn't wait to go home.

I wheeled into my room, grabbed a hoodie from my closet, and pulled my backpack out from under my bed, when there was another knock at the door.

"What?" I shouted. God, couldn't people just let me get on with my life?

"Oh, I'm sorry, I was just looking for my friend Alice Choy, but I guess she's been replaced by some rude girl."

"So-hyun!" I cried happily. "I was literally just coming to see you!"

"Oh yeah? What's up?" So-hyun walked in smirking and flopped down on my bed, but when she saw that I was crouching over my backpack, her face dropped. "Wait, why are you packing . . . ? You're not moving out, are you?"

"You mean you didn't hear yet? I thought the rumor mongers would have gotten to you by now."

"I just figured I'd come straight to the source," she said with an anxious-looking smile.

I caught So-hyun up on my meeting with Mr. Kim, and when I finished, she collapsed backward onto my mattress and let out a huge sigh of relief. "Thank the fuh-reaking lord!" she said, raising her arms up to high heaven. "Oh my god, I was literally bracing myself to say goodbye to you on the way over here."

"So you thought I was going to disappear, too?"

"I mean, yeah, the thought had crossed my mind . . ." she said.

"Wow, and I thought I was the one being overly dramatic about the whole thing."

So-hyun shoved me in the leg with her outstretched foot. "So are you relieved or what?"

"You honestly have no idea. I mean this V stuff still sucks, don't get me wrong, but at least I still get to perform at the Dream Concert."

So-hyun propped herself up on her elbows a little bit so she could see me better. "So, *I* actually have something to tell *you*."

"What?" I asked.

"This morning Olivia texted me."

"Wait, really? Let me see."

So-hyun slipped her phone out of her sleeve, opened up her messages, and held the screen up to my face.

OLIVIA

Hi to whoever's phone this is. My sister is Alice Choy.

Can you please tell her to call me? Thanks.

Oh, by the way this is Olivia Choy.

"She is the cutest," said So-hyun when I was done reading.

"Yeah, she can be," I said with a sigh. "Cool if I call her back?"

"Duh, of course. You need me to leave?"

"No, it's OK. Stay."

I stood up next to my bed and sort of tapped my thumbs on the side of the phone. It was stupid, but I was kind of nervous about calling her. Her text didn't come across as very friendly. What if she wanted to talk because she was really, really pissed about something and just wanted to yell at me?

Finally, I hit call.

"Hello . . . ?" said Olivia. Her voice sounded small and far away.

"Hi . . . it's me," I said tentatively.

"Alice, oh my god, are you OK?" she asked. I could hear her pressing the phone right up to her mouth.

"Yeah, I'm OK!" I said. "I guess you saw all the stuff about me online?"

"Yeah. I can't believe it. Alice, literally everyone is talking about you!"

"I know. It's a lot."

"Some of it isn't very nice, though . . ."

"I know," I said. "But everything's going to be fine." I didn't want her to worry too much about it.

"You're really OK, though?"

"I'm really OK."

"Well . . . I saw you on *M Countdown* last night. Mom and Dad and I watched it together. I, like, literally couldn't believe you were there! I kept having to get right up to the TV and squish my face against the screen to make sure it was really you."

I sat down next to So-hyun on the bed and pushed my hair back behind my ears. God, it felt so good to have her talking to me again. "Yeah? Did you die when I poked Joon right in the stomach?"

"Ummm, yeaaaaaah! I can't believe you did that! . . . Are you guys actually dating, for real?"

"Ha, no," I said with a laugh. Even my own sister believed what V wrote about me. "I would tell you if we were. He's just my friend."

"Your *friend*? You guys are *friends*?"

"Yeah, pretty good friends, actually," I said, thinking about his secret.

"AHHHHH!" yelled Olivia.

I pulled my knees up to my chest and rested my chin on them. "Hey, so I actually got the whole day off . . . since it's Saturday and you don't have school . . . do you maybe want to hang out?"

"Really?" she said.

"Yeah, really."

"Yes!"

"OK, awesome," I breathed. "There's this burger place in Samseong-dong that a lot of the kids here like. Can I send you a link and you can meet me there around noon?"

"Yeah, totally!"

"K, good, see you soon."

"Bye!" she said.

"Bye," I said.

"Well, that went better than expected," said So-hyun when I hung up. She was still propped on her elbows with her legs kicked out, watching me.

I melted onto the mattress next to her and threw my arms and legs out, spread eagle. "Ughhh, you have no idea."

The restaurant was called Brooklyn The Burger Joint, which was a pretty funny name for a place located in Seoul. It was known for this thing called a cheese skirt. It was basically a cheeseburger with so much cheese on it that it melted way off the edges of the bun into a sort of cheddary tutu. There were probably over a million pictures of it on Instagram.

I got there twenty minutes earlier than I meant to and parked myself outside the restaurant, leaning against the window. I definitely didn't need to bring a sweater; it was really hot outside, and everyone was out shopping and going to brunch in T-shirts and sandals. I leaned back against tzhe cool window and just let the sunshine pour over me. It felt incredible to be outside the academy, all on my own.

"Hey!" said Olivia as she walked up to me. She was wearing a helmet and pushing a white-and-green rental bike.

"Hi!" I said. "You rode a bike here!"

"Just from the subway. But, yeah, I'm basically a whole different person now," she said, grinning.

"Wow, I'm so jealous."

We walked over to the bike station across the street, and I held her helmet while she docked her bike and locked it into the hub.

When she was done, she took her helmet back and we kind of just looked at each other, not knowing what to say.

"Liv, it sucks that we haven't been talking," I finally said. "What's going on? Why have you been so mad at me?"

Olivia looked down at her helmet straps and wrapped them around in her fingers. "I dunno . . . It's just that when you left, I didn't really have anyone to talk to."

"What do you mean you didn't have anyone to talk to? What about your school friends?"

"I don't really have any school friends," she said simply.

"No way, that can't be true."

"It's true, I swear!" she said. "I don't really fit in at school. A lot of the kids treat me like I'm some kind of freak, just because I'm from the US. There's one girl who calls me Miss America—and not in, like, a nice way."

"Oh," I said quietly. Olivia was usually so good at making friends—she could find something to talk about with anyone—it was shocking to hear that she was being treated like the school outcast. "God, I had no idea."

"Yeah, well, I wasn't sure I even wanted to tell you . . ."

"Why not?" I said, taken aback. "We talk about everything."

"I know, but you had so much going on at the Star Academy, it didn't seem like you had time to talk about any of it . . . or even really cared."

"Of *course* I care! How can you think that?"

"Well, ever since you left, you never once checked in on me. You never even asked me how I was doing." She had the helmet straps all twisted around her fingers now in a tangled mess.

"Olivia, I asked you how you were doing all the time," I argued.

"No, you didn't! We only ever texted about all the stuff going on with *you*, how the other girls made you cry, or how Top10 was being hard on *you*. It was like the Alice Choy show, 24-7!"

"Oh, come on, that's so unfair," I said, taking a step back from her on the sidewalk.

"It's true, though. That's what it actually felt like." Her voice was getting all choked up like she was going to cry.

"OK, then why didn't you tell me any of this when I saw you in Dong-Incheon? You just ignored me and pretty much treated me like shit."

"Well, how was I sup*posed* to act when you just abandoned me!" She stopped all of a sudden and clenched her eyes shut, squeezing big tears out between her eyelashes. It was the same squished cry-face she used to make when she was a baby.

"Liv, I didn't abandon you!"

"But you did! You left me all alone . . . all by myself!" she cried.

Watching her cry, her hands wrapped up in her helmet, I remembered the day of the photo shoot, how I was so hungry I practically hung up on her when she told me about the school fundraiser. And then I totally forgot about it until she brought it up again later. God, I was such an asshole.

I bent down to console her, but I didn't have anything to wipe her tears with so I just rubbed her little shoulders while she cried. "Look, it's true. I probably could have been a lot better about checking in with you. I guess I've been pretty self-absorbed the past few months."

"I was really mad at you," she said.

"I know; I could tell. But you have to tell me when you're mad, OK? You can't just ignore me like that."

"O-OK," she choked out.

"And you know I only left in the first place because I thought it would make you proud, right? You're like the whole reason I'm famous now. Or infamous, or whatever you want to call it."

"Really?"

"I mean, I wouldn't even be at the Star Academy if you hadn't pushed me to do it," I said.

"No way. You didn't need me; you did it all by yourself," she sniffled.

"That is so not true. It's been complete hell not being able to talk to you. I've barely been surviving." I reached down and gently unlaced the straps from her fingers. "I need you, OK? I can't do this without you."

She smiled up at me, her face all puffy and wet. "OK."

"And you know you're not a freak, right?"

"I know," she said, wiping at the tears on her face.

"I mean, maybe just like a little, tiny bit."

Olivia punched me softly in the stomach, then wrapped her arms around my waist and planted her head right into the spot in my chest where it always went. I hugged her back hard.

"Oh!" exclaimed Olivia, pushing away from me. "I almost totally forgot!"

"What?"

"Hang on one sec." She crouched down and reached into her backpack, and when she stood back up she had a brand-new phone in her hand. "It's just a crappy pre-paid, but I thought you could use it until Top10 gives you your phone back."

"Holy shit, Olivia! How did you get this?" I took the phone from her and literally hugged it.

"I told Mom your phone got taken away so we went to SK Telecom and bought it for you."

"See, this is exactly what I mean! What would I do without you?"

"I dunno, probably be a total mess?" she said.

"Oh, most definitely."

Eventually, we went inside and each ordered a cheese skirt. It was probably the best burger I'd ever had.

It tasted like pure happiness.

INTERNAL SERVER ERROR

"The Fix" cannot be displayed because an internal server error has occurred. Please try again later.

HTTP ERROR 500

Thirteen

"WHAT DOES 'BOIKOT' MEAN?" I ASKED.

Seol stuck her tongue out the side of her mouth and squinted one eye, thinking about the translation. Eventually, she crossed her arms into an X shape and said "No more!"

"A-List boikot . . . A-List *no more?*" I tried.

Seol shook her head, and her short blue hair fanned out like a brush at a car wash. "Mmm . . . no listen to A-List," she said.

"Don't listen to A-List?"

Seol shook her head again. "No . . ."

I shoved a pillow in between my back and the wall and brought my phone up closer to my face. Seol and I were hunched up on my bed reading DaumCafé, this platform that hosts a bunch of fan forums, and whatever *boikot* meant, I really wasn't getting it.

"A-List boikot . . . boikot . . . Oh! Boycott A-List!" I exclaimed.

"Yes!" Seol nodded vigorously, and we high-fived, excited that we finally understood each other.

"Oh. Shit."

#BoycottA-List

The Dream Concert was tomorrow, as in the day after today, as in the biggest moment of my life was less than twenty-four hours away. V's blog had been inexplicably shut down for a week, so we had to rely on social media for updates on the anti-fans. It was way worse than I thought. The hashtag was all over Daum, Twitter, Instagram—everywhere we looked. Mr. Kim was practically giddy about the amount of publicity we were generating. There were whole forums dedicated to discussing the merits and faults of my performance at *M Countdown*. It was humiliating, but it was exactly what Mr. Kim had hoped for when he asked me to flirt with Joon.

#BoycottA-List.

What did boycotting us even mean? It wasn't like we were a store that you could picket in front of and convince other people not to shop in. The Dream Concert only had one stage, and all the idols had to perform one after the other. What would the antis do, walk out of the arena during our set and come back in when it was over? God, the thought of it made me want to crawl under my bed and live with the dust bunnies and dirty socks for the rest of my life.

Just then, the door swung open and Aria came in. "Hi," she said, sighing, like the effort of saying that one little word was just too much for her. She shuffled over to her bed and dropped her backpack on it like it was a bag of rocks. It was hard to explain her mood since *M Countdown*. Joyless, maybe? Or like a part of her had given up. The other girls were always trying to cheer her up and get her excited about our debut, but whenever the Dream Concert came up, she just got silent and depressed. "Come on, we're going to be late for our lesson with So-ri," she said.

"Coming," I said, tucking my phone under my pillow.

She walked about three feet behind me up the stairs, dragging her feet. In the past week, I'd tried to start the conversation about a hundred times, the one where I explained why I behaved the way I did at *M Countdown* and why there was a deeply embarrassing selfie of Joon and me all over the Internet, but I could never bring myself to actually do it. It probably wouldn't have made any difference to her anyway.

"Nǐ hǎo! Over here!" sang So-ri. She was waiting for us at the top of the stairs. Tiny wisps of gray hair stuck out at all angles from under her baseball cap, and she had a huge smile plastered on her face.

"Alice-yah, you look like you need a map," she said as I came up the last couple stairs.

"A nap . . . ? What do you mean?"

"A *map*. I mean you look lost, chica!"

"Oh, sorry," I said, trying to shake all the doom and gloom off my face. "What's going on?"

"Today," she said, clapping her hands, "we do our lesson in the studios!"

So-ri scurried ahead of us down the hall to one of the big studios that can fit a full band inside. It was all ready to go for us when we walked in, with two microphones and two music stands set up inside the soundproof booth. Behind the mic stands were a huge drum kit and a couple abandoned guitars.

"Are we recording something, Seon-saeng-nim?" asked Aria.

"No, no. We just have fun today. I want you to sing in the nice microphones so you can hear how good you sound. Is the last time you sing together before your big day—why not?" She flashed us her signature So-ri eye twinkle. "Into the booth, please."

Aria and I filed into the booth and put our headphones on so we could hear ourselves. Our mic stands were positioned so we'd have to sort of sing at each other, but when So-ri wasn't looking, Aria turned hers to the side.

Our lessons had been going fine. We rehearsed enough one-on-one and with the other girls that when we sang together it sounded OK, at least technically speaking. And whenever So-ri asked how the movie-watching was going, we just said it was good and didn't elaborate much.

So-ri situated herself behind the big sound engineer console on the other side of the glass window, leaving Aria and me alone in the booth together. It was so quiet that I could hear the oxygen passing in and out of Aria's lungs when she breathed. It was so quiet that I could hear individual strands of her hair moving against one another when she ran her fingers through her ponytail. There must be a mathematical relationship between silence and awkwardness, because the awkwardness level was off the charts.

So-ri played a little electronic keyboard through our headphones and warmed us up.

"Remember the duet about the mommy and the home?" she said when we were done. "I want you to sing that again." We turned to the music stands in front of us where So-ri had put sheet music from the first duet we ever sang together. "Same parts as last time. Ready?" she asked.

"Ready," we both said.

So-ri played us our opening notes, and I pulled in a deep breath from my belly.

"There was a house not so far from my ooown . . . Not a one lived there, t'was nobody's hooome."

My voice started out in a quiet place, and so did Aria's, even though I could hear everything so clearly through my headphones.

Chords together, chords together, chords together. The words repeated themselves in my head as I tried to close my vocal folds.

So-ri's voice came on in my headphones over her piano, "Do not worry how you sound. Only focus on listening to each other!"

I stood up straighter and pushed through the next verse, trying to lose myself in our voices.

"*Home is a trouble . . . A place to forget . . . Home is a heart . . . Forever in debt.*"

It felt like a hundred lifetimes since Aria and I last sang this song, back before Miss Jackie was hell-bent on humiliating me, before V had almost ruined my barely begun career, before I became the bane of Aria's existence. I mean, Aria and I actually had *fun* the first time we sang this song.

"Too much thinking! I see your brains working in there. Just sing!" said So-ri.

"*In the years of their absence, a deep quiet bloooomed. The home 'came a house . . . 'came four empty rooooms.*"

I tried to stay in the moment, but the microphones only amplified all the struggle in my voice, and hearing Aria so clearly in my headphones was extremely distracting; it was like she was inside my brain. The lyrics were too depressing and my voice felt too raggedy. *I* felt too raggedy. Singing wasn't helping me forget about my problems; it just made me even more aware of how shitty I felt. If So-ri thought this would get us out of our heads, she was wrong.

Aria gave a little sigh when we finished, and I shut my eyes so I wouldn't have to admit to So-ri that whatever Grand Gift of Song she was trying to give us hadn't worked. When I did finally venture to look through the window, she had this tragic little smile. She already knew.

So-ri hopped off the chair behind the console and waddled into the booth. "Chicas, how do you feel, hmm? Nervous for tomorrow?"

"I'm feeling fine," said Aria. "We've been practicing our set every single day at tech rehearsal, so it feels like we're ready."

"And you, Alice?"

What I really wanted to say was: I'm completely terrified of the antis. Please, please don't make me go out there tomorrow. "Yeah, I feel fine, too," I said instead. "I really just want to get on that stage."

"You know, it is OK to be scared," said So-ri. "Even though I perform on hundreds of stages—even me—I have stage fright."

I shifted my weight from one hip to the other. "I mean, maybe I'm a little bit nervous," I confessed.

"I'm fine," Aria said again.

So-ri examined us with this look that was forty-five percent skeptical, forty-five percent sad, and ten percent something I couldn't really identify. "No more singing; I want to talk to you about something. Come, sit down." We helped So-ri pull out the little leather stool from behind the drum kit, and then we both sat down on the floor next to her feet.

"So," she began, "back when I am younger, in the nineteen eighties, after all my big records and big tours, teu-ro-teu-style music is not so popular anymore. Everyone want ballads and city pop. My producers, they are very worried that if I keep performing teu-ro-teu I cannot keep selling records. So they ask me to work with a new artist who is getting famous. Her name is Lee Young-ja."

Aria inhaled sharply as if she knew the name, and So-ri nodded at her like "Yes, *that* Lee Young-ja."

"She is very good, but we have a lot of trouble. She wants me to try something new, a new kind of singing. But I am very stubborn.

I do not want to listen to her because I think I know best." Her voice was getting louder, and she wagged her crooked finger as she made her point. "My albums sell millions of copies; people all over the world know my name—why should I listen to this woman who has so little experience? Why should I start doing this kind of singing that is so hard, when for so long my way is best? I want her to be more like *me* and listen to *my* way . . . So, as we go along, things get more and more difficult because I will not listen to Young-ja. I am too proud . . ." So-ri trailed off, and she clapped her hands into her lap.

"What happened between you two, Seon-saeng-nim?" asked Aria quietly.

"We make an album together. But it was just OK. The producers decide it is not good enough, and so it is never released," she said, shrugging. "For me, after a while, I stop selling albums. Maybe a few here and there, comme ci comme ça, but no one remembers So-ri Tae anymore. So then I start teaching. It is a good life," she clarified, holding her palms up, "please understand. But there are no more fans, and so I stop singing." So-ri's voice wavered the tiniest bit, but she pressed on. "And Young-ja? She found a different partner—three of them, actually."

"Starlite," said Aria. She was staring up at So-ri now, rapt with attention.

"That's right." So-ri nodded. "Her group name is Starlite. One of the very first K-pop groups."

I raised my eyebrows at So-ri in surprise; I had no idea that K-pop went back that far.

"Together, they sell so many more albums than me," she said wistfully. "Matter of fact, Starlite is still touring all these years later."

"But you're a legend," I said, unwilling to let that be the end of the story. How could So-ri ignore all those years when she was at the top?

"Yes, a legend. But what is that worth? Do I still sing for people—the thing that I love so much? *No.*" She spat *no* out bitterly like she had something rotten in her mouth.

Done with her story, So-ri placed her hands on her knees and eyed us. All I could do was watch my own knees knock against each other. She didn't have to spell it out for me; it was obvious that I was supposed to be So-ri in her story, the girl who was so proud that she was destined to work alone for the rest of her life . . . or maybe never work again. I peeked over at Aria to see what she might be thinking and was surprised to find her tearing up.

It was dead quiet in the studio as So-ri let her story sink in a little longer, then she spoke again. "You two are such hard workers; you fight so hard for this role. I see this because I have this same fight inside me, too." She was clutching her chest, right over her heart. "You do not know any other way—singing is who you *are*."

So-ri leaned down toward us and hooked her fingers under our chins so that we had to look up at her. "But you must not let the fight get in the way of everything you work so hard for. If you want to get right in your art, you two *must* get right with each other, you understand?" Her lips were pressed firmly together in a grimly serious look. It was almost as if she were speaking to her younger self.

"Tomorrow you will have so many eyes on you. Not only fans, but Yuri and Hayan and Seol. They look up to you, too. It is a lot of responsibility I put on you. And you know why I make you both leaders?" she asked.

Aria and I shook our heads mutely.

"Because I know you are *strong*," she said, answering her own question. "Remember what I say—there is power inside you, but you have to know how to use it. It is the only way you will get through tomorrow."

So-ri eventually dismissed us, and I drifted down to the second floor with nowhere to go, really. I ended up in the common area, looking for any kind of distraction, when the elevator dinged open and MSB and their entourage unloaded into the lobby. The guys were all dressed in matching red-velvet suits; they looked like human versions of those heart-shaped boxes of Valentine's chocolates.

The last one out of the elevator was Joon. It was the first time I'd laid eyes on him in person since *M Countdown*, a whole week before, and I raced after him, wanting to catch him before he crossed the threshold into the boys' wing. "Joon, hey!" I called.

Joon stopped with his back to me, his shoulders lifted then sagged as he sighed. "Hey," he breathed, turning around to face me.

"I've been looking for you all over the place. I wanted to explain what happened at *M Countdown*."

"Can we not do this here, in the middle of everything?" Joon stooped down into his suit so that his collar almost touched the bottom of his ears.

"Um, sure. Sorry."

"It's OK," he said, scanning the area. "I just don't think it's good idea for us to be seen together."

He was right; everyone was still talking about us. And not just the other kids at the academy but all the talk shows, radio stations, and entire South Korean Internet couldn't *think* about anything except Joon and me. It felt like he had made an appearance on every single talk show in the country, just to reassure the world that he wasn't dating me. (Because god forbid anyone as famous as Joon would date a nobody like me.)

"Can we go somewhere, then?" I asked. "So we can talk?"

Joon sniffed and pulled at the black-satin bow tie around his neck. "Yeah . . . OK, meet me in the garage in ten. I gotta change out of this suit; this bow tie is killing me."

"K."

Sunlight was still streaming through the concrete pillars in the garage, even though it was getting late. I anxiously paced around one, going around and around in a circle and dragging my finger-tips over the warm concrete as I waited for Joon to emerge.

He showed up dressed in an oversize white tee and baggy jeans, just like a regular kid. It always amazed me how quickly he could transform between idol Joon and normal Joon. Maybe there wasn't really as big of a difference between the two as I thought.

"Hey," he said.

"Hey," I echoed.

"My car's over there. I'll meet you on the corner so the security guard doesn't see us leaving together."

I never really paid attention to cars, mostly because I grew up in a city where I didn't have to. My friends and I didn't even get our driver's licenses because we could just get around on BART and Muni, so the idea of driving around with Joon was exciting, espe-cially since he had this shiny black sports car. I could tell it was expensive—or at least it seemed expensive with its leather seats and loud engine. And of course, tinted windows.

We drove slowly, not saying anything, just feeling the warm air stream in from our cracked windows. After a few blocks, he pulled into a parking garage, taking a ticket at the little kiosk as we entered, and parked in a spot that had a view of the Han River.

"Is this where you take all your dates?" I asked, attempting to make a joke.

Joon smiled faintly. "Yeah, once or twice maybe." There was a tiny basketball the size of an orange in one of his cupholders; it was stop-sign red and had a Seoul SK Knights logo on it. Joon picked it up and tossed it in the air a couple times. "So what did you want to talk about?"

"I just wanted to explain that whole mess that went down last week."

"Uh-huh."

"So, all that flirty stuff? You have to know that's not me at all. Mr. Kim told me I had to flirt with you onstage. I would never have done that if they didn't ask me to."

Joon cupped the ball in between his hands, studying the sword in the Knights' logo. "Did he tell you to post that picture of us, too?"

I hesitated. "No, he didn't. I put it on my Finsta; I thought no one would find it there."

"But they did find it."

I lifted myself up higher in my seat, kind of surprised that he was pushing back on me. "Look, I messed up, OK? I didn't mean for anything bad to happen."

"I know you didn't *mean* for it to happen, but it did," he said. "There's a reason I have an Instax; you know that, right? We're not like other kids; we can't just take selfies on our phones and post them wherever we want. We actually have to keep our private lives *private*."

"I know, I tried to, but my Finsta was hacked. How am I supposed to control that?"

"Alice, our social media gets hacked all the time. That's what happens when you become famous. You can't control the hacking, but you *can* control what you post online. That thing that happened to Soo-li? That could have happened to me. Or to you."

"I get it, but it's not my *fault*," I said. I was getting a little fed up with the whole blame Alice Choy routine. Was it my fault some stalker hacked into my private account? Was it my fault that Mr. Kim forced me to embarrass myself on live TV—or the fact that the anti-fans were totally overreacting about it? I slumped onto the car door with my arms crossed, and Joon went back to tossing the ball in the air.

"I get it that you're not responsible for what other people do," he said slowly. "And, don't get me wrong, what you're going through really sucks—it probably feels like the entire Internet is coming after you right now."

"Yeah, it does."

"OK, but this isn't just about you. You hurt a lot of people whether you meant to or not. You kind of have to get over your own feelings and make this right."

I wanted to jump out of his car and just run, but this was Joon—he trusted me and I trusted him. If I ran away now, all that would disappear. A tiny sob was working its way up my throat, but I choked it back. "I don't know what to do," I whispered finally.

Joon caught the ball and closed his fingers around it until it disappeared in his hand. "For starters, you could say you're sorry."

It occurred to me that this was what Joon looked like when he was hurt—a little crumpled, grinless, the beautiful creases in the corners of his eyes turned down—and I was the one who made him feel this way. He was waiting for me to say it, and it was obvious that I had to—so why was it so freaking hard to say?

I knocked my knuckles against the window a couple times, then sat back up. It was like pulling a chewed-up piece of gum off my back molars; it just didn't want to come out. Finally, I said it. "I messed up. I'm sorry, Joon . . . I really am."

Up went the ball, then back down into Joon's hand. He shook his bangs off his forehead and dropped the ball into my hands. "It's OK, Alice. I forgive you."

"Thank you, Joon," I said, my voice barely above a whisper.

"What did I expect from a rookie anyway?" Joon smirked out of one side of his mouth, and a little dimple formed in his cheek. Nothing so small had ever been such a big relief.

I laced my fingers around the ball and tucked it up under my chin. "Goddamn rookies," I said.

"Goddamn rookies," he repeated, chuckling. It was so easy. Joon had to be the most forgiving person on the planet. It was just one more thing to add to the huge pile of things I loved about him.

"So . . . you doing OK?" he asked. "I'm sorry that Mr. Kim made you do that; he's such an asshole. He doesn't care if we're getting good or bad press, as long as his idols bring in the big bucks."

"Yeah, I'm OK, I guess," I said, tucking a strand of hair behind my ear. "Scared, though. Seems like I really upset the BoMS."

"Yeah, some of them aren't very happy with you right now. Or with me, really. But you know, they're just trying to stay loyal to MSB."

"Yeah, I know. But do you think there's anything I can do to make it better?" I asked.

"Eh, I don't know," he said, his knee bouncing up and down. "I'm gonna have to work hard to make it up to them. But you know what I *do* know?"

"What?"

"Whatever the antis have planned, the BoMS will do the right thing. Our fans have the biggest hearts. They would never allow a group of haters to bully you guys or ruin your debut."

"But they're not our fans, though; you really think they'd help us out?"

"They all banded together and got V's blog taken down, didn't they?"

"Wait, they did? I just assumed she deleted her account because of all the negative comments she was getting."

"No, she was being toxic, so they got her kicked off for violating Naver's rules. I know my fandom. They'll come through for you." Joon's faith in his fandom was never-ending; no wonder they loved him so much.

"How about you, you nervous about tomorrow?" I asked.

"About the Dream Concert? Nahh. It's our third time in a row on that stage. I'm actually pretty pumped."

"Yeah, but you're *headlining*."

"Headlining just means you're last to the after-party," he said with his giant Joon grin. "You got any plus-ones coming?"

"Yeah, my whole family is coming tomorrow. You?"

"My mom never misses a show. She always makes cookies for the guys, and she brings them in these little Tupperware bowls. It's pretty cute, but they must have a hundred of those bowls by now."

"Aw, that's so sweet," I said.

"Yeah, she's the best."

It was getting dark inside the car. The sun was almost completely gone, and there was only a faint orange-gold streak bobbing in the river. I leaned my elbow on the leather armrest and planted my cheek in my hand, watching the streak get shorter and shorter.

Joon waved his hand in front of my face to get my attention. "Hey, what's wrong?"

"Nothing. Not really . . . I just always imagined I'd be a little more excited the night before the Dream Concert."

"You mean you're not having the time of your life sitting in a creepy garage with me?" he teased. He rocked his shoulder into mine, and I shoved the ball back into his arms.

"Oh, believe me, this is thrilling," I said, smiling, "but yeah, it hasn't been the best day."

Joon rolled the ball up his arm and popped it off his bicep back into his hands. "Is there something else going on? I mean, besides the antis?"

"Well, it sounds cliché," I said, rubbing my arm, "but it used to be that singing made me feel . . . alive. It was supposed to be the light at the end of the tunnel, if the tunnel is waking up at five a.m. every morning and eating cabbage for every meal. It was the thing that made everything else dim in comparison, you know?"

"Yeah, I know."

"But today in class with Aria? It didn't feel anything like that."

"What do you think happened?" he asked.

"I'm not really sure. Training has been really hard, and I've been a little distracted. I guess singing has become a bit of a chore, just like everything else at the Star Academy."

"I'm not surprised," he said knowingly. "Entertainment companies have a way of taking the joy out of things we love."

"Yeah . . . I guess. But I think, more than that, *I've* taken some of the joy out of it. I don't know; I've been pretty resistant to a lot of things these past five months, and I'm just thinking about what you said, that I've hurt a lot of people. I think . . . I think I might've really hurt Aria."

"To be honest, I've kind of noticed a change in her," he said.

"You have?" I said, shifting in my seat so I could get a better look at him. "I have, too, but I didn't know you guys really knew each other."

"Yeah, I mean, we've been training in the same academy for almost seven years now."

"*Seven* years?" I gasped. I was stunned. I knew she'd been at the Star Academy for a few years, but I didn't think she'd been training for that long. Seven years was almost half my life. "Wait, that means she was . . . twelve when she started at the academy?"

Joon bounced the basketball lightly in his palm, doing the math. "That sounds right. She had a lot of trouble back then, and it took her a long time to get as good as she is. But like I was saying, I've just noticed that she seems kinda down or something. Normally, she's pretty intense, but I think that's because she just wants to debut so bad. I mean, she literally never stops training."

"Yeah, tell me about it."

"I've always wondered if it was hard for her when you came in and got to debut right away. I mean, if I'm being totally honest, I was pretty shocked when So-hyun told me that. Some people train for years and years and never debut. That's like every trainee's worst fear."

The memory of Aria and me in our first costuming session randomly popped into my mind. I cringed remembering how I just stood there, completely oblivious, thinking that I somehow deserved to be a main singer just as much as she did. "And it wasn't like I tried to make it any easier on her . . ." I said under my breath.

"Huh?"

"Nothing," I said with a sigh. The more I thought about how uncooperative I'd been over the past few months, the more I started to get this weird sinking feeling, like someone had pulled my plug and all my bathwater was draining out.

"Anyway," Joon said, arcing the basketball up in the air so it sank right back into the cup holder. "We better get outta here before it gets too late, yeah?"

"Yeah . . . I think I'm going to walk back, though."

"You sure?"

"Yeah, I have some stuff I need to think through."

"OK."

As I got out of the car, Joon rolled down the passenger-side window. "Hey. Thanks for apologizing; it means a lot."

I bent down so I could see his face through the window. "Yeah, 'course. Thanks for not being mad at me anymore."

"Nah, I can't be mad at you," he said. "See you on the big stage tomorrow."

"Yeah . . . see you."

THE FIX

[This page has been translated from Korean.]

05.22

CATEGORY: ANNOUNCEMENT

Taking a Break

For the past week, netizens swarmed Naver with complaints about my blog in an attempt to get it shut down, and it worked—I was blocked from posting since my explosive *M Countdown* review. The post was *so* explosive that some have even gone a step further, by messaging me hate mail and death threats. I won't lie: it's been a terrifying week, but thankfully those messages have been in the minority. Many of my longtime readers wrote in, as well, and they helped me understand some things.

Here is what I've learned.

I used to be in love with K-pop, but then we had a nasty breakup. Instead of moving on with my life, I decided if *I* couldn't have K-pop, no one should. So I did what bitter exes do: I found ways to drag it through the mud. I won't lie, for a while it felt good, but you can only push an ex so far. Eventually, they'll lash out, and lash out it has.

Just like this blog, there are real people behind K-pop and they don't deserve to be terrorized. You might find that statement laughable considering my Scoop post was the start of all this. Or you might find it ironic that I suddenly care about idols only when my own skin is on the line. You might even think I deserve what I got. All I can say is that this incident woke me up, and I regret letting things get this bad before realizing the errors of my ways.

So now what?

I'm not quite sure what the answer to that question is, but I won't be doing my regular daily posts for a while. I'm cutting all the bullshit and snark to say that I hear you; I broke the rules, the ones written in fine print on Naver but also the unwritten ones between you and me, my dear Readers. You're angry, and I need to figure something new out.

+ V +

COMMENTS ══════════════════════════════════════

LOCKED

Fourteen

OUR GREENROOM WAS A CLAUSTROPHOBIC concrete tomb. I'd expected the backstage area at the Dream Concert to be this luxurious place full of leather furniture and buckets of champagne, but I was utterly wrong. Today, the Seoul World Cup Stadium was transformed into a K-pop extrava-palooza, where all the entertainment companies were playing nice and letting their idols share a single stage. Every other day of the year, the stadium was used for professional soccer matches, so "backstage" was just a bunch of concrete rooms connected by one big underground tunnel (though I heard that MSB's greenroom was actually a converted locker room). The closer you got to the stage, the more famous the groups got. Somewhere way closer to the action were groups like Ruby-Red, 6IXA, and G2K. Of course *we* were as far away from the stage as you could get.

I leaned against the wall vaguely stretching, while Yuri and Seol got their make-up touched up in chairs behind me. Hayan had been stalking around nervously all afternoon, occasionally snapping in and out of choreo, and Aria just sat in a chair with her legs crossed, watching her foot slowly point up and down. The crowd above us chanted and stomped their feet so loud that you could hear them through the bleachers, through the concrete, through the ceiling, all the way down into our room. The only thing I could think about was that any number of them could be antis.

"Na watta!" said a voice as rough as a cat's tongue.

So-hyun stood in the doorway with one hand planted on her hip and the other held in the air as if she were holding an invisible silver platter. She was all made up, her pigtails curled into perfect ringlets, and she was wearing a pale-pink skirt with ruffles so flouncy she could barely squeeze them through the doorway. She looked like an actual celebrity. It was a dumb thing to think—she *was* a celebrity, after all—I'd just never seen her like this in real life.

"What are you doing here?" I said excitedly, rushing over to her.

She held up the laminated badge around her neck. "What's the point of this ARTIST pass if I don't get to go wherever the hell I want? Besides, no one is gonna stop me; Miss Jackie is running around like a cobra with its head cut off right now."

"I don't think that's how that phrase goes," I said, stifling a laugh.

"In her case, it goes like that," she said flatly. So-hyun threaded her arm through mine. "Come on, let's get you out of this dressing room. It's depressing as hell in here."

"Great," I said.

We stepped out into the tunnel, and So-hyun stopped, spinning me around in a circle so she could see my entire outfit.

"Um, girl. You look *iconic*."

"Hardly." I laughed. I was wearing a black-and-white jumper with tiny short-shorts and thigh-high boots. The secret was that all our outfits were coated in UV paint, which you couldn't see unless we were under black lights. I was starting to get used to getting all dressed up, but I still didn't feel like I was totally owning it like So-hyun was.

"*You* look so good," I said.

"Oh, gawd. I feel absolutely destroyed. If I have to go to one more fansign, I swear my freaking wrist is going to pack up its bags and walk out on me. I mean, I love our fans, but a girl can only shake so many hands in a day, ya know?"

"Yeah, I don't have that problem so much . . ." I sighed.

So-hyun hooked her arm back around mine. "I guarantee you: after tonight, people will be killing for your autograph."

"You have way too much faith in me," I said.

"Excuse you! I have the exact *right* amount of faith in you. You're going to slay tonight, so get over it."

We headed off toward the stage but only got few feet before we ran into Joon. "Alice! Been looking for you all over the place!" He was wearing a pair of ripped Levi's and a red leather motorcycle jacket, and he looked amazing.

"Hey, why? What's up?" I said.

"Well, I think this one might belong to you?" Joon moved to the side, and behind him stood Olivia, who was all decked out in black-and-white A-List swag, her eyes as big as dinner plates. She looked like a lost toddler in an airport.

"Oh my god, Olivia!" I said. "I didn't know you were here already!"

Olivia, her eyeballs glued to Joon, nodded once, but it was obvious she hadn't heard a word I said.

"Joon," I said, delicately nudging Olivia in his direction. "This is my sister, Olivia. She's a huge fan of MSB."

Joon was in idol mode and bowed graciously. "Thank you so

much for supporting us, Olivia. Your fanship means the world to me." He took her hand into both of his and shook it solemnly.

Something started to happen to Olivia's body. It was like her little skeleton couldn't handle the moment, and she started to quiver all over. I put my hands on her shoulders just in case she keeled over. Joon didn't need a second Choy sister to faint on him.

"So, what's your favorite song of ours?" asked Joon.

"Um . . . 'Light Up' . . ." she whimpered.

"That's one of my all-time favorite songs! When we sing it tonight, I'll be thinking of you."

Damn, he was *good*.

Olivia swallowed and nodded slowly, unable to say anything.

"OK, I gotta get warmed up. Wish me luck out there, Olivia. I hope we make you proud!"

"Good . . . luck!" squeaked Olivia.

Joon squeezed her hand one more time, then winked at me and headed off back the way he came.

Olivia blinked after him, and when he was completely out of sight, she let rip a piercing scream. "EEEEEEEAAAHHH!"

I clamped my hand over her mouth. "Olivia, oh my god, you can't scream like that here!"

"JOON KWON HELD MY HAND, ALICE. JOON KWON HELD MY HAND!" She was practically hyperventilating.

"OK, OK, breathe," I said, rubbing her back.

Olivia took a deep breath. "My hand . . . Joon Kwon . . ."

"I know, I know. He's Dreamy McDreamboat. You have no idea how distracting it is that a boy like him can pop up out of nowhere whenever he pleases."

Olivia held her right hand close to her face. She took a few more deep breaths, then seemed to actually see me for the first time. "Wow, Alice, you look really good. I've never seen you dressed like this before," she said, touching the sleeve of my jumper lightly.

I pulled the top of one of my thigh-high boots up. "Eh, I feel little silly, but thanks."

"You don't look silly at all! You look like a real idol."

"Well, thanks. I hope I live up to it," I said. "I see you got your backstage pass."

Olivia looked down at the ALL ACCESS badge around her neck. "Um, yeah, it's like the best thing that's ever happened to me."

"You're welcome," I said, beaming down at her. "Oh my gosh!" I cried, slapping my forehead. "You guys haven't met yet . . . this is So-hyun!" So-hyun had politely stepped back to give us some room but now was back by my side. "She's the person you texted the other day when you were trying to get ahold of me," I said.

"The little sister has arrived!" exclaimed So-hyun. She scooped Olivia up in her arms and gave her a big bear hug.

"Y-you're in XOKiss . . . !" stammered Olivia. Her body started to tremble all over again, so much so that she could barely control her arms as she hugged So-hyun back.

"I was just about to take your sister to the stage," said So-hyun to Olivia, who seemed totally accustomed to talking to quivering middle schoolers. "You can come with us."

So-hyun steered us down miles of tunnels, past two different levels of security who waved us through when they saw our badges, and past dressing rooms guarded by even more security guards. The crowd got louder and louder as we approached the entrance to the stage, until finally we came upon a pair of heavy doors that vibrated like a hoard of wild elephants was going to burst through at any second. So-hyun pushed through them, and a wave of sound exploded into our chests.

"This way!" she yelled over the thudding bass.

She took us right up to the edge of the stage, and we parked ourselves next to a couple of towering speakers that literally shuddered every time the bass dropped. Olivia clamped her hands over her ears and I did the same. Ten feet away, the members of EL3MENTAL danced their asses off, while the audience collectively lost their minds.

From our vantage point, we could see all the way across the stage and beyond the curtains on the other side, where other idols and their famous friends sat watching the show from a little stand of bleachers, as if they were normal audience members. The thought *Celebrities are just like us* flashed in my mind, but then I remembered which side of the stage I was on. I was no longer an "us," I was officially a "*them.*"

So-hyun waved me over to a black drape, the flimsy barrier between the backstage and the masses. I walked up to it, and she pulled it back a couple inches.

"Welcome to the Dream Concert, Alice Choy."

"Holy *shit.*"

In the weeks leading up to the concert, whenever I tried to imagine what sixty thousand people actually looked like, what I pictured was ten times smaller than what I saw on the other side of the curtain. The crowd was so massive that it moved like water surging in the ocean, or like treetops swaying chaotically in the wind—there were just so *many* of them.

The sun was setting and light sticks were just starting to pop out against the darkening sky. I expected them to be scattered randomly like a bottle of rainbow sprinkles, but instead each section of the arena seemed to glow one solid color.

"How come the light stick colors are all clumped together like that?" I yelled into So-hyun's ear.

"Oh! Because each fanclub gets their own section! See over there," she pointed toward the upper-left side of the stadium, at a frenzy of hot-pink light. "Those're our babies, the HeartBeat." There must have been at least two thousand people waving her group's heart-shaped light sticks. So-hyun covered her mouth with both hands and sent off a big MWAH in their direction. "God, our fandom is the best!"

I scanned the rest of the stadium, looking for any sign of our light sticks. There was a whole rainbow of different colors splotched throughout in the arena—a pool of neon yellow, three different shades of green, MSB's electric blue, EL3MENTAL's orange-red—it went on and on, but I couldn't see a single patch of white.

As if reading my mind, So-hyun tried to reassure me. "I bet your fans are waiting to turn their light sticks on until you actually get onstage," she said, smiling encouragingly. "Hey," she said, letting the curtain drop back into place, "you wanna go sit over on the other side of the stage and watch the show?"

I looked down at Olivia, who still had her fingers in her ears and a gigantic grin. "Sure," I said to So-hyun.

We turned away from the stage and headed over to the bleachers just as the big metal doors flew back open. Out stormed Miss Jackie with the girls and So-ri right behind her. The staccato click of her heels was so loud that you could hear them over the roar of the crowd.

"Harmony!" she reprimanded. "A-List goes onstage in less than ten minutes. You will *not* walk off again without a chaperone; do I make myself clear?"

Before I could even answer, she hauled me over to the opposite side of the stage where the girls were all getting fitted with their wireless microphones. So-hyun waved at me from afar and pointed at Olivia to show me she would hold on to her during the show. Miss Jackie planted me next to one of the sound technicians, and he started to clip a battery pack onto the back of my jumpsuit.

"Let me finish that," So-ri said to the man in Korean. The man bowed deeply and gave her the battery pack, and I wondered if he might recognize her.

"Hello, la bonne étoile." So-ri smiled up at me, and there was still something vaguely sad about it.

"Hello, Seon-saeng-nim."

"How you feel today? Ready?"

"Yeah, I guess I have to be, right?"

"Hmm, yes!" She chuckled. So-ri ran a thin beige wire through the back of my jumper and looped it over my left ear. It tickled the hairs around my neck and sent a shiver up my back.

"You *are* ready, Alice. And when you go out there, I want you to just fly, OK?"

Now it was my turn to smile sadly. "I'll try," I said.

So-ri took a clear piece of tape from the sound guy and taped a tiny microphone the size of my pinkie to my cheek. "Just remember, it takes two wings to fly." She pressed the tape into my cheek one more time, just to make sure, then wished me luck. I looked at her face, with the deep creases around her eyes and her permanent smile lines, and I knew what I had to do.

The girls were huddled around in a tight semicircle, watching EL3MENTAL finish their set. It was now or never.

"Aria," I said, sidling up to her at the side of the stage.

"What?" she said. She didn't even look at me when she said it.

"Can we talk?"

"Why?"

"I just . . . I need to say something to you."

"Fine," she said. We edged sideways away from the other girls and behind some equipment where it was a little quieter.

"OK, what is it?" Aria swept the hair back from her face, and I was struck by just how immaculate she looked. Her skin was perfectly smooth, almost glowing, but the usual fire in her eyes was gone.

"Look," I said, "Joon told me that you've been training at the Star Academy for something like seven years?"

"I have . . . So what?"

"Well, I had no idea. I had no idea how long you've been waiting for . . . this." I gestured toward the stage where EL3MENTAL was starting up the final song of their set.

"Well, of course . . . It's been my dream to perform at this concert, ever since I was a little girl. Every rookie wants to perform at the Dream Concert; didn't you know that?"

I didn't know that. I swallowed something back and looked down at my ridiculously tall boots.

"I mean, Alice, do you know how many times Top10 has told me I was going to debut?"

I shook my head.

"Three times before A-List. I trained with three different

groups, and all of them were canceled before we ever debuted."

"Wow," I said under my breath. "That sounds like it would be pure agony."

"It was. I cried for days. Every single time."

Everything made sense all of a sudden—why Aria was so worried when I told her I had never trained in dance, why she acted so weird when So-ri made me a main singer, and why she cried after *M Countdown*. She had been trying to debut for most of her life, and I had almost ruined it for her every step of the way. That sinking feeling I got when I was talking to Joon was shame—I was ashamed that I never really understood what was on the line. I remembered how badly Aria wanted me to watch the video of our routine even though we were all exhausted. And what did I do? I avoided her in the bathroom like an immature little kid. I was embarrassed for being so oblivious, like I'd been walking around naked for the last five months and everybody knew it except me.

"I can't believe how lucky I've been," I said quietly.

"Extremely." Aria crossed her arms, but it wasn't because she was mad or anything.

"I really didn't mean for things to get so bad between us, you know?" I said.

"Me neither." She sighed. "We could have made a really amazing group."

"Aria . . ." There was that chewed-up piece of gum again, stuck right on my back molar. I lifted my eyes to meet hers and exhaled. "I'm really sorry."

Something like surprise flashed behind Aria's eyes, but then her face immediately softened. "I'm sorry, too, Alice."

"You know . . ." I said, fidgeting with the zipper on my jump-suit, "we're probably only going to make it out of here alive if we figure something out together."

"You sound like So-ri," she said, half smiling.

"Is that such a bad thing?"

"I guess not; but what can we even do?"

"I don't know . . ." I said. "But anything's better than going out there feeling all alone, right?"

"TWO-MINUTE CALL FOR A-LIST. TWO MINUTES," someone yelled in Korean.

"Hey, come on," I said, motioning toward the girls, "we have to at least do our preshow ritual."

Aria followed me with a bemused little smile and we pulled everyone into a tight circle. She told the girls what we were going to do and then she looked up at me and said in English, "Do you want to lead us?"

"Absolutely," I said, smiling at her. I pressed my hands into the letter A, then stuck them out in front of me. "AAA—" I called out. The girls put their hands into the circle next to mine, with Aria throwing hers in last. "LIST!" they all chanted. Then we did our point dance, tapping our fingers onto our chests and throwing out peace signs, just like Seol did at *M Countdown*.

We didn't laugh this time. I think we all felt slightly self-conscious about the whole thing, but I was still glad we did it. At least we'd be on the same page before we walked out onstage together. Aria looked like she might be revving up for a pep talk, but before she could say anything, the lights faded to black.

An epic rainbow of light sticks kept the stadium lit up like Times Square on New Year's Eve. The crowd screamed sixty thousand people loud as the members of EL3MENTAL bowed and waved, then walked past us off the stage.

It was showtime.

It was all moving too fast now. The five of us fell into line, with Aria in front, then Hayan, Yuri, Seol, and me at the end. A man pulled back the black drape for us and waved us forward. Aria threw her head back in her full-blown Aria way, then she took her first step beyond the curtain.

We walked out to our marks and stood motionless on the dark stage. In the in-between moment before our set began, I stared out into the audience, which felt even more massive without the curtains to hide behind. It was so big it made me feel claustrophobic—or whatever the opposite of claustrophobic is. I had no idea what the crowd would do when the lights came on, and the not knowing was what scared me the most.

As I peered out at the bleachers, a sign sprang up in one of the stadium sections; it was flimsy and made of poster board, with something written on it that I couldn't make out.

Then another and another.

My heart was pounding so uncontrollably that I could feel it beating into my neck and my cheeks, like my whole head was throbbing. My eyes wouldn't focus enough to read what the signs said, but it was too late anyway; the stage lights and speakers burst to life, and then so did we.

There were no cheers. There was no applause.

There was only silence as the five of us danced across the stage.

Then, like a rolling power outage, the light sticks began to wink off, section by section, until the stadium went completely dark. It was more than black, like a photo negative, the crowd appearing like a gaping hole. Like someone had taken a pair of scissors and cut out the part of the arena where the audience used to be.

My feet kept moving as if they were on autopilot— step-ball-change, step-ball-change, hip-shimmy-down, hip-shimmy-up, arms above head. I sang, but I couldn't understand the words that were coming out of my own mouth; they were just meaningless syllables.

I twirled past Seol, who was smiling but had eyes full of fear. It was a look that made no sense on her face, and it made everything seem even more terrifying. This whole time, I thought the anti-fans would do, I don't know, *something*. Walk out on us, or boo us, but this—this nothing—was so much worse. This was the end before we even had a beginning, a silence in the shadows. This was what it was like to have no fans at all. We might as well have been at home, singing for no one.

We made it through the first song like that, performing for nothing, not even a single clap. Then the second song, and somehow we made it to our last song, our single "2day/2nite."

The stage lights lowered and I stood next to Aria on the blackened stage. If she was scared, it was impossible to tell; her breath sounded even and controlled, and something about it gave me a tiny bit of courage. I wanted to undo everything I'd done to create this nightmare; I wanted Aria's debut to be like she always imagined it, but I didn't know how. There was really only one thing I could do.

I covered the microphone on my cheek with my hand and turned to my right. "Aria . . ." I whispered to her, but then the first chords of our single blasted out over the speakers and we danced away from each other.

"*NAE-GA ILEO NASSEUL TTAE NEON SALAJYEOSSEO . . .*"

We sang and danced through two verses, to the backdrop of a

raging silence. At the chorus, we met up again at the middle of the stage, the black lights flared on, and our costumes glowed neon.

"TURN OFF THE LIGHTS . . . AND TURN TODAY INTO TONIGHT . . . TURN OFF THE LIGHTS."

The intense heat of the spotlight focused on me and warmed my face as I closed my eyes and centered myself. It was finally here, the moment I'd been waiting for, my solo. I took two steps toward the silent audience, just like I was supposed to, but instead of opening my mouth to sing, I reached back behind me and held my hand out to Aria.

I didn't care how Miss Jackie or Mr. Kim were going to react, and I didn't care if I was giving up my one big moment; Aria had been waiting a lot longer for this than I had, and I was done messing everything up for her.

Aria hesitated, then took my hand and stepped up to the front of the stage with me. Without missing a beat, we started singing together.

"NOBODY KNOWS WHAT THE NIGHT WILL BRING . . . YOU HAVE TO TRUST ME . . . COME ON, BOY, IT'S JUST ME."

I had no trouble with my vocal chords now; they sat right in the balance between closure and release, and the result was an immense power coming from my stomach and lungs. I closed my eyes and suddenly I was soaring. It was that same heartbreak feeling that I had lost way back before I signed with Top10. My voice reverberated through my lungs, down my arm, and up into Aria's, connecting into one single voice. I felt the last five months of my life, all the crying, all the anger, all the hurt, come free and fly off the stage, over the darkness, above Seoul and out into the world—gone. I was singing and I was happy.

When I opened my eyes, a spark of light flashed on in the mezzanine. There were a couple more glimmers, then a wave of white light rippled out, pooling out into the rest of the stadium. It didn't look like it was coming from light sticks, though; it was something else. As I danced away from Aria so she could have her solo, I squinted into the audience and realized what it was—everyone in the arena had their phones in the air.

"ULINEUN ONEUL BAM-E MANNASSDA. HAJIMAN NEOLEUL ANEUN GEOS GAT-A."

Stepping backward, I danced my way to center stage where the other girls were waiting for me.

"TURN OFF THE LIGHTS . . . AND TURN TODAY INTO TONIGHT. TURN . . . OFF . . . THE LIGHTS!"

Just like we rehearsed, Hayan leaned into me and I lifted my right arm up onto Aria's shoulder, right as the last crash cymbal rang out over the stadium. Our chests rose and fell together as the stage lights faded to black, leaving us glowing by the light of the White Ocean.

[This page has been translated from Korean.]

05.23

CATEGORY: REVIEW

Something New

When San Francisco native Harmony Choy used to close her eyes and imagine a career in singing, she probably never envisioned herself walking out onto the Dream Concert stage. That would have been someone else's dream. Perhaps that's what Aria Yu, the lead member of A-List, saw when she pictured herself debuting as a Top10 Idol. Aria has had more than seven years of training at Top10's famed Star Academy under her belt, but Harmony has had less than one. Debuting with one of K-pop's elite entertainment companies with so little training is a privilege that few in the industry can claim.

What neither could have anticipated was the rude welcome that greeted them on Saturday night. It was a moment that was a week in the making, requiring absolute coordination on the part of A-List's anti-fans and was ultimately born, I'm ashamed to say, on this very blog.

At approximately nine p.m. last night, anti-fans stood up with signs that read BE QUIET and LIGHT STICKS OFF. Obedient fanclub members fell in-line, unwittingly aiding the antis in their diabolical scheme, and the sixty thousand some-odd K-pop fans who packed the sold-out Seoul World Cup Stadium quieted themselves as if everyone had gone home for the night.

The five members of A-List—Harmony, Aria, Yuri, Hayan, and Seol—stepped out into a pitch-black arena, a breath-taking sight that can only be described as a Black Ocean. A-List made a valiant attempt to perform their way through the tense blackout, but their performance was stilted at best, awkward at worst. No doubt driven by sheer panic, their dancing was joyless and robotic, almost as if it were over-rehearsed.

It was a performance that should have spelled certain death for K-pop's newest rookie group, but then came another moment as spontaneous as a power outage. It took perhaps longer than it should have for the crowd to comprehend the horrific success of the antis' plan, but after the initial shock wore off, fandom message boards began buzzing with a new one. Few in the stadium had A-List's light sticks in hand, but the clever Dream Concert–goers realized there was another way to represent their diamond-white lights: by using their phones. Within mere minutes, the fandoms coordinated an arena-wide response to the antis in a spectacular show of unity. No amount of training could prepare an idol for something as disastrous as A-List's Black Ocean, but the fanclubs gifted them a different kind of ocean, one created by sixty thousand cell phone flashlights.

Originally slated for a solo during "2day/2nite," the group's final song of the night, Harmony made the split-second decision to share the spotlight with Aria instead. At times both brightly buoyant yet enigmatic, Harmony's voice is one capable of capturing the hearts and ears of even the most cynical critic. And adding Aria's own crystalline voice to the mix, the two left the audience spellbound.

The debut is a seminal moment in any trainee's life. It is the moment when the world decides whether they'll cheer for you. This year's Dream Concert should have been remembered for its darkness, but Harmony, Aria, and their fans ensured it would only be remembered for the light.

And cheer they did.

● 312 COMMENTS >>

Acknowledgments

It's the cliché of all clichés, but I do mean this quite literally: *Idol Gossip* would not exist if it weren't for my editor, Susan Van Metre. I've had countless editors in my career, and none have felt more like a writing partner than you. You knew that a novel was hibernating inside me way before I did. Thank you, Susan, for trusting me to bring it to life.

Patricia Nelson, I knew you were the agent for me and this book the moment you said "sensitivity readers." I am eternally grateful for your guidance and your endless insight about the YA lit world.

Many thanks to Lindsay Warren for asking the hard and necessary questions early on, and to Emily Stone, Maggie Deslaurier, Sarah Chaffee Paris, and Martha Dwyer for catching an infinity of little issues and errors in my first drafts; your keen eyes astound me. Jamie Tan, you were one of the first people who made me feel like I had written something exciting, and I am so thankful you're representing this book. I really did cry when I first saw Alice's half-Chinese, half-Caucasian face—thank you, Maya Tatsukawa and Angelica Alzona, for such a gorgeous and striking cover. And to the rest of the team at Candlewick, I thank my lucky stars daily that my work is in your hands.

Haeryun Kang, you were my eyes on the ground in Seoul when I couldn't be there myself. To all my sensitivity readers, bless you for all your good and necessary notes. And special thanks to Hee Chung Chun, who allowed me to breathe an enormous sigh of relief after our first meeting.

Andersen, the biggest K-pop fan in my life, this book would have been garbage without you. Mark my words, you will be an editor one day. And to Gabriella Schmidt and Paola Landaverde, the very first real live, actual young adults to read my manuscript—you two are the BEST!

Thank you, Mohum, and everyone else at Kirukkiruk Residency for introducing me to K-pop and South Korea; and everyone at Radiolab for helping me produce and report "K-poparazzi," without which Susan never would have found me.

BOUNCE, my fives, you listened to me fret about the writing process for years and jogged my brain when I got stuck. Stella, special thanks to you for demystifying the publishing world and taking a picture of me every time I reached a milestone.

So much love to you, Momma, for reading every single thing I've ever written—you are the reason I have confidence in my own writing. Big love also to Dad, Mary, and Olivia for showing me what commitment to one's art looks like.

Damiano, my love, you've made so much space in our life for my ambitions, and never failed to bring me food whenever it got late and I hadn't gotten off my chair for hours. This book is half yours.

And to all the K-pop fans, stans, and armies: I've spent years reading your words on forums and blogs. Thank you for sharing your world so generously.

About the Author

ALEXANDRA LEIGH YOUNG currently produces *The Daily* podcast at the *New York Times*. She produced tours for pop bands for three years before moving to South Korea as a freelance journalist. An assignment on K-pop for NPR's *Radiolab* became the basis for *Idol Gossip*, her first novel for young adults. She lives in New York City.